PRAISE FOR

Bright Angel Time

"To get a sense of what Martha McPhee's affecting first novel is like, imagine *Rabbit Run* or *Revolutionary Road* written from the point of view of an 8-year-old child....Ms. McPhee shares her father John McPhee's gift for fine, lapidary prose. Blessed with a poet's ear for language and a reporter's eye for detail, she proves with this volume that she is also a gifted novelist, a writer with the ability to surprise and move us."

—Michiko Kakutani, *The New York Times*

"Gorgeous...The voice of the young narrator trying to find her center is compelling and lucid. In this well-rendered tale of misplaced dreams and forgotten realities, McPhee's prose is as delicate and lovely as an angel's wing."   —*US*

"This is an original, peculiarly American story of a family unhappy in its own way....McPhee writes with assurance in her first novel. Her story flows smoothly, and she dissects her characters kindly."   —*People*

"*Bright Angel Time* is a gorgeous novel with subtle things to say about America in the wake of the first divorce boom....McPhee writes such lovely sentences that you want to do more than just underline them: you want to cut them out."   —*Newsweek*

BRIGHT ANGEL TIME

BRIGHT
ANGEL
TIME

MARTHA McPHEE

A HARVEST BOOK
HARCOURT, INC.
Orlando Austin New York San Diego Toronto London

www.HarcourtBooks.com

Grateful acknowledgment is made to *The New Yorker,*
The North Atlantic Review, Open City, and *Redbook*, in which
part of this work originally appeared; to the Yaddo Corporation and
to the MacDowell Colony of the Arts for their support.

Grateful acknowledgment is also made to Mark Svenvold for permission
to reprint "Erosion." Copyright © 1990 by Mark Svenvold. First published in
The Atlantic Monthly. Reprinted by permission of Mark Svenvold.

Published by arrangement with Random House, Inc.

0-15-602934-0 (pbk.)

Library of Congress Cataloging-in-Publication Data
Bright angel time/Martha McPhee.
Previously published:
p.   cm.—(A Harvest book)
ISBN 0-15-600586-7 (pbk.)
1. Sisters—United States—Fiction. 2. Divorced women—
United States—Fiction. 3. Mothers and daughters—United States—Fiction.
4. Family—United States—Fiction.   I. Title
Ps3563.C3888B75   1998
813'.54—dc21   98-15053

Text set in Sabon
Printed in the United States of America
First Harvest edition 1999

A   C   E   G   I   K   J   H   F   D   B

*For Mark
and for Pryde and John*

Erosion

They are small and flat, riverbed stones
that can hardly believe the long journey,
the grand lapidary of wind and water,
has led them, finally,
to a snug fit in the soft delta
of the palm, to be rubbed and rubbed again
in the recesses of the pocket.
They are unlikely companions, one polished,
the product of some refinement,
tear-shaped and, it seems, a bit frail,
the other, an earnest little piece of a mountain,
cut and tumbled from the scree one day,
a rock nouveau, a rock's rock.

There is justice in the world,
and the rocks are quite prepared
to ride it out in this bag of notions,
forever amongst car keys, chapstick,
an occasional ticket stub—
because if it weren't here,
it would be as it is elsewhere:

the world grinding itself to dust.

—Mark Svenvold

BRIGHT ANGEL TIME

THE GENTLEMAN

Mom learned to fall backward into the arms of strangers without hesitating or looking over her shoulder. She learned to fall freely, with her muscles relaxed and her mind open, inhaling the bitterness of sweat along with stale cigarette smoke, inhaling the thought of freedom with her hands by her sides, her fingertips clutching the fabric of her dress, her reddened lips turned up in a smile. At first she was afraid to fall. She wanted to look behind. She bent at the waist and fell awkwardly, buckling at the knees. But eventually she succeeded, and fell freely into waiting arms that received her, catching her under the armpits, catching her with fingertips pressing into the soft flesh of her breasts. A human pillar, she fell and fell and fell, until she fell in love with Anton. Anton was her therapist.

It was the spring of 1970. I was eight years old; my sister Julia was ten, and my sister Jane had just turned twelve. It was several months after Dad had left and a few months before we knew Anton well enough to leave everything behind and follow him to California—to make a new life on the road with his kids, in a turquoise camper—with no plans. In 1970, you could do that. Dad had needed a love that Mom was incapable of giving; Dad was a geologist who needed time for his work and he'd fallen in love with a woman who could give him both love and time. But already, by now, Mom had the hope that with Anton she could lead us to a new life that was bigger and better than the one that came before.

Mom had curly hair, golden curls the color of sand. She was thin, with a big bust, a gap between her teeth and green, green eyes. She wore shiny taffeta dresses with big flowers and no sleeves. Some had matching jackets, some had matching sweaters. The colors were living colors that made me think about summer: peach, lemon, strawberry. Her skin was ivory and smooth and there was no hair on her legs or under her arms. It was comforting skin, the type that showed no signs of stress, honest sincere skin that wrapped her in an extra layer, protecting what was inside.

Mom did her falling with a group of other patients in a house she referred to as "The Farm." Anton was an itinerant therapist of sorts and he'd come to our town to spread the Gestalt word and his idea of women's liberation. He started the local chapter of NOW and organized sit-ins in pubs that excluded women. But his specialties were lonely housewives and clergymen; he taught them all to fall, and to him our mother fell.

We didn't meet Anton right away. We were on the outside, near the road, with a lemonade stand that Mom helped us set up so that we'd have something to do while we waited for her. We went on Saturdays, arriving early, before the others. Mom left us with three crisp dollar bills in an old cigar case filled with shiny pennies and small bits of tobacco. The dollars were meant to appease us so that we wouldn't complain about bad business at the end of the morning, when she would emerge from Anton's with her face swollen with tears.

Daffodils and forsythia were in full bloom and the scent of the long onion grass filled the air. A gentle mist lifted from the ground toward the sky, and all around were trees. The house was gray and chipping paint, and it stood at the end of a short dirt driveway pocked with potholes. Ivy climbed up the walls, and the windowpanes were smoky and unpolished. One window was lit—a window on the second floor illuminated by a blue light.

"He's a priest," Julia said. The words came from her mouth in a steam of warm breath. As she spoke, her left eyebrow rose. Julia's hair curled like Mom's in small ringlets, sausages, that fell gently just below her ears. Her dark blue eyes gleamed. We stood by the lemonade stand, a little chilled, dressed alike in our yellow rain slickers and yellow boots, studying the blue light. A car rushed by on the road, blowing air over us. "A Jesuit priest."

I hadn't quite pictured him as a priest. A man dressed in a cope and cassock wasn't what came to mind when I tried to imagine Anton.

"He's not a priest anymore," Jane said. Her braids hung heavily, pulling her face long. Beads of mist glistened in her hair. "He's a Gestalt therapist now."

"Duh trois," Julia said, acting smart. That meant no kidding in her vocabulary. She said she knew everything.

"Mom's falling in love with him," I said.

I didn't know what a Jesuit was then, but I could tell by the way people looked when Mom told them he'd been a Jesuit that it was important. Awe seeped over their faces like a stain. I did the same with my face, pretending I understood. Gestalt was another one of those words that impressed people and that I didn't know but used as if I did. I told teachers and classmates, anyone who'd listen, that he was a Jesuit and a Gestalt, and just using the words made me feel big.

"Gestalt therapist," Jane would correct.

We were serious, serious to the point of solemnity. The air was blue, wet and cold against my face and suddenly I felt unusually clean. I thought of us as buttercups, standing in the onion grass in our yellow jackets and boots. We looked odd and out of place at the head of Anton's driveway: odd because we were clean, as if there were something jarring and peculiar about being clean and being there. Everything about us was clean: behind our ears, the napes of our necks. We smelled of lemons and witch hazel and our clothes smelled of bleach and starch. Our cotton bobby socks were clean, soft as feathers around our feet; our jumpers were clean; our shirts were clean; even the grosgrain ribbons tied around our hair were clean. I had the urge to run deep into the trees and roll around in the bitter and decaying leaves and then I began to laugh. I pointed at the blue light. "Do you think they're fucking?" I said. Julia had taught me that word. I looked at Jane and Julia and they laughed. "Ka-te," they said. But we were bored. We laughed hard and loud and I worried that we would disturb Mom and Anton. Then I hoped that we would. I hoped that Anton would come to the window and tell us to be quiet so that we could have a peek at him. I hoped he'd raise the window and rest his palms on the sill and call us each by name. Jane, Julia, Kate—and the sound of our names would come to us, the warmth of his reprimanding words making us want to obey him.

"He's a philosopher. And he's writing a book," Jane continued.

"He's got five children," Julia said.

"He's married," I blurted.

"Kate," they said. We weren't supposed to talk about that.

"He's a Texan and a poker player," Julia said. "And he's a big, big man with a big, big head." Her eyes widened and her nostrils flared. "And he's generous."

"And he likes to eat." Excitement flooded our voices.

"He earns over thirty thousand dollars a year playing cards," I said. I liked saying "cards" instead of "poker." It sounded more professional.

"How do you know that?" Julia snapped. She hated it when I knew something she didn't know.

But the image of Anton that I held and hoped for was that of a distinguished man, tall and slender with silver graying hair and long protective fingers, a gentle man.

The familiar coughing of a muffler warned us, and Jane yelled for us to run. We darted through thistles deep into the forsythia. Surges of panic excited us, shooting up our spines. We thought we could vanish. We were surrounded by thickets and rough branches, and the ground was soft and gushy and speckled with the greens, whites and yellows of fallen blossoms and ragweed.

Jane parted several branches so that we could spy on the patients. First came Delilah, Anton's secretary. She didn't look much like a secretary in her miniskirt and stovepipe patent-leather boots. Her hair was long and it wrapped around her shoulders, dancing with the leather tassels of her jacket. She parked between Anton's Cadillac and our station wagon and vanished into the house like Mom.

"She's a hippie," Julia said.

Then the rest of the people came. There was something strange about them, though the women weren't that different from Mom. I guess it was because the clergymen didn't look like clergymen, dressed like normal men in pants and T-shirts, and the women were all so similar. Their hair was nicely brushed and curled, held back with bows or bandeaux. They wore wraparound skirts or slacks and bright argyle sweaters with initials embroidered on the front. One by one they drove in, parked with a screech, and rushed from the car to the door as if pulled by some mysterious force. Mom told us not to sell lemonade to the patients. She said some of the housewives were the mothers of our friends and it might make them self-conscious to know that we knew they were in therapy.

We watched until the last car came and the last person went inside the shack. Then we emerged from the forsythia, coming into a new space that was somehow larger than before, filled with new things. A telephone pole shot into the sky, blossoming into a network of black wires that webbed their way in and out of the trees. Planks of wood leaned against the side of the house, disorganized and ugly. I imagined rusty nails in hidden spots and thought about tetanus and rabies and lockjaw. Jane had read about lockjaw. Lockjaw from rusty nails, lockjaw from stepping in animal excrement, lockjaw from licking our dirty fingers. She warned us that lockjaw was easy to contract at a farm. She told us that our jaws would convulse and our muscles would spasm and our mouths would lock shut permanently.

"A car's coming!" Julia sang, running across the road. The first car to stop all morning, in fact the first car ever to stop for our lemonade. Julia's smile was electric and her cheeks rosy. As the car approached, she waved her hands furiously. Even when she was clumsy she moved with grace. She threw off her slicker and rolled up her sleeves. I followed her. Jane stayed behind: she was above selling lemonade. She said the only reason she came along was to baby-sit us. Ever since Dad left she'd pretended she was our mother.

Not so long before, Julia had made me her best sister.

"This is a secret pact," Julia had warned. "Can't tell anyone. Specially Jane." We were sitting on the bathroom counter with our feet in the sinks, washing them before bed. The neon light buzzed overhead, making the bathroom incredibly bright. In the mirror our skin was ugly, betrayed by the light, pasty and pale.

"I won't tell Jane," I promised. Jane and Julia fought a lot and I swung between them like a pendulum. I liked doing that. For the most part I always had someone on my side.

"Jane's a bitch," Julia said. "I'm the one who always does special things for you." She stuck my fingertip quickly with a needle, and then stuck herself. Small beads of blood popped from our skin and she clamped our fingers together to mix the blood, pressing them hard until they turned purple. When I thought it was all over she put my finger in her mouth and hers in mine. "We can become so close," she said. "By drinking each other's blood we can become each other."

The black Lincoln Continental was dull, dirty. I stood on one side of the road and Julia on the other. The car slid quietly between us, an ocean liner gliding through the sea. Julia disappeared and I heard the soft mechanical murmur of an electric window going down.

"Kate! Kate!" Julia commanded suddenly, appearing at the front end of the car. "Get a cup of lemonade. This gentleman wants a cup of lemonade. He'll pay us twenty cents!" She looked at me from across the hood. "And he's gonna pay us to do him a favor. Get him a cup!" Her smile was big.

She snatched the lemonade from my hand and passed it into the car. Her arm vanished for a second and then reappeared, a dollar bill clutched in her fist. I wanted to look into the car, but she wouldn't move from the window. Hog, I thought.

"Look, Katy." She held the dollar up. "He wants us to watch him change. He needs to fix his car and he wants us to make sure that nobody peeks at him while he's changing into his old clothes." She spoke fast, with assurance.

"Where do we have to go?" I said, suspicious. I wasn't going into any woods with this man. Mom had warned us about men who raped and killed. "Raped and killed": she said it a thousand times, so we'd listen. But Julia was older, Julia knew everything. I watched the dollar in Julia's fist, wondering how much he'd pay us, hoping it would be more than just a dollar, thinking I'd bargain with him if he didn't offer more.

"Nowhere. Just here," she said. She grabbed my arm and together we leaned through the car window. I felt warm and special.

It was dark inside the car, and thick dust lay on the dashboard, broken with fingerprints. In several places stuffing poked out from rips in the seat. The radio was turned on, music struggling through static. Stacks of browned newspapers littered the backseat, plastic-foam coffee cups spilled from paper bags lying on the floor. I imagined there must be a lot of coins in that car.

The gentleman looked oldish, and his skin was leathery and wrinkled from too much sun. He had very little hair: a halo of white fringe and a large freckled bald spot. From his nose dangled something disgusting that I couldn't make out and I thought I should tell him.

"This is my best sister. She's my very best sister, my blood sister," Julia said, speaking as if she had found something great like blue sea glass on the beach. I knew I should feel privileged that she was including me.

"You have something coming from your nose," I said.

"Kate," Julia snapped. *Kate* sounded like *hate* when she said it that way.

"She's just young," Julia apologized. I hated it when she said things like that—I didn't feel young.

"Uh-huh," the gentleman said, and stared at me. The whites of his eyes were yellow, filmy. I thought he'd wipe his nose, but he didn't. It was as if he liked having something hanging there. I couldn't look at it. "That's a . . . real nice, really quite nice."

There was a strange smell in the car: a smell of old milk and smoke.

"It's a pleasure to meet you, little missy. You're just as charming as your sister." He reached for my hand and kissed it on the knuckles. His lips were wet and his whiskers pricked my skin. I was afraid the thing would fall onto my hand, but it didn't.

"Now, uh, yes, I could use another cup of this lemonade." His words drew out long and he stumbled over some of them. "How 'bout gettin' me another cup of this lemonade. Yeah . . . why don't you, uh, run along?" His eyes caught ahold of mine as he handed me the cup.

"But aren't we going to help you? Don't you need to fix your car?" I asked. The engine was still running, the car vibrated.

"When you get back, pretty miss."

"Go on, Katy." Julia shoved me gently until I drew away from the car. I could imagine her saying, "You've gone and ruined everything and now I'll have to fix it." I was mad I'd mentioned the nose.

I walked back across the road, leaving Julia with the gentleman. I wished I'd told him I thought he had snot coming from his nose. The only reason I didn't was because I was trying to be polite and the only other word for snot I could think of was booger. My arms felt heavy swinging by my sides—awkward and uncomfortable, as if I couldn't carry myself properly, and I was afraid that he'd be watching me. I could feel his eyes on my back and it made my legs twitch. Julia can get the gentleman a cup of lemonade, I thought. Julia can watch the gentleman change.

Jane was picking forsythia, placing the boughs in the crook of her arm.

"Jane!" I yelled and she turned to me.

"What's wrong," she asked, screwing up her eyes. "Didn't you sell any lemonade?" Her face looked alert, ready to react.

"Julia's so selfish," I said. That's what Mom always said to us when we asked for too much.

"You're just figuring that out?" Jane said. Her shoulders slumped forward. "I've been trying to tell you that for centuries."

I helped her pick forsythia, twisting the branches to break them off. They splintered into green and white flesh and I yanked and yanked. There was a difference going from Julia to Jane. Jane was quiet and she didn't poke at me all the time and boss me around. Unless she was mad at you, she'd just let you be. Sometimes she'd speak and say something really smart, you could tell she thought a lot. Nothing got by Jane. Sometimes I thought I'd rather be Julia and I tried to be just like her. Other times it would be Jane I imitated. Now I imitated Jane. I even put on her long face. But, God, I wished I hadn't mentioned the nose.

Five, ten minutes passed. I looked back at the car, glad to make Julia wait. It drizzled and the rain made sounds in the leaves. I practiced making long faces, stretching my mouth this way and that, raising my eyes.

"What are you doing with your face?"

"Nothing."

We heard a car door slam, wheels screeched, burning rubber churning over pavement. The Lincoln Continental vanished in a cloud of exhaust. "Raped and killed" flashed across my mind, but Julia stood where I had left her, frozen for a minute, with her hands in her hair. Slowly, she began to cross the road toward the house. Slowly, she leaned down for her ribbon which lay on the road, and then she rose and erupted into tears.

Mom rushed from the house onto the little front porch. She stood there for the instant it took Julia to run screaming to her. Jane and I followed, stopping a short distance from the steps.

Mom's taffeta dress was wrinkled at the waist and her lipstick was gone. Her arms opened, and Julia collapsed into them. Mom rocked her, her hand caressing the back of Julia's head. She looked past Julia's curls to Jane, asking her with a look—what happened? They had a mysterious way of communicating that was all their own, but I could tell that Jane was in trouble. Her face became long, her eyes grew big and dense, taking over her face until it seemed she was just two enormous brown eyes. The rain plastered her hair to her skull. Even her braids hung limp, like two fraying ropes. The flowers drooped in her arms.

"Eve? Eve, is everything all right?" The faces of three women appeared at the upstairs window. Their hair was messy like Mom's, their ribbons and bandeaux were gone. Their smiles were panicky. I stared at them, hoping I'd recognize somebody's mother so that I could make her feel uncomfortable, but I couldn't.

"Don't worry," Mom called to them. "It'll be all right. Jane just wasn't watching the girls."

Instantly I wished I hadn't sided with Jane. I was afraid I'd get Mom's silent treatment now too, and Julia would be favored for days.

The screen door creaked open slowly and a man appeared. Anton: he was as big as Julia had described. Big round head. Big tall body. Big fingers. I thought about poker and the thirty thousand dollars a year. Then I thought about God—I don't know why. Maybe because Julia had mentioned that Anton was a priest. I didn't know much about God, but watching Anton appear I just thought about Him and then the thought vanished and I felt spooked and I smelled the stink of rotting toadstools that came from a grove of sycamores not far from the forsythia.

Anton squinted, a deep furrow ran across his brow, as he squatted next to Julia and Mom. I could hear his joints crack. His hair was thin and graying. Thick sideburns striped his cheeks, and his shirt was an explosion of oranges, yellows, purples and greens. The sleeves were pushed up right below his elbows, and he wore a pair of faded jeans that hung low on his hips.

"What's wrong, babe?" he asked.

What's wrong, babe. Babe. His words rushed through me. Babe. The tenderness. His southern accent sounded somehow tough and strong yet protective, like his presence. He was bent down close to Julia, running his fingers through her hair. Her face was a mess of tears and drool. Mom stood watching, pressing her thumbnail into her lip.

When Anton's mouth touched Julia's ear, her crying stopped. His lips on her ear, whispering into it. I felt as if those lips were touching my ear, wet and warm and soft, and I shivered, feeling that pleasure a whisper sends through your entire body, all the way to your toes. Julia sank against him and he pulled her deeper into him. She looked so tiny against him. They whispered back and forth and I wished that I were her.

"Everything's all right," Anton said, rising. He loomed above us. His hand fanned out on top of Mom's head. On his finger there was an enormous turquoise ring. I thought of Julia's hand reaching inside that car. I thought of my hand with the man's whiskers pressing into it. I wanted to know what the gentleman had done. I almost hoped he'd done something gross, because I knew if he had I'd hear about it in detail, and if Julia had learned something from it I knew she'd try to teach me. Anton noticed Jane and me watching, and he winked. "It'll be all right," he said, a little louder; he was talking to us.

We fell quickly to Anton, more quickly than Mom. We were limber, falling freely, and our world opened up, suddenly becoming brighter. Mom wanted it that way; she said Anton would love us, she promised to God it would be the truth. And we fell and fell and fell, we fell for the pure sensation of it. At first we were young enough not to hesitate or question, not to look behind.

WAITING

Our father had left us the summer before, on the day the men landed on the moon. He had made a promise with us that morning: he would bring the TV out to the yard on the end of a long extension cord so that we could stare up at the moon while watching the men walk on it. He was going to tell us about the geology of the moon, but instead he ran away with the wife of his childhood friend to make a new life of his own.

Hot and overcast. The air was opaque and thick, but soft. A visible heat swelled like waves around us, shimmying up our legs. All the trees were still, the way they are before a storm. Our big white house and the bright green lawns, a small pocket in the woods. The excited voice of a newscaster crackled through static on the radio and Jane kept fidgeting with the dial. She had set the radio up in the kitchen window so that we could hear outside. July 20, 1969. Three-thirty, four.

Jane, Julia and I were dizzy with excitement, running through the sprinkler on our front lawn. The water fell in crystals and we leaped through them, catching them on our hot skin. Mine tingled and I was happy.

"By the time we're thirty," Julia said, raising her left eyebrow (she could do that; she said she had double-jointed muscles in her eyebrows), "we'll be going to the moon for vacation in spaceships." She clapped her hands and kissed me and I kissed her back and then we twirled around in circles holding hands. Thirty seemed so far away. But Dad had said that time changed as you grew up, it passed more quickly. Years became months, months became weeks, days turned into minutes. Now I was impatient. Julia said that people were already making reservations to go to the moon and the spaceships were all booked up for years.

Mom watched us from her garden. She was pulling up weeds just the same as every Sunday, nearly hidden among the columbine and purple delphinium. A card table holding a watermelon stood on the lawn nearby. We were waiting for Dad to come back from a tennis match before eating supper. Mom and Dad had made a special supper for a picnic on the lawn—southern fried chicken with thick, crusty skin, and chocolate-wafer icebox cake. I hoped it wouldn't rain.

"It's getting late, Mom," Jane said. "Where's Dad? The *Eagle's* gonna land soon."

"Don't whine, Jane. He's coming, dear. Just be patient," Mom said. "He'll be here any minute." Mom wiped her brow. Her hair was pulled back with a red bandeau and she was sweating. She looked down the driveway, squinting, straining to hear. It was a long driveway of red gravel that sliced through the trees to the road. Then we heard a car.

"Jane," she said, "can't you fix that radio? I can't hear a thing he's saying." She started digging again. A heap of weeds were piling up by the edge of the garden. Daylilies surrounded the house and the shutters were freshly painted.

A pale blue Ford sedan roared up the driveway, screeching to a halt. It was a familiar car, but it wasn't Dad's. Maybe Dad had borrowed a car. We always borrowed cars when ours broke down. But Brian Cain stumbled out of the driver's seat, flailing a letter. Brian Cain was my father's friend. He and his wife, Camille, came to cocktail parties at our house and always left before our bedtime because he got so drunk. I wondered why he was here now. His hair was white and thick and he was a big man with a potbelly that spilled over his plaid Bermuda shorts. All his flesh was loose, as if it might fall off like meat off a boiled chicken. He stood at his car door, trying to steady himself. His eyelids were red and swollen and his cheeks puffy. But the hand with the letter kept swatting the air. He slammed his car door and my stomach jumped.

"They've run away," he screamed. "Eve! Ya hear me, Eve? They've run away." His voice echoed through the trees, against the house, louder than everything, even the radio static. "I'm gonna kill tha bastard." He stumbled toward my mother. Her face wavered. We were frozen, watching, as Mom rose from the dirt, and walked in slow motion toward him.

"Brian," she said. "Brian." Her legs were long and blotched with dirt. She wore her bathing suit, the one with the short skirt patterned with enormous daisies. Little palm prints of dirt stuck to her cheeks. Dirt was in her fingernails, between her toes. "Calm down. What's happened?" The humidity had curled her hair.

Brian was crying. Jane and Julia and I stood there solemnly. The sprinkler fanned back and forth, spraying us and the water seemed suddenly cold and unpleasant, prickers piercing my skin. I wished that Dad would come.

"I gotta shotgun and I'm gonna kill the fuckin' bastard," he screamed. Then he poked at the letter with his index finger, stabbing it. "I'm gonna find 'em and kill 'em both." He turned over the card table and the watermelon smashed into the grass. Raw pink swarming with black seeds like flies. Water seeped into my ears, clogging them, muffling sounds, everything seemed blurred.

"Go inside, girls!" Mom said quickly. "Brian, let's talk about this. Brian." She was talking faster now. "Jane, don't just stand there, take them inside."

Jane led us to the laundry room and locked the door. That's where we hid sometimes when we were playing games. That's where Mom and Dad sent us when we misbehaved at the dinner table. I felt giddy with that feeling of excitement, of getting away with something bad, squirming to get hidden.

"What about Mom?" Julia said. "Do you think it's true? We shouldn't leave her there."

"Yeah, what about Mom?" I said, looking at Jane. I realized I was shivering.

"Shush. Mom's okay," Jane said. Her eyes looked wide and remote as she wrapped a towel around me. The laundry room smelled of everything clean: of lemons and ammonia and bleach and detergent. Our clothes were neatly stacked in three piles. Summer jumpers and underpants with pink balloons. But folded you couldn't distinguish whose pile was whose. I started to laugh. White blouses, just pressed, danced on their hangers in a breeze sneaking through the window.

Julia pulled me close to her. She was crying, and her skin was spongy and wet and I laughed some more. Then Jane began to cry too, wrapping her arms around Julia and me. But I couldn't stop laughing. My bathing suit was too small, and the straps were slicing into my shoulders. I buckled at the waist, wheezing uncontrollably.

We handed clothes down among us and I found this suddenly funny. Julia's bathing suit would become mine and Jane's would become Julia's. I wondered if Jane would get Mom's suit with the daisies. I wanted that suit. I loved that suit.

"Stop laughing, Kate," Jane yelled into my ear.

"Where's Dad?" I demanded. "When is he coming home? He promised about the moon." But they didn't answer me, they just cried.

Dad had fallen in love with Brian Cain's wife and they had run away together. They went on the summer vacation that we'd planned to take as a family—first to Maine and then to Nova Scotia, it was to have been a working vacation. Dad had given me a rock chisel and a prospector's pick for that trip because he was going to teach me to help him. At the moment, though, we had no idea where he was. We thought he just needed time away from us. I remember now, how he would buy time from us. When we cried he gave us crisp dollar bills and begged us to stop. Time and peace were worth money to him. He knew about time: its brevity within the larger scheme of things. Dad wanted peace. Mom couldn't give it to him.

We didn't understand then that Dad's departure was larger than time, that it had to do with the love that Camille Cain had for him and that Mom did not.

Later, that vacation would be included in Mom's long list of things that Dad had stolen from us.

Dad could lift me up easily and set me on his shoulders. On his shoulders I became so tall and dizzy, I could see and touch the tops of things. I was above everything; only the trees were taller. I was above my mother and sisters, swirling around in the field behind our house. The air felt different up there, colder, fresher. I would say, "Run, Daddy, run" and clasp my hands around his warm neck. His hands were tight around my ankles. "Run, Daddy, run." And Dad ran and ran and ran while I felt the wind against my face and I kept my eyes open wide.

For a long time after my father left, I was afraid of getting big. I was afraid that when Dad came back I'd be too big for his shoulders. Jane and Julia already were.

At first, we expected Dad would come back any day. The four of us lay on Mom's bed and waited. The ceiling fan stirred overhead, slowly and rhythmically, cooling us. Mom kept all the windows closed.

While we waited, we watched television. Before Dad left we hadn't been allowed to, but now things were different. We watched the *Million Dollar Movie* and the *Late Movie,* and then the *Late Late Show.* We didn't talk much. We didn't want to disturb Mom. She was so tired. We just lay there, all of us, waiting to fall asleep. Some nights we watched until the station went dead and the bedroom became blue with electric TV light. Glasses half-filled with water and bottles of aspirin shimmered on Mom's bedside table next to a picture of her father. The channel purred a magnetic hum. I tried hard to fall asleep before the others. I was afraid of being left awake alone.

In the mornings we slept late and ate breakfast in bed. Jane put Mom's eyelet apron on over her pajamas and cooked enormous amounts of creamed chipped beef and made large pitchers of orange juice. Julia and I arranged a silver tray with doilies and flowers in a vase. We hung half-moons of oranges from the rims of the glass and rolled the silverware up in napkins. We sprinkled lots of parsley on the creamed chipped beef. When the tray was ready, Julia and Jane carried it together to Mom's bed. Every morning was the same. We wanted to keep it just that way.

After several days, we started trying things.

"Let's write him letters," Mom said. She sat up abruptly and looked at us across the bed. It was early afternoon. I was lying on my stomach picking at the cold food on the breakfast tray while Julia examined my scalp. She was looking for things, she said. She was always examining me with Q-tips: my belly button, my ears. I don't know what she was hoping to find on my scalp, but her fingers felt good in my hair.

The curtains were drawn, but light leaked through the seams. Jane was at the foot of the bed making a food-shopping list.

"If we tell him how much we miss him and how much we love him, he'll come back." Mom's eyes were puffy and red, but she smiled a wide, hopeful smile. "I love my little girls," she said. "He loves his little girls." My heart started to race. I thought maybe Dad didn't know how much we missed him.

So we wrote, furiously, on pads of white paper. Crayons and Magic Markers spilled out of their boxes, getting lost in the folds of snarled sheets. We worked with determination, pleased. You could hear pens scribbling over the page. Godzilla roared across the television screen in a landscape filled with giant rocks. I wrote

"I love you," just "I love you," at least one hundred times all over my blank white page.

"This is stupid," Jane said. "You promised that we'd go food shopping." She stood up and tossed her pad on the bed. Light from the television made her nightgown transparent, and I could see her thin legs and large underwear. Her eyes were big and dark. Mom said Jane had Dad's eyes.

"Write, Jane," Mom said. "We need you to." Mom rested her back against the headboard. It was upholstered in lavender fabric printed with large tulips, just the same as the spread, and it seemed to swallow her up.

"He's not coming back," Jane said. Everything clenched inside me. I could feel the crumbs in the bed. I stopped writing. It was so easy for Jane to ruin things. She sat down and started scraping all the leftover creamed chipped beef onto one plate. It had turned thick and wobbly like Jell-O. The little flakes of beef had curled, dried up again. But still I wanted her to leave it alone. I was hungry. I was always hungry.

We never did send the letters. They stayed in the bed with us, accumulating along with books and television guides, newspapers and rubber bands.

Sometimes we had fun in Mom's bed. We fell in love with movie stars. Mom with Laurence Olivier. Jane with Omar Sharif. Julia and I fought over Clark Gable. A week of Cagney turned into a week of Cooper. And then came three movies with James Dean. The men had long since returned from the moon.

In mid-August we finally heard from Dad. He sent us a package. It sat on the kitchen counter while Jane decided what we should do. Sunlight caught its glossy paper and it shone. The box became a golden box and the bold black letters of Dad's print shouted out our names.

Jane was at the stove in Mom's apron, stirring creamed chipped beef. Julia stood at the sink, which was piled with pots and pans and glasses and plates, trying to retrieve and wash plates for our breakfast.

"Let's just open it," I said. I couldn't understand why Jane wouldn't. My chest pulsed and I could feel my thumbs throb. It seemed the box was throbbing too.

"We shouldn't open the box," Jane said. Her hair was long and out of braids, her face red from the heat of the stove. The spoon in her hand was covered with a thick film of cream. "Or maybe we should open it and smash whatever's inside and send it back to him."

"That's absurd," Julia said, moving toward the box. She liked big words. She was a show-off. Of the four of us she was the only one with brushed hair and the only one out of her nightgown. She was wearing her pink leotard and toe shoes. I agreed with Julia, though at first I didn't believe that Jane could be serious.

Jane ripped open the package and inside were three presents wrapped in cheerfully colored paper. Jane reached for one of the presents and Julia grabbed her arm and they started to fight. Their faces went red and splotched. They pulled at each other's hair. But all I could think about was the present. It seemed to grow. My impulse was to grab, so I grabbed the present marked for me and ran.

"Traitor," Jane screamed. "He doesn't love us anymore, Kate. You either!"

I ran through the hall, up the stairs to my room, and flopped down on the bed. Inside the box was a Madame Alexander doll, Scarlett O'Hara with her green eyes. *Gone With the Wind* was my favorite movie; I'd seen it fifteen times. I didn't even know Dad knew that. Scarlett's hands held a rock for my collection of rocks and minerals. An ugly gray rock with thin lines of quartz running through it. Within the quartz were the tiniest flakes of gold. It was a nugget of the rock that gold comes from, and Dad's note said that it was from South Africa, from 6,800 feet down in the ground and he'd been there to get it himself.

I held the doll and the rock and remembered Dad's hands. They were strong, with long slender fingers and not too much hair. Dad and I had a game. I squeezed his hand four times. He then squeezed mine three times. I squeezed his twice. He squeezed mine once, long and hard. Each squeeze was a word. "Do, you, love, me?"

"Yes, I, do." "How, much?" And the last squeeze indicated how much. Sometimes he'd squeeze so hard it would hurt.

I got sick. Fever crept beneath my eyes, making it hard to move them. My body ached and my lungs grew sore. It was a familiar feeling. I had had pneumonia seven times since I was born. It was one of those queer things that I was proud of. Julia and Jane were sent away to a college friend of Mom's who lived in the South. Mom couldn't handle more than one sick child and after a while she couldn't even handle one. She said the doctor said that it would be best if I went to the hospital. She said not to worry, that going to the hospital didn't mean I was any more sick than I'd been before. She said that he said it would bring my father back.

I spent two weeks in the hospital and Dad did not come back.

In early September I went home. My sisters were still away. I crawled into bed next to Mom and her arm wrapped around my stomach, pulling me into her chest. The sheets were gentle and smelled of so many things: of Mom's honeysuckle perfume, of detergent, of sweat.

The house was quiet. The television was off. Outside, the sun was sinking into the trees and the sky was striped with paths of color, turning first orange then violet and then a deep red. Every so often Mom would wake and stare, blankly, listening. A web of creases surrounded her eyes and they were swollen. "I love you, little Kate. You love your mother, don't you?" I'd reassure her and then she'd fall asleep again, pulling me with her, deeper against her chest. I lay there trying to keep my eyes closed, but they were heavy and static seemed to sizzle beneath the lids.

Then I heard the sound of wheels rolling over gravel, rolling slowly, cautiously. It was already dark on that side of the house. Carefully, I slipped away from Mom and went to the window. A car was sneaking up the driveway, my father's white Volkswagen. Instantly, I was flooded with joy. I shoved the window to open it, but it wouldn't budge. I wanted to scream out to him. I could see him. He stepped from his car, rising tall above it. I could see his head of black curly hair.

"Dad's back," I shouted. "He's back!" I clapped, turning to Mom, but she was already at the bedroom door, locking it. I shouted at her, *why?*, and my stomach lurched.

"Quick. Be quiet. He's just here to get things," she said. "He's been here before." Her voice was angry and sharp. She wrapped her arm in mine and we moved close to the door. In her other hand she clutched the phone.

Dad's footsteps pounded into the rug as he climbed the stairs to the bedroom door. The banister creaked. Blood banged in my ears.

"Eve," he said, knocking. "Eve. Open the door. Don't be foolish." His voice was impatient, but I could feel he was trying to be calm. "We need to talk."

"Go away," she said. "Go away or I'll call the police." She started dialing on the phone.

Almost instantly they were fighting. Their voices vibrated in waves into my skin. My eyes were wide and stinging.

"You never loved me, Eve. Always your father, always your father. I could never live up to your father." The picture of Granpy stood on Mom's bedside table; it had been there since I could remember. He was a tall, distinguished man with graying hair and a strong jaw. He'd died when I was six, two years before Dad left.

"That's too easy, Ian," Mom screamed. They were both screaming at once. About Camille Cain, then about us, then about money.

"I'm going to come in there, Eve. I'll smash this door down if I have to." The room was a mess. The drawers of Mom's bureau hung open and clothes streamed out of them. Dangling bras and underwear. Her taffeta dresses. Her purse strap. Her robe. Books and papers and magazines littered the floor. The slow stir of the ceiling fan made the papers rise and sink as if they were breathing. Mom was a clean person. She loved being clean. She loved washing behind our ears and scrubbing our necks. I felt embarrassed for her.

"Kate was sick, damn it," Mom said.

"You spend up a storm. What do you think? That money grows on trees? You put the children in the hospital and run up thousands of dollars in doctors' bills. What do you think I'm made of?" I could hear the panic in his voice. I couldn't breathe properly. I had to concentrate to breathe. My tongue felt too big for my mouth. "I won't work another day in my life. I'll go to Hawaii and live on the beach. I'm not going to be burdened with all these bills that you run up carelessly."

I felt all this was my fault.

"Daddy," I blurted out. I wanted to explain. There was silence, loud silence. Mom and I sank down into the rug, which was prickly with little things. It hadn't been vacuumed in weeks.

"Kate?" he asked. "Is that you, Kate? Sweetie?"

"I was sick, Daddy," I said. "Really." I swallowed. I needed to swallow.

"Oh, baby," he said, drawing out the words. "I didn't mean . . . " He stopped. I could hear him on the other side of the door, sinking down as we had. I pushed my cheek into the hard wood door. Maybe his cheek was pushed into the hard wood door too. "Baby. Open the door for Daddy."

I thought if I just let him in everything would be all right. I could explain. I thought if I opened the door they could work things out. He would come back. Everyone loved Mom. Waiters and store clerks and teachers, the mothers and fathers of our friends, they all fell in love with Mom because she was always so interested in them and their lives. It was impossible to believe that she didn't love Dad or that Dad didn't still love her.

"Kate," he said. Kate. Kate. It rang in my ears. I reached for the knob and as I did, Mom clutched my arm. In her hand my skin was soothed. Her hands were soft and warm and gentle.

"Tell him no, Kate," she whispered in my ear. "Tell him you don't want to see him."

I said, "No, Dad." A thick lump caught in my throat and my mouth became dry. "No Daddy, we don't want you. We want you to leave, Daddy." Then I started screaming it. "Leave, Daddy." My face burned. In fact, my whole body burned. I screamed blindly. "Leave, Daddy." And then I heard him cry. I wanted to hear him cry.

The police came discreetly, without flashing lights. Two solid men in solid blue suits. I heard them coming up the stairs and I heard the crackling of their walkie-talkies. I heard them ask my father to leave. From the window in the late evening light I saw Dad being escorted to his car, a shadow between two solid figures, his arms linked in theirs. Gently they set him in his car. And just as quietly as he came Dad drove away.

ANACONDA

Anton pinned money to our bedroom doors. Fives. Tens. Twenties. Once we got a fifty. The bills smelled acrid and wonderful, and there was something dusty about the way they felt on your fingers. I loved their smell; it got into my hands just as garlic does and I started to sniff my hands all the time just to smell that smell.

Monday nights were Anton's poker nights and Tuesday mornings, early, when it was still gray and misty outside, I'd check my door. Finding the money sent a rush through me, like the thrill of finding an Easter egg—the good kind, stuffed with cash.

It was spring now and Mom was out of bed all the time because Anton was coming around a lot. He drove a turquoise Cadillac with windows that hummed like flies as he put them up and down. He played high-stakes poker with hundred-dollar antes and thousand-dollar chips. He played with a group of real estate pirates and a local policeman who didn't ticket Mom the time he pulled her over. Practiced men, who played in the Islands and Las Vegas. Some of the men were worth three hundred million dollars, Anton told us. "I play with a man, Mickey Eager, worth so much he doesn't trust the banks," Anton said, squinting and winking. He was always squinting and winking. It made you feel he was including you in something big and mischievous. "Keeps all his money in gold Krugerrands—fifty thousand of them—buried in his backyard."

There was something dazzling about a man worth so much money. My father had told me that a human body wasn't worth much. He said maybe all told the value of the individual pieces—the heart, lungs, liver, kidney—would be worth a dollar and a quarter in a scientific laboratory.

Julia put her money from Anton toward ballet lessons. With mine I bought rocks and minerals for my collection. Jane left her money tacked to her bedroom door in one long snaking strip. Only a few bills disappeared, borrowed by Mom for groceries. Jane didn't trust Anton anymore. She said he'd never leave his wife. His wife was a Texan oil heiress and also a nun. She'd been a nun when Anton was a priest and while they both served God they fell in love. Jane and Julia called her "the wife." I called her "the nun." I liked "the nun" better. I liked thinking of her in a black habit with those wide strips of white banding her face and neck.

The first bill on my door had been small. A five. But it seemed large at the time, and beautiful, scrolled with important fives, fives all over it. And the memorial. Thin white lines webbed over green like lace. A red pushpin tacked the five to my door and when I saw the money I felt suddenly guilty because I wanted to steal it. The hall was quiet and cold. It didn't occur to me the bill was mine. Mom's door at the end of the hall was locked, bolted now because before Julia was always trying to pop the lock with knitting needles and straightened-out clothes hangers, trying to prove that Anton spent the nights. Julia said you could smell it when Mom had had sex. She said sex smelled like bad breath.

Nothing got by us. In the mornings, from the school bus, we'd see Anton's Cadillac hidden beneath a willow tree, down an overgrown lane not far from our house. It reminded me of a boat I'd seen, sunk in the shallows of a lake.

In the hall, I thought about the three of us behind that door, in bed with Mom, watching the *Late, Late Show* after Dad had left—how we didn't do that anymore. The house creaked, scaring me. I stared at the five-dollar bill, my skin in goose bumps. I noticed Jane's door and then Julia's, each with money pinned there the same as mine, so I snatched the bill.

"Act smart when he's around," Mom would warn. "He's an intellectual, a thinker. He's a philosopher writing the definitive treatise on the psychology of love."

All over town Anton spray painted I LOVE YOU EVE in bold blue paint. Drizzles of paint slithered down street signs, polka-dotted the pavement, decorated the windows of stores and the water tower that loomed over town. I LOVE YOU EVE. He'd been writing his treatise for ten years and was still on chapter one.

"He's married," Jane said. We weren't suppose to talk about that, but Jane did all the time.

"Don't be difficult," Mom said. She pushed her thumbnail into her lip and thought, running her eyes over us. The nun lived in Europe with their children. Mom worried about her coming back. She didn't tell Julia or me that she worried. She told Jane, who told Julia, who told me. Mom confided in Jane as if they were sisters and sometimes it seemed Jane really believed she was Mom's sister.

"If he leaves the wife he'll have nothing, because she won't give him any money," Jane said to us when we were alone. "Especially if she can prove he's had an affair." I didn't like thinking about Mom as an affair. Dad's girlfriend, Camille, with her long ginger hair, was an affair. Julia said Camille "oozed sexuality" as if sexuality were something liquid. I said that this reminded me of bulldog ants I'd seen on a nature program, which oozed infertile eggs called "omelettes" to feed their young.

"That's absolutely disgusting," Julia said.

"If the nun goes back to the nunnery," I said, "she'll leave Anton her money." It was really an ashram in India that she was considering, but I liked "nunnery" better. "You can't take money to a nunnery unless you donate it, and I don't think anybody would throw away all that money." That's what Julia had said. I liked using Julia's thoughts. They made me feel smart.

"We need to protect Mom," Jane said, giving us her serious look.

When Anton started coming to our house for dinner he always brought enormous boxes filled with wonderful food—Hydrox cookies, ice cream, doughnuts, slippery steaks of such a brilliant red I was afraid Mom wouldn't let us eat them. Mom didn't care much about food, and since Dad left we'd eaten creamed chipped beef for dinner every night. It was pasty and gooey, like plaster of paris, and it was slopped over well-done toast and was very salty because we always forgot to rinse the beef. The food Anton brought glistened like birthday presents in its cellophane packaging, and we tore into it greedily.

The thing about Anton and Mom was that they really knew how to have fun together. "We have the same sense of adventure," Mom would say. And they always included us on their adventures. In the beginning he and Mom would take us for late-afternoon drives, so that Anton could get to know us, scaring us with stories. They drove us to the site where the murdered Lindbergh baby was found. They drove us to the home of a woman who'd chopped off her mother's head. It was strange to be scared by Anton; it made us feel protected.

At dinner one night, Anton told us that he came from a family of murderers in Corsicana, Texas. His grandfather, Johnny Darling, had killed at least three men—two black men, shot in the forehead for tipping their hats at his wife, and a white man, his brother-in-law, shot square in the back for writing an article for the *Corsicana Star* in defense of the black men. For the first two Johnny Darling was charged five dollars for disturbing the peace. After the latter, he skipped town.

"You wouldn't believe him," Mom said brightly, "but he's got the article from the *Corsicana Star.*" A big smile spread across her lips; she was proud.

"It's true," he nodded. "It's true." He sat forward in his chair,

Dad's chair, at the head of our kitchen table. His eyes sparkled and he fingered his chin, resurrecting stories and details. I hoped we were acting smart. You could always count on Julia to act real smart. Jane slumped back in her chair and Mom shot her a look. For Mom, sometimes, it was as if our whole world depended on what Jane thought, as if Jane knew all the answers. "Clairvoyant," Julia would say.

In town Anton had a reputation. People were divided. Some thought he was grand. "Unique," they'd say. "An individual with charisma—he'd give his soul to help you out." Others suspected him and didn't want their wives doing therapy with him. They said he had "multiple" wives. "Multiple wives," Julia would repeat, flexing her left eyebrow. And from the multiple wives he had multiple children, who were scattered about the world.

"They're just jealous," Mom would say. That's what she'd always say when someone criticized her.

Anton was a lot of things, but to me he was a poker player and I liked cards. I could shuffle evenly and quickly, and could deal with one hand. I knew a lot of games, but I didn't know poker yet.

Anaconda high and low. Up and down the river. Five-card draw. Seven-card stud. Hold 'em—a Texas game. Anton taught us the different varieties one evening over dinner. He said it would be good for us to learn poker. Poker made you tough, and we needed to be tough and to trust.

Anaconda: *Eunectes murinus*. I learned that name at a Coney Island freak show. The snakes could live up to twenty-eight years and grow over forty feet long and the females could give birth to seventy-two babies at once. Though they were strong enough to crush a doe, they ate only small animals and birds. "The hug of death is how they kill," that's what the freak showing us the snake had said.

"Whichever game you play, babes, it's all in the face," Anton said to us. "You have to know how to hold the same face all the time regardless of your hand. Mickey Eager's the only man I've ever known to consistently hold his face." I thought about the

Krugerrands and tried to hold my face still. "An inscrutable face that gives no hint of your thoughts or feelings."

The kitchen smelled of lemon polish. Mom's Christmas cactus thrived on a windowsill, in full crimson bloom. The long stems fountained over the pot like narrow green ribbons cut with pinking shears. The fire hissed. The five of us sat at the table eating steaks and grits. Big slabs of steak, trimmed with thick translucent gristle. The steaks reminded me of Dad. Dad loved steaks. I remembered how he'd said when he died he wanted us to have a feast and eat thick juicy steaks with peppercorns to celebrate his life. I wondered where Dad was now.

After dinner we played a few open hands of poker to learn the rules. Julia asked a lot of questions about the rules. She always asked a million questions to look smart. The rules were a cinch. It was holding the face that was the difficult part, and already mine was twitching.

"Keep your face straight, stupid," Julia said. She wore her ballet outfit and sat next to Anton, flirting with him. He kept fingering the fabric of her tutu, telling her how pretty it was. Mom liked us to flirt with him.

"Fuck off," I said. I wished I were wearing my tutu instead of the velvet dress.

"Kate!" Mom said. But the tone of her voice was light and I could tell she didn't care. There was a lot she didn't care about anymore. She didn't care if we licked our fingers or if we put our elbows on the table. "Elbows off the table, Mable," she used to say. But I knew she wouldn't be caught dead saying something as stupid as that now.

Jane had her stubborn mouth on and was silent. She didn't like to flirt. Julia said Jane didn't know how.

"Don't mind Jane," Mom said to Anton, smiling. "She's just shy."

"If you have a good face you can bluff and bluffing's a lot of fun. There's a lot to it, but it's really quite simple. A matter of simple psychology," Anton said.

He asked us if we'd brought our money. My face dropped. He

winked and smiled and then Mom smiled and knit us together with her eyes. Anton pulled out his wallet and gave us each a twenty-dollar bill, which relieved me. The money was new and clean and I clutched it in my hand. Money seemed like nothing to Anton. Dad never gave us money like that, just handing it out as if it were nothing. Mom said Dad was "cheap" and all they fought about now was money.

We exchanged the twenties for stacks of different-colored chips. They were glossy on one side. The other side was soft, like a rabbit's foot. We stacked the chips in towers in front of us, turrets of gold. The twenties lay in a glorious heap by the carousel of chips that Anton had brought. I was going to win it all. Of the three of us I was the generous one. Jane didn't care about money and Julia kept close hold of hers. The one time she had loaned me money she'd charged me interest. Julia peered over her chips at me and flexed her left eyebrow. I'm going to win it all, I thought again.

Anton turned the lights off and the kitchen went velvety dark, leaving only the two lit candles in the middle of the table. Everything familiar vanished for an instant, and reappeared in the murky gray shadows. The room became a poker room, a casino. I imagined Las Vegas and the Islands, and the real estate pirates, sitting around a smoke-shrouded table with their whiskeys, their thousand-dollar chips clinking. The candle flames moved and twisted, although the air was still. Wineglasses on a shelf glittered neon. I thought about the thirty thousand a year Anton earned playing cards and of what it could do for us. No more creamed chipped beef, I thought.

After three closed hands we were hooked. It turned out I had a knack for gambling. All you had to do was bluff and keep your face straight. Even Jane was hooked. She tried not to show it, but she was concentrating on Anton's words just as carefully as the rest of us. A giddiness rushed through us as our turrets of chips diminished and grew. Even Mom had changed, although she had said, "I don't want to play. You play for me." Her green eyes glittered, flirting with ours. She had the same magical radiance that winning or almost winning brings. We would do anything for her now.

Raise by raise the pots grew. We were bluffing like crazy. Lying freely and openly did something for us, made us feel we were getting away with a lot, like we had something on each other. I won two hands with pairs—sixes and eights. Suckers, I wanted to say, but instead held my face straight, using my arms as a scoop to sweep in the chips. The next hand, I had a pair of fives. I bluffed fiendishly with my knack. I had an inscrutable face. I bet. Anton raised. I raised again. Everyone folded. I could feel the blood in my veins.

"Let's see," Julia said, reaching for my cards.

"No, no," Anton said, stopping her. "She doesn't have to show." That was the best part—you could bluff and get away with it, and no one would know. With gambling there was always something more, something better just within your grasp, just in that next hand, which made even losing enjoyable.

"But you can't bluff all the time, babe," Anton said, winning a hand I had tried to bluff. He gave me a stern, instructive look and gathered his chips. "That too sets a pattern, and you don't want to be read."

After that hand he won several in a row. Our turrets shrank. He left his chips in a messy pile. Mom smiled. She was tipsy. When she had a few glasses of wine the world would seem utterly perfect to her. Dad used to tease her for getting tipsy on one glass. I tried to remember how he'd tease, but couldn't.

"You see now, babes, a lot of subtlety goes into the game," Anton said. His eyes sparkled and the candlelight caught a gold filling in his mouth. A wonderful seriousness spread over his face. He wanted us to learn—to be tough and to trust. "Once you learn to bluff you need to learn how to read bluffs," he said. "You can win regularly if you know how to spot nervous tics." He pulled a silver cigarette holder from his breast pocket and took out a skimpy cigarette that looked almost like a match. "Say you see a player turn his ring while betting high, you wouldn't be a fool if you challenged him." He touched his ring, the turquoise so large it looked dangerous. Then he took a long, deep puff and held it inside for a while. He exhaled and cleared his throat.

"So likewise, the other players will be looking for your tics. It's the tics that'll give you away." He paused again and studied us. His big round head seemed suspended on his neck like a globe. I loved him. "A friend of mine in Texas, Bobby O'Donnell, had an ear tic that gave him away. It was involuntary, but he insisted on a good game of cards."

Anton's voice became particularly thick and cottony as he remembered Texas—long, powerful, drawn-out vowels. He half smiled. I looked at the heap of money. I was impatient to win the game. "Lost his entire ranch, two thousand acres, in one poker game. Lost every last acre and also the house, down to the bearskin rug. Bobby was a terrible card player. There's another lesson here. Always remember, never start off with more money than your opponents when playing high-stakes poker." His eyes sharpened and he shook his head in disapproval.

"See, Eve," he said. "If you were playing, your tic would be your thumbnail against your lip."

Mom smiled and reached for his cigarette and took the tiniest puff.

"And Julia." Anton looked at her. "You twist your hair." She was twirling a curl into a sausage. She quit and sat on her hands. I stopped too; I was picking at my knuckles.

"Kate, you fiddle with your fingers." He grinned at me and squinted. I hadn't realized we had all these ticks and my dress felt suddenly tight.

"And Jane." They stared at each other for a long time and I thought any minute Jane would break into a smile. Then her face changed and became serious. God, I hoped she wouldn't get difficult. A smile waited in Anton's eyes as they continued to stare. "Jane," he said, "you press your palm into your cheek." Jane kept staring, until at last he looked away. I thought of the four of us with our tics, all ticking at once around the table. Mom's thumb rubbed her lip and Julia twirled her hair. I started to laugh.

"It's not funny, it's sad," Jane said. She looked down at the table, staring at the litter of dishes and dried-up bits of steak and fat. "I don't like this." She got up and excused herself from the game, shoving her chips back in the carousel without getting any money for them.

"Babe, don't get discouraged," Anton said gently, dealing the rest of us another hand of draw. "You're doing fine. You're a good player." Tender like a father.

"It's a school night," Jane murmured. "I have homework to do."

"You should pay attention to him," Mom said smiling. She sipped her wine. "He makes a living at this." Jane ignored her and cleared the table noisily.

"Just let her quit," I said. She loved to make a scene. She liked it when we begged her to do stuff. I bet she wanted Anton to beg her.

"Don't mind Jane," Julia said. "She's just antisocial."

Jane turned on a lamp and then sat down by the fire to read. We ignored her.

The poker game went on. I was almost feeling pretty, playing cards. My velvet dress felt good. I thought I'd wear it to school when I'd get some of my friends to play. I'd take the rich ones down by the brook behind the school. I could almost hear the water in the creek rippling. The sky would be blue with a few lazy clouds. Billy Keaton came to mind, with his eggplant head and the wad of cash he carried around in the front pocket of his jeans. He loved to show it off, fanning it between his fingers, flapping it against his palm. I was going to win that wad. Thirty thousand a year. I wanted to be tough. My palms sweated. My temples ached just thinking about all that money.

Julia dealt a hand of Anaconda and I got a pair of tens. She bet, and I raised her. My first card was another ten and a chill raced through me. I studied Anton. His face was as straight as a quill. I studied Julia. Her left eyebrow rose. I thought she must be bluffing. It was a big pot. The next two cards were a one-eyed jack and the Suicide King—the king of hearts with his sword pointing into his skull. They looked glorious together—three tens, king high. "I raise seventy-five cents," I said, and slid three red chips into the pot, letting them clink against the other chips. I loved that sound.

I rubbed my knuckles and then quickly stopped, hoping nobody had seen me. Julia raised. I raised again.

"It's eleven o'clock," Jane said. She came to the table, looming over it. The candlelight lit her face, making it spooky and beautiful. Her big eyes beamed. "It's time for bed."

"Bug off," Julia said and we began our showdown, rolling our cards over one at a time, betting with each roll.

"Let them finish the hand," Mom murmured to Jane, watching the game. I hated it when the two of them started acting like Moms together. Jane cleared the rest of the plates, clattering dishes on top of each other. She loaded the dishwasher. My three tens lay on the table beautifully with the jack and the king. "Three tens, king high," I announced and turned to Anton, smiling. He smiled back, but said that with three of a kind, high cards were irrelevant.

"I have a full house. I won," Julia said turning over her last card. She had three twos and two threes. That's not fair, I thought. Julia's the cheap one. She can't win. Quickly, she swept the chips to her pile.

"Time for bed," Jane said again, flicking on the overhead lights. My eyes stung from the brightness. The room became just a kitchen again, but I didn't care.

"Good job, babe," Anton said to Julia. My face dropped and all that possibility inside vanished. I had only a handful of chips left. I felt ugly. I thought hard. Then I filled again, thinking I'd take Jane's chips. Nobody was using them. I decided I'd take a loan from Anton. That would be fair. I'd win it back. I'd win the next hand, I could feel it.

"Anton?" I asked. He looked at me. "Could you loan me ten dollars of chips?" I held him with my eyes. Mom laughed.

"Come on, Kate," Jane said. I hated her.

"I don't think it's right for Kate to be gambling," she said to Mom. "It makes her greedy."

"Bitch," I said. I could tell she wanted a fight. "Can I borrow ten dollars?" I asked again.

"You lost, Kate. Game's over. Time for bed," Jane said. Her hands rested on her hips. Her hair, released from its braids, was loose and wild. Her face was pale in the bright light.

"Good night, sweeties," Mom said to us. She gave me a look that told me to go with Julia and Jane.

I said I wanted to play another game. Anton put down the cards and counted out Julia's chips. I hated Julia.

"We'll play another game tomorrow night," Mom said. Her expression was pleasant. She was happy we wanted to play.

"That's not fair," I said.

"Don't be a poor loser," Julia said.

"You're coming too, Mom. It's late," Jane said.

"I'll be up in a bit. Now do as I say."

"No. You promised you'd read to Kate, and besides it's already late." Jane turned on the dishwasher. There was something wrong with it that made it chug and cough. We were all fighting, we all hated each other.

"Anton," Jane said, "I think it would be better if you went home now."

"What's the big deal?" Julia said to Jane. "You know Anton spends the night." I thought of Anton's Cadillac hidden down the overgrown lane.

"They sleep together," I announced. "You know that." I liked saying "sleep together" instead of *fuck*. It was more grown-up.

"Shut up," Jane said to both of us.

"Fuck off."

A glass slipped out of Jane's hand and shattered. Silence. I could still hear the sounds of glass flying everywhere.

"Enough," Mom said. Long and slow. For a moment there was more silence. I was afraid to look at her.

"I have had enough of you, Jane," Mom said, speaking slowly. "You have been an embarrassment all evening." She stood up. "Why don't you tell Anton why you're being so impossible?"

Jane murmured that it was a school night. Her voice was small.

"A school night?" Mom said, staring at Anton. Her face flushed.

I felt sorry for Anton being caught up in one of our fights. I was afraid he wouldn't like us anymore. God, I wished Jane would just behave. She could drop it right now and everything would be fine.

"Jane," I said, but Mom didn't let me speak.

"You see, Jane doesn't want me to have a life," she said.

"Eve," Anton said gently, "Jane hasn't been difficult. Don't antagonize her."

But Mom pressed on. "She's been difficult all right. I want you to hear what she has to say. She thinks she's so smart, understanding everything."

"Come off it, Mom," Julia said, wetting her fingertips to put out the candles. I thought she looked stupid in her ballet outfit. I bet the only thing on her mind was cashing in the chips. Greedy pig, I thought.

"Don't tell me to come off it," Mom snapped.

"Mo-m," Jane said, drawing out the word.

Mom grabbed Jane's arm and yanked at her. I knew what that felt like.

"Jane's afraid of you, Anton," Mom said. "Why don't you tell him, Jane?"

Mom kept repeating her name. You knew you were in big trouble when she'd keep repeating your name. It was eerie the way she did that—as if the name became something she possessed, something that didn't belong to you. I was glad she wasn't mad at me. For the most part I tried hard to stay out of trouble.

Mom yanked Jane forward. Jane looked like a little girl suddenly. Younger than me. Her shoulders slouched forward as if she were carrying something, and suddenly I felt tremendously sad.

"Tell him you think he'll never leave his wife, Jane," Mom said. She pushed Jane toward Anton, still holding her arm. "You see, Jane thinks she's so smart. She tells me you're never going to . . ."

"Mom, shut up," Jane said, shaking herself free.

"Eve," Anton said again. For a moment there was quiet. I could hear Jane breathing. I thought about the nun and looked at Anton. Just looking at him made me feel awful. His eyes were big and afraid, and he was alone standing there. His face didn't seem so lively anymore. He fingered his ring.

"We can talk about this all together, babe," Anton said softly to Jane. "These are big questions and it's late now but we need to talk about these things, babe. It's right to talk about this."

He looked at Julia and me. His eyes were deep and sad. I thought about his children. I imagined he missed them. I thought about Dad and the day he left and felt a knot in my throat, wondering what it was like for him when he chose to leave. I thought about the nun and how she'd call sometimes, the international beeps giving her away. The three of us would press our heads into the receiver, hoping for something that would explain what was happening, give us a clue about what was coming next. We'd listen until she'd hang up.

"We'll have to have another poker game again soon," Anton said, finishing off his wine. He placed a kiss on the top of my head and his fingers rubbed my neck. Then he did the same with Julia and Jane. He hugged Mom quickly and went out. Suddenly I had the feeling that he really did need us, and that made me feel closer to Mom. I felt he needed her too, and that she wanted to be needed. There was still a smell of Anton in the room, a faint scent of rain and smoke.

Headlights flooded the kitchen and then faded as Anton backed his car down the driveway. Mom turned off the dishwasher and the kitchen went silent. "Are you happy, Jane?" she said, her eyes hard.

"You're drunk and stoned," Jane said.

"You are wretched!" Mom screamed in a whisper. Her face was all pink. "Why can't you be nice to my guest? Why can't you just once let me have a life? You don't know how it is? Do you have any idea what it's like with no one to help you out? No one to share your life with? Have fun with? How could I have such a child? Kate and Julia aren't like you."

Julia and I stood still.

"Your guest is a creep," Jane said, quietly but vehemently. "A married creep."

The hand of Anaconda was a mess on the table. The money still lay in its glorious heap. I wondered if Julia would get it all, or if Mom would keep it.

"Get out of my sight," Mom said.

"What are you going to do, hit me?" Jane darted from the room, slamming the door. "He's not going to marry you," she hollered. A ruler and a flyswatter clattered to the floor. I was sorry for Jane. I was sorry for Mom. I was afraid I'd have to take sides.

MORE

After Dad left we were worth thirty dollars. Mom said as much, standing in the kitchen. Early mornings, the dawn sky drained of light. Pale. Mom was pale too in her pale blue robe. She pulled it tight around her neck, clamping it shut with her fist. "Thirty dollars a week. That's nothing," she'd say. "Do you know what thirty dollars a week buys?" The three of us had our heads bowed over large bowls of Cream of Wheat, cereal sunk beneath too much milk and pools of melted brown sugar. But we had to finish all of it before leaving for school, for Dad who waited in the driveway to pick us up. He had won three mornings a week in court. His first victory. And he drove the fifty miles from New York, where he lived now, to our house to drive us the five miles to school. So many mornings just like this, before Anton. Anton came later, in the spring.

Mom in her robe with sleep pressing heavily into her eyes. After eating the Cream of Wheat, we had to do the dishes, then wait while Mom finished packing our lunches, then wait while she ran her fingers through our hair and twisted it into braids, tied little bows at the ends. She moved around calmly, assuredly, determined to make Dad wait. "You need clothes, you know. Thirty dollars a week barely pays for food. You're growing. I can't do it on thirty dollars a week." I thought of Dad in the car, having driven all that way. His plans for the Chocolate Shoppe shot. She'd do anything to delay, to steal back that extra minute she believed was hers.

When just enough time was left to get us to school before the bell, she would release us. Before leaving, we'd tell her a dozen times that we loved her, drilling the words into her to reassure her that going to school with Dad didn't mean we loved him more. We marched out the door, all alike and clean in our yellow slickers or our red duffle coats. We moved cautiously, as if on a tightrope, feeling Mom's eyes on our backs and Dad's on our fronts, pulling us taut. "Thirty dollars a week" tumbled through our heads. In the car my cheek would recoil gently from Dad's warm lips. His soft curls would tickle unpleasantly. "So your mother's finally let you go." I was stiff at first, and quiet, with a pout, as if Mom could see or somehow feel the pout and know that I wasn't betraying her. No matter how hard I tried, after a few miles I'd warm up and by the time I got to school I didn't want to leave.

"I'm not going," I said. The seat belt strapped me into the backseat. Jane had already been left at another school. Julia sat in the front, looking over at me, thinking of ways to tempt me. Outside, other kids spilled off the yellow buses, bright and cheery, their knapsacks dangling over their shoulders. Station wagons driven by mothers with curlers in their hair dropped off children. Quickly. The kids eager to go, slamming the doors without looking back.

"You can come to homeroom with me and we'll sing the national anthem together," Julia said, her eyes hopeful. I ignored her. I hated the national anthem even more than I hated the Pledge of Allegiance. I always got the words wrong and the one time I had gone to Julia's class the kids had looked at me as if I were queer. "What's your big problem," I'd wanted to say, but didn't.

My fingers rolled my lunch bag into a scroll. Rolling and unrolling. It was a plastic bag from a loaf of bread, transparent, revealing what was inside.

"Katy," Dad said. "I love you, Katy." He hugged me, a big hug, and he pressed his lips to my forehead. I wanted to stay in his arms, in his car, forever. My toes pinched in my boots. My socks had fallen down and bunched under my feet. Kids swarmed near the entrances to the flat green school like bees buzzing around a hive. It was a lime-green school of concrete the color of which reminded me of the skirt my teacher Mrs. Jackson wore. She liked to take me into her office and ask me how I felt, and she'd stare at me while I said nothing, as if she liked watching me bleed.

"I'll be back Friday. We'll go to the Chocolate Shoppe. I promise," Dad said, releasing me. Then he offered me a dollar because he knew how much I liked the hot lunches in the cafeteria. They cost thirty-five cents, with milk forty. A dollar would be enough to last until Friday. It did something for me, buying those lunches in line with other kids.

"Can I have two dollars?" I asked. I thought I'd give the other to Julia because I knew she'd never ask. She never asked Dad for anything. He gave me two.

Then Jane stopped coming. She marched down the driveway past us and onto the bus, without even looking or nodding at Dad. The fat driver—so fat he'd have to be buried in a piano case, Julia would say—sucked shut the door, sucking Jane inside, where she sat upright, staring straight ahead. "He abandoned us," she would say to me and Julia, sounding like Mom. "He asked for it," she would say. To him she would say nothing. Dad stood in the driveway, dappled dark and light in the shadow of trees, watching her go, having pleaded with her until he cried.

Sometimes he'd break in half at the steering wheel. He'd pull over by the side of the road, bend his head into the wheel and cry. "Dear God, just let me have my girls, just let me love my girls." I'd be in the backseat watching Julia kiss him and pat him, listen to her tell him how much she loved him. Her head of blond curls would blend with his dark ones as she kissed him, bowed over him like a parent, soothing him. But I'd be thinking about the time, looking at the second hand on the dashboard clock as it spun around and around, thinking about the Chocolate Shoppe and the woman who served us, her funny thick accent filled with Vs and her checkered apron with the clean white bib of lace. She always drooled an extra dollop of whipped cream over our hot chocolates. I wanted to get to the Chocolate Shoppe in time to have two. As Dad cried, I thought about the comic books and the candies I'd have him buy me. I rocked myself, my weight resting on my palms.

I wanted to get. Get, get, get. Anything get. When he won weekend visitation rights I had him take me shopping for an extra dress, a pair of shoes, rocks and minerals for my collection. I had him give me extra quarters for the Magic Fingers box that vibrated the beds in the hotel rooms we'd stay in when he took us on surprise trips. Hershey, Pennsylvania. Atlantic City. At first I wanted to share with Julia, who didn't ask, and then I didn't want to share at all. At the chocolate factory I insisted we tour the place twice to watch the Olympic-sized pools of undulating chocolate and the silver machines that spit kisses. At the Arcade in Atlantic City we went on every single ride and played every single game. I marched around like a brat, dizzied by my determination and that creepy arcade music and the spinning of wheels, rubber flipping over nails. The clapping of waves and a cold, lonely boardwalk. Sunny skies with fast-moving clouds. Never enough. "Thirty dollars a week." A dress, a shoe, a rock, a stuffed animal. He gave. He lost Jane. He wasn't going to lose me. More. I wanted to be worth more.

THE PROMISE OF ANTON

We slept in gas stations all across America to get to Anton. It was early July and we were running away from Dad, who was about to move back to town. We drove fast in our green station wagon, toward Big Sur. Anton was giving a workshop at Esalen on "Romantic Love and Sexual Equality."

We felt we had won. Even Jane felt we'd won. The nun had gone to India to join the ashram and Anton had promised he'd marry Mom.

All over the car were maps: maps of each state we would pass; one map of the entire country. I had collected them before we left. I loved maps. I was afraid of getting lost. I knew where everything was—the Grand Canyon, Monument Valley, Yellowstone. For months I had wanted to go to the Grand Canyon, simply because the Thanksgiving after Dad left, he had planned a trip to take us there. He had bought tickets, even for Jane, but at the last minute we didn't go because Mom said we'd do badly in school if we missed any. She said we wouldn't learn our multiplication tables and if we didn't know them, then we'd never get into college.

It seemed impossible that one road could connect all that land, but it did. On the map of the country, I drew one solid red line from my town in New Jersey to California. It went straight across Interstate 70, one bend up at Denver to 80. I imagined us on that red line and felt safe: that red line like the string through the sleeves of my winter jacket attaching the two mittens.

At midnight Mom would pull into a land lit by neon and the bright orange and red lights of trucks. She never stopped earlier. It was a waste of time, she said, her body leaning forward, eyes hard on the road.

The stations were always the same, glowing islands in black fields of grain. The starry sky became lost in the milky haze of lights. It was darkest near the bathrooms, so we parked there. Mom fixed our beds, unrolling the sleeping bags over the front and back seats. Her hands smoothed the fabric down as gently as she did our bedspreads at home. The four of us curled into each other and tried to fall asleep: Mom and Jane in the front, Julia and I in the back. All night long truckers came and went. Night belonged to the trucks: the sighing and revving of their engines was a comfort, a lullaby.

That first night in Ohio, I told Mom that I didn't like to stay in gas stations. They were dirty. We couldn't change into our nightgowns, brush our teeth or wash our hands. The bathrooms smelled so bad it was hard to breathe.

I was asleep when we arrived and woke up to the gears grinding. The car filled with light, turning our skin red. Wind still blew in my ears. Then the engine died and the fan whirred off. Julia was asleep next to me, a heap against the door. Through the windows came air, alive, thick with gas and warmed tar.

Outside, trucks crowded the station. I counted eighteen lined up at the edge of black space. One cab light was on and I could see the naked chest of a man getting ready for bed. Big and white. I was sorry for him, sleeping in the station. Pumps stood dull in gray silhouette. In the darkened window of the convenience store Coors and Coke signs flickered.

"What do you think?" Mom asked. She opened her door and the

overhead light shot on. Sounds from outside became distinct: the steady drone of electricity; the ice machine churning; trucks thundering past on the highway.

Suddenly I was alert. "We're not sleeping here," I said. I really didn't think we would. Across the road a sign blinked HOTEL, unfolding one bright red letter at a time. H.O.T.E.L. When we traveled with Dad we always slept in hotels. In hotels I collected things: pens, folders filled with writing paper and postcards, menus, chamois for polishing shoes, bags for laundry. I liked the miniature bars of Ivory and also the keys: ordinary keys attached to big plastic plates with the hotel's address printed in gold. I stole keys just to mail them back. I loved the idea of mailing the key, of it traveling naked without an envelope or a package to conceal it.

"Just keep sleeping, Kate," Julia said without opening her eyes. Her hair was messy but her pink ribbon was still tied in a perfect bow. The car swarmed with junk, maps over us, bags at our feet. The ceiling was close and the vinyl sticky.

"Shut up, Julia." I spat.

"Don't start, Kate," Mom said, glaring back at me. I noticed little wrinkles were appearing beneath her eyes.

"I'm not starting anything."

"I'm tired. Don't nag," Mom said.

"Don't be selfish, Kate. Grow up," Jane said, turning to glare at me. That was her new thing, don't be selfish. Grow up. She was perched in the front, cheek pressed close to Mom's, as if she and Mom were one, acting like mothers together. It made me mad.

"Why can't we stay in the hotel?" I said. "We always used to stay in hotels. Normal people stay in hotels. Dad stays in hotels."

"You're being a child," Jane said.

"I am not being a child," I yelled.

"Oh come off it," Julia said to both of us.

But then Mom's voice turned as sharp as a slap. "If you think *he's* so *normal,* then go home. It's his fault, Kate. He didn't give me a chance, Kate. He's cheated *us,* Kate." She got out of the car and slammed the door. The light went out and the sound of the door smashed into my ear. Julia gave me a protective look.

In a second Mom was back, heaving the sleeping bags in on us. "I'll send you home if you love him so much. I'm trying my hardest to plan fun things for you. But I'll send you home. This isn't easy, you know. What has your father done for you, Kate? What? Tell me! What has he goddamn done for you?" At first I was afraid she'd wake the truckers. But then I didn't care.

When Mom finished yelling, she gave me the silent treatment. I shriveled in the cold. I was alone, leaning against the door. Jane and Julia pretended to be asleep. Outside, the trucks swarmed at the exit coming off the highway for the night. Bright polished trucks: orange trucks; green trucks; white and sparkling; smooth like an ice-skating-rink trucks. All the lights of the semitrailers twinkled. They were majestic, almost beautiful. A carousel, a caravan of twinkling lights.

I thought about my father trying to call us and how the phone would ring in our empty house. I was mad that we'd left. I was mad that we hadn't said good-bye.

In my suitcase I had the gold rock he'd given me for my collection, and I wanted it now. It was deep down in my suitcase with my prospector's pick and my chisel. I'd brought my tools, all but the rock tumbler, because Dad had always said that the West was where geology was happening. He had always said it was so active you could see it out there, see the world being made, unlike in the East, where the activity had happened millions of years before. Dad had wanted to take us to the Grand Canyon so that we could contrast East and West, so that we could see layers of time and a cross section of the earth's history—read it in the canyon walls. He had spent hours lecturing us about the geochronology of the Grand Canyon, preparing us. He said that the story of rocks could be read there like words in a book. He loved those words, those names, and he'd repeat them to us over and over just to hear the sounds of them—Vishnu Schist, Coconino Sandstone, Muav Limestone, the Toroweap Formation and Bright Angel Shale. He'd sing them to us like a song, his face radiant and thrilled and we in turn came to love them. Bright Angel—that name was wonderful, though it didn't sound as if it could be the name of a rock, a shale from the

Cambrian period that represented seventeen million years of time, or a creek named by John Wesley Powell, the one-handed geologist who first explored the Colorado, as my father had explained to us. Rather, the name sounded like something spiritual, that seemed to hold a promise, something named by God.

I dug blindly through our luggage in the back, making noise. I had to have my rock. The gray, ugly rock that was a nugget of the rock that gold comes from. I thought about Dad in South Africa traveling the 6,800 feet down into the ground to get it for me himself. It always seemed peculiar to me that gold was the ugliest rock in my collection. The rock was there in my suitcase and when I found it I held it tightly in my hand until my palm hurt.

Julia's warm body snuck next to mine. I felt her hands on my arm and her lips coming close to my ear. "You're my best sister," she whispered. Double load, thirty-six wheeler trucks. Tubular trucks. Ice trucks. Oil trucks. Milk trucks. Tiny trucks without their eighteen-wheeler load. So tiny they looked muted and malformed. Powerless midgets. And I think I almost fell asleep.

"Kate," Mom said. A long time had passed.

I didn't answer.

"Oh, Kate, I'm sorry. I'm sorry for yelling." Her voice came from the front seat. I couldn't see her head. "Katy, speak to me." Just voice. Soft voice. "You still love your mother, sweetheart?" A car raced up to the pumps and screeched to a halt. Music blared from the radio. The first car all night, except for ours. It cheered me for a second. The driver went to the closed convenience store and banged his fists on the door. In a flash he was back in his car, screeching away. Vanishing into highway. I hoped he would run out of gas.

"Can we go to the Grand Canyon?" I finally asked. At first I wanted to make her mad again. I knew that she'd know why I wanted to go to the Grand Canyon. But she didn't get mad. She sighed, relieved that I'd spoken, happy to have me back on her side again.

"Oh, Kate. When we get to Anton we can do anything. When

we get to Anton everything will be different. You'll see, honey. He has a beautiful family. It will be fun. I promise."

That's what she said all across America. And there was so much hope in her voice and smile that we believed it. Even Jane believed it. I remembered poker. I still had some of that money; I had twenty dollars; I'd turned it into a traveler's check. When we got to Anton there would be money and beds and kids and we'd travel to exciting places. First to Esalen—a camp by the ocean, Mom said, with fun things to do for kids: horseback riding and swimming. There would be naturally heated pools, endless gardens and flat lawns for croquet. Then on to Disneyland, Hollywood, and Sea World—anywhere we wanted, the Grand Canyon, anywhere. Anton had five children—Nicholas, Caroline, Sofia, Timothy and Finny. "There's a boy for each of you," Mom would say, smiling and happy, looking young again. She really wanted it to work. There was nothing more in the world she wanted. "A boy for each of you and you'll all fall in love. I promise."

We slept in two Essos, a Jenney, a Chevron, and a Gulf. Five stations, that's how long it took. I wrote the names down on a pad. I wrote everything down: the states we passed through; the towns we stopped in, even if it was just to have a sandwich—Buckeye, Terre Haute, Junction City, Denver, Laramie, Elko, Winnemucca. I wanted to remember. There was so much I had already forgotten.

During the day the road became ours again. Dark endless space turned into fields of sunflowers and corn, wide and open like the ocean or the sky. And the trucks turned suddenly dull, all their polish and majesty replaced by stains of exhaust and black trails of fumes. By day the trucks were something to flirt with. We stuck our hands out the window and pulled on imaginary chains so they'd blow their air horns as we sailed past.

We woke early. Mom would get a cup of coffee from the convenience store and the key to the bathroom. A heavy sleeplessness lingered on our eyelids, but we were young and it soon washed away.

During the days, Jane sat in the front doing needlepoint. She was making a pillow with yellow finches and apple trees. Julia and I, in the back, licked S&H Green Stamps into their little books, making the paper crinkly and substantial. We would only let Mom go to gas stations that gave stamps. The signs hung alone on their own pole like a flag, red letters surrounded by a green that was a prettier shade than the green of money. "We're gonna get something for nothing," Julia said. We were saving for a lawn mower—279 books. We had six and a whole lot of time.

On an old cassette player we listened to "Ob la di, ob la da" over and over to learn the words by heart. Julia fell in love with Ringo Starr and none of us cared. We let her have him.

I grew used to being in the car with the window open and the wind against my face and the steady rhythm of the wheels rolling over all that highway. I thought a lot about Anton. I wondered if he were waiting for us to get to him.

"Kate?" Mom said. "Do you still have the twenty dollars?" We were at a service station in Junction City. It was early and we had just woken up. Mom's head was bent over her purse and she was thumbing through her wallet frantically.

My face twitched. "Yeah," I said. I wanted to wash my hands. Julia and Jane were in the bathroom.

"I think I'm going to have to borrow a little bit of it. I'm running low. Is that okay, sweetie? I'll pay you back when we get there." She didn't look at me. She just continued to fumble through her wallet as if hoping to find something hidden.

I paid for the gas all by myself. It cost $6.75. We got lots of Green Stamps and Mom took the change. I remember what I was wearing, a long beige dress with eyelet trim and blue satin ribbons. I was always wearing pretty dresses. It was dirty, though, filthy actually.

There was a lot of candy by the cash register, displayed on racks, colorful and infinite, but I didn't want any of it. I thought I'd never eat candy again. The woman at the counter was spindly thin with blue-powdered eyelids. She had stringy black hair. I can still remember, signing away that check to her, how it felt. The sharp point of the ballpoint almost ripping the waxy paper of my American Express cheque. My one and only, my first travelers' traveling check, a beautiful purple blue with elegantly swirling script. Even "cheque" was spelled more gloriously, with a *q*. It was like signing up for something big. I was almost nine. I felt large then. Swollen. Grown up. Better than my sisters.

Just outside Junction City. The land was flat, a blanket of yellow wheat and corn. Enormous sprinklers fanned water, and silver puddles collected big as ponds. A strong wind beat against our car, nearly visible, making it sway back and forth. It was early, six-thirty. The road was empty.

"This wind is giving me a headache. How can people live out here?" Mom asked. A farm popped up by the side of the road, unprotected by trees, a big white house near a barn with a red silo. An island in wheat fields. Behind it in the distance a black cloud exploded into the sky like a giant mushroom. Smoke flooded the horizon, streaming high into the air in one violent rush.

"What do you think that is?" I asked.

"I'm not sure," Mom answered.

"It's an oil refinery gone up," Julia suggested.

"There are no oil refineries here," Jane said.

"It's probably a dump in some town."

"Do you think we'll be able to see it from the road?" I asked.

"No," Mom said.

We were silent. The fire cloud burst again.

"It's a bomb," I said. "A nuclear bomb." And I laughed.

"Kate!" Mom said.

"They test them out here. I saw it on a postcard."

"That's Nevada, not Kansas."

"It's a creepy postcard."

"If it's a nuclear bomb," Julia said, "everything around will remain the same except us. We'll disintegrate."

"Julia," Mom said.

"I'm glad there's no war going on," I said.

"There is a war going on," Jane said.

"I know, but not here," I snapped. I'd forgotten about the other war that we saw on TV at school.

We drove for nearly an hour before we got to the explosion. The black cloud grew bigger and denser the closer we came, taking on colors: orange, red, yellow, even blue.

"Do you feel your bodies disintegrating?" Julia asked.

"Oh, God, it's an accident," Mom said. She pushed her thumbnail into her lip and the wind snarled her hair.

Traffic appeared out of nowhere. For a few miles we crept along until we saw it: an eighteen-wheeler was lying on its side in the median, charred. People had pulled their cars over to the shoulder and were taking pictures. Ambulances and police cars swirled their blue and red lights and their sirens hollered on the wind. Around the truck the grass had turned charcoal and amber.

"Do you think he's dead?" I asked.

"I think he's fried," Julia said, lifting her left eyebrow.

"Julia," Mom said. But we were laughing, a nervous kind of laughter. Then Jane stopped and started to cry. "It's so sad," she said. I thought about the shirtless man in the middle of the night.

"Look, look," Mom said. "He's all right." She pointed to a man squatting near an ambulance. A nondescript man, head in hands, blue jeans, T-shirt, baseball cap. He could have been anyone.

Then Mom looked back at us, a thin quivering smile parting her pinkened lips. My stomach turned hollow.

We were in the middle of Kansas, halfway between Esalen and home, halfway between Anton and Dad, on my irrelevant red line, suspended in Mom's hopes and beliefs, suspended in the promise of Anton.

"The guy's dead," I said. I knew it. Absolutely.

The traffic thinned and the car picked up speed. Home vanished beneath the pavement, crumbling into the heap of debris that was our past. A part of me wished I could have remained suspended in Mom's dreams, cradled, anonymous, high above two worlds.

THE LARGER SCHEME
OF THINGS

Dad had told me that in the larger scheme of things he wasn't much older than I. I was eight. He was thirty-eight. Age spots spotted his hands. His hair was graying. Thirty years was a universe of time. When I thought about getting big, I thought about being Julia's age or Jane's age. I thought about middle school, being twelve or thirteen. I thought about clothes belonging to Jane and Julia that would someday belong to me. Julia's white cardigan with the embroidered strawberries. Jane's silk brocade shirt with silk-covered buttons from China.

When my father was eight, the Japanese bombed Pearl Harbor. He was given a colorful armband with wings sewn on it by the U.S. Air Warning Service so that he could go along with female volunteers to a field near our town to keep on the lookout for German aircraft. The field was on a hill with miles of visibility, and while the women monitored telephones, relaying information, my father stared at the sky reporting to them what he saw. He knew all the names of the aircraft of the day. He'd recite them to me proudly, remembering them still. Fokker-Wulf 200; Ju-87; Messerschmitt ME 109—the best of the German fighter planes—and the Heinkel bomber.

Twenty-four years earlier, during World War I, Dad's father lost his left hand in combat. Lost, I was told, lost as if somehow that hand could be found. Thirty years before that, Grandpa's father came to America from Scotland, leaving behind his father and family—farmers who used the letter X to sign their name.

Dad said the universe was 15 billion years old. When Dad left Mom, they'd been married for twelve years. Jane was now twelve years old. Dad said a star could die the day you were born, but its light was so many years away from earth your lifetime would pass long before that star's light went out. He said my children's and their children's lives could come and go before that star's light vanished. I wondered how many dead stars were still giving off light. Mom's father died the summer before Dad left, at the age of sixty-five. As an eight-year-old, he was the model for the Buster Brown Shoe boy. His family owned the company, but lost it in the stock-market crash of 1929. At eight, my mother's mother had been a cowgirl on the Montana plains, while my father's mother, at the same age, had been an Italian princess. Four hundred years could pass before a star's light went out.

Mom said she was only ten years older than Jane was now when she had given birth to Jane, as if that made her somehow Jane's age. Only four years older than Jane was now when she had met Dad. Sixteen years was twice as many years as I had. My oldest cousin was sixteen, so far away from me in age he scared me. When Mom was eight it was discovered that she had a split vertebra and her mother told her she would never have children.

Dad said that 4.6 billion years ago the earth was formed out of the sun, and not long thereafter came the moon. He said that at first the earth was lifeless and may have become a globe-girdling sea, and that 3.2 billion years ago bacteria began to form in the seas. The first signs of life fossilized in rock of that same age, and much later calcium carbonate formed. "Hard stuff," he said, tapping his teeth. "Teeth are made of calcium carbonate. The Empire State Building is made of calcium carbonate." I thought about his teeth, a little bit crooked, a little bit yellow from coffee and the cigarettes he used to smoke, and I thought about the Empire State

Building shooting into the sky like hope and I thought of all those billions of years and then thought again of my oldest cousin, trying to distinguish the difference. Dad said that 570 million years ago life was abundant for the first time, and that 65 million years ago for some unexplained reason most life on earth was destroyed, killing the dinosaurs, wiping the slate of nature clean. I thought of those big machines that clean ice-skating rinks, slowly, rhythmically gliding over the ice, smoothing out the incisions that skate blades make. He said that nature takes care of itself, coming back bigger and better than before. I thought of a wet sponge running over a chalked-up blackboard, cleaning up the mess of numerals my math teacher could make. Dad said that the blue whale was bigger than a house, and had, in the Eocene Age, surpassed the dinosaurs in size.

One hundred thousand years ago came the first Homo sapiens. Man Wise. Wise Man. Fifty million years from now the earth will be unrecognizable. One billion years from now the sun will devour the earth with heat, and both will be extinguished. One year our father was married to our mother. We ate dinner at the same table at six sharp. The next year he was gone.

Dad said man works so hard to be immortal, creating his arts and his monuments, developing his technologies, worrying about making his mark when actually he is insignificant, simply a guest on earth, here for a moment. He spoke as if he weren't man. He said that children are our only immortality. I thought of my sisters and myself standing alone in a desert at the end of time, but I didn't understand, since at any moment we could all be wiped clean.

ESALEN, THE NEW LIFE

I wanted a new name. We were beginning a new life. Actually I only wanted a new nickname. My father had given me a hundred nicknames. For my seventh birthday he'd had a birthday cake made for me with my nicknames scrawled all over it. Minky. Minky Pibulous. Flea. Flea Flea. Fleabert. Kitty. Kitty Kat. Missy. Missy Mort. Kay. KK. Katydid. Kandy. Tita. Titatoad. Toad. I wanted to be called Toad.

"Toad. Call me Toad," I had said to my sisters and Mom, as we drove across the country. I had had a baby-sitter nicknamed Booger, and she was so beautiful, with aqua eyes, a sharp nose and a southern accent, that it made even her name the most beautiful name in the world. "Call me Booger," she had said, the words sliding out gracefully in that soft accent.

"Call me Toad," I repeated. On that road anything seemed possible. The slate was clean.

"All right, Toad," Mom had said. "Toad Kitty is." Toad made me feel pretty, like Booger. I had thought about Scarlett and had considered Cinderella, but chose Toad because I only wanted a nickname. Kitty was Mom's nickname for me. Kate and Katy were Dad's. Mom said he called me Kate after an old girlfriend.

"I think you should be called Mongoloid," Jane said. Julia agreed with a nod. They were always making up names for me. Anything I said could become my name. If I said I wanted Green Stamps they'd call me Green Stamps. "Okay, Green Stamps." "Okay, Nickname." "All right, Gas Pump."

I didn't know what a mongoloid was. Julia explained. Know-it-all, I thought. She'd recently read the entire dictionary.

"I'm not a mongoloid," I said.

"Little Mongy," Jane teased, looking back at me from the front seat.

"Big-bosom-blood-balls-early-period-nipples," I shouted. The words came involuntarily and fast like bullets and I was proud of the nickname. "That's your nickname, Jane." Jane had just gotten her period. Julia had shown her how to use tampons. Julia hadn't gotten her period yet, but she'd been practicing for it for years.

"Toad!" Mom gasped and smiled. There was road in front of us. Road behind us. Slick black road as far as the eye could see.

After five days in the car we finally got to Anton. We met at Esalen in the late afternoon of a perfectly clear blue day. He waited next to his camper—a turquoise Chevrolet Del Rey perched on the back of a pickup truck. A Honda 70 hung from the front grille and a Honda 50 from the back.

Over a month had passed since we'd seen Anton. He was smaller than I remembered, though still large and handsome, with his side-burns striping his cheeks and his sparkling blue eyes. He was shirt-less, and wearing lime-green Bermudas that didn't match my image of him. On his head was a fraying leather cowboy hat. The air was fresh and briny and in it I felt suddenly stunned after having been in the car so long.

A new session was beginning and people swarmed the parking lot, arriving in expensive cars. They were hippie people with long hair and bell-bottoms and pins that declared PEACE and LIBERATION. Some of them whistled hellos to Anton, telling him they looked forward to his workshop: "Romantic Love and Sexual Equality."

Redwood and eucalyptus rose tall into the sky and sun sliced down in tubes, thick with pollen and dust. In the distance, through the trees, I could see a garden, and beyond the garden a sliver of the Pacific. Julia, Jane and I stood next to the camper feeling awkward, adjusting to that strange sense of the new, worried that things would be different here than they had been with Anton at home; it was clear that this was no camp for kids. Music rained down from invisible speakers, welcoming us, it seemed, to this new world.

Anton hugged Mom. She stood tall and thin, her hair a mat of tangled curls, in a flower-print shirt and new blue jeans. Anton hugged her and she disappeared. Her arms drooped by her sides. She could give up, finally. She'd arrived. His big hands fanned out across her back and he kissed her hard and she kissed him hard and they claimed each other. He claimed her.

"Jesus," Jane said. And all the belief in Anton that Mom had encouraged in Jane died again and I worried she'd be in trouble soon.

"It'll be all right," Julia said, and she darted into Anton's arms. Her shirt lifted up her back as he hugged her. Flirt, I thought. Then I wanted her to flirt, I thought all she'd have to do was flirt and things would be as they had been before.

"Hello, babes," he said with a wide grin. For an instant his gold fillings flashed.

I wanted a kiss. And then I wanted my twenty dollars. I wondered if I should ask him for it now. But I didn't. I'd wait. We'd arrived.

Two foreigners came to drive our green station wagon back across the country and when Jane protested, saying we'd have less freedom, Mom just sighed. She had surrendered and the camper was to become our new home. We were to fit in with Anton's children and, since we would all love and trust each other, there would be no need for another car. I looked at the tiny camper and thought of our big white home in the woods and wanted to protest too. But Mom was happy and I thought of all that distance we had come and I was tired and I wanted then to be happy.

With the car went my maps and my solid red line and I knew

that things would never be the same as before. It was Anton's world that we were entering now.

Anton's children were hippie children and strange, different from us. They drank beer and wine and smoked cigarettes. They listened to Bob Dylan, Neil Young, The Rolling Stones. For them the Beatles (our music) were passé, over, unhip. They were sophisticated kids who spoke about grown-up things—abortion, Vietnam and Nixon. Exotic and cool, confident kids—millionaires with airs, a certain way they looked at you, a certain strength in their eyes that made it seem they thought they owned the world.

We met them at the Esalen baths on the day that we arrived. A thin mist veiled them, their legs dangled in the water. Four were blond and one, the youngest, Finny, was dark. He had olive skin and thick, black curly hair that was long like a girl's and you would have thought him a girl, but he wore no clothes. The only thing connecting him to his brothers and sisters were his eyes. They all had magnificent blue eyes, cornflower blue like a late-day sky. Anton's eyes.

"Try to love them as if they were your own sisters and brothers," Mom had said to us on the long drive across the country. "They need you to." She had told us they were suffering since the nun went to the ashram. We were to love them as we loved each other. Love them instantly. I wondered if they had been instructed to love us too.

The tubs were perched on a wooden platform halfway down a bluff, suspended in midair, it seemed, above the jagged rocks below. Waves crashed against the rocks, foaming and swelling, then receding into an instant of calm. The baths oozed hot, sulfurous steam and its gaseous smell mixed with the spray of the ocean. The sun was low, behind thin clouds; peach and violet ribbons spread across the sky. The ocean was red.

My sisters and I stood dully at the edge of the Esalen baths. Our clothes alone revealed the differences between them and us. The others were sloppy in fraying cutoffs and bikinis and lots of silver jewelry; we were neat, my sisters in some matching outfit or other,

I in a red velvet dress. Jane and I had our hair in braids and Julia's was tied back in the pink ribbon. Mom had brushed our hair before we'd arrived, dragged the comb through it for the first time since we'd left home, yanking it nervously as she leaned over us from the driver's seat. We were parked on the shoulder of the Pacific Coast Highway, all of us a little giddy and eager to arrive. The ocean was fifty feet below, and cars were rushing by, rocking us each time they passed. Mom wet her fingertips with spit and rubbed our faces clean.

"It'll be fun. We're doing the right thing," she said, gnawing on her lip. She spoke fast, trying to convince herself. "You're going to get on with Anton's kids. They're good kids. Loving and religious." It scared me that she was trying to convince herself, as if somewhere she really didn't believe. I thought of the children in the Sunday school classes we attended before Dad left, all nicely dressed with pink faces and straw bonnets, and wondered if Anton's kids would be like that. Religious kids went to parochial schools and we always thought there was something strange about them. They thought a lot about death and God and Jesus, and in the word *parochial* alone there was something strange, like a disability. If they were like that I wouldn't be scared; I'd be able to boss them around. I thought I'd be able to love and trust them.

But now, at the baths, our hair was still dirty, itching and plastered to our skulls, but neat. Mom had stayed behind at the parking lot with Anton to take care of things, check in.

"We're the Fureys and I'm Sofia. Sofia means wisdom," said one of the girls, coming toward us with a smile. She was a strong girl, and beautiful, with deep dimples and at the corner of her mouth a dark hairless mole. She offered us her hand and then introduced us to the others: Caroline; Nicholas; Timothy; Finny.

The Fureys. We'd thought about their name a million times. Anton Furey. The Fureys. A glorious name, pronounced *fiori* like flower in Italian, that's what Julia said. Furey like fury, is what Jane said. We wondered if Mom would take that name when she married Anton.

"We call Finny 'Bone,' " Sofia said pointing to the naked boy. He was tiny, I imagined about five. "Bone for his bones because he rolls a fine bone. Do you know what a bone is?" Julia said yes and explained that it was a hand-rolled marijuana cigarette.

Sofia acted as if she owned the place and told us to come into the water and we did, after changing into our suits. Jane held me close in front of her like a shield. She could be so shy. I let her hold me, pretending I was the shy one. I liked protecting her. The idea of loving all these people frightened me. I wondered what would happen if I didn't. I slid beneath the water. It was hot and made me dizzy. I needed to pee. I'd never thought about loving my sisters. I just did.

"Watch out for amoebas," Nicholas, the oldest, said to me as I emerged. He had a big half smile just like Anton's, and beautiful teeth. Watching him was like watching a younger version of Anton, and he flirted with us as Anton had back at home. "They live in sulfur baths and if you put your head under water . . . "

"They crawl in your ears and eat your brain," the little naked one, Finny, finished Nicholas's sentence. Nicholas tickled him, scooping him up in his arms. It was clear Nicholas liked to tease. I wondered what it would be like to have an older brother who teased and loved me. Jane, Julia and I listened to them. Since it was Anton's world we were entering, it was also theirs—more theirs than it would ever be ours—and they knew it. We sat on the edge of their world, wondering how we'd fit in. We were all quiet for a moment, and awkward in the quiet. Then Timothy farted. He wasn't much older than me. He had a boxy head and long teeth. He laughed, picked his nose, examined the snot and wiped it on Finny, then farted again.

"Do you go to parochial school?" I asked. None of them looked like a religious kid to me.

Sofia let us know that they went to free school in Dallas, "Erehwon. Nowhere spelled backward." That "Erehwon" was a word that they would trumpet. They loved the fact that it spelled "nowhere," that it was their school—the best school in the world, everything about them had to be the best. Timothy told us that they could study whatever they chose to at Erehwon. Mostly, he said, they chose to play football or stay in Europe with their mother and not go to school at all.

"*Erehwon* was a book about a utopia by Samuel Butler," Julia said. The Furey kids all looked at Julia. I hated when she showed off. I was afraid they wouldn't like her.

"That's right," Nicholas, the oldest, said. "A utopia was Dad's big idea for our education. But Dad refers to it as 'Now Here backward' instead of nowhere."

"Dad has lots of big ideas," Sofia said and rolled her eyes.

"We're Catholics," Caroline said to me. "We don't go to parochial school, but we *are* Catholics." She was soft and gentle and seemed so old and wise. She looked about thirteen. She tucked her hair behind her ear and smiled warmly and with that smile she welcomed us, made us feel comfortable—like we belonged. I fell in love with her instantly. She asked which religion we were and I tried hard to remember. I wished we were Catholic just to be like her.

"Presbyterians," Jane whispered.

"Presbyterians," I repeated out loud.

Sofia did most of the talking. She told us they were millionaires and that they had flown here from Europe. I could tell she was the kind of person it was better to pretend you liked, stay on the good side of. "Our grandfather was in oil in Texas, so Mom's a millionaire, but she left it all to us when she went to India."

We know, I wanted to say. Your mother's a Texan oil heiress and also a nun. But I didn't, because Julia said it made you weaker if you knew too much about someone, as if you were curious and interested in other people because they were so much more fascinating than yourself.

Sofia didn't seem to be suffering very much. In fact, none of them seemed to be. I thought of all the money Anton used to carry around. Then I thought about my twenty dollars.

"We're Europeans, of course," Sofia said and then explained that each one of them came from a different country and that each one of them had a different passport to prove it. She was French, Caroline Dutch, Timothy German, Nicholas was "almost" African because he had "almost" been born there, and Finny was Italian. "But Dad and Mom are both Irish, so of course we're also Irish."

"The fighting Irish," Timothy said proudly. That was another thing they'd trumpet, the fact that they were Irish.

We'd lived in Europe too, several times, because Dad was working there. Once for five months when I was three years old. We'd sailed on the *QEII*, since Mom was afraid to fly. I remembered, or at least I thought I remembered, that trip, I'd heard about it so many times. One night we all turned green and threw up into little paper bags that Dad had knotted to the posts of our bunks. I remembered it clearly. I wanted to remember simply because Dad was there. On the arid island of Arran, in a dark stone church by the edge of the Firth of Clyde, I was baptized by the cold hand of a Presbyterian minister. For a long time I thought that made me Scottish.

"I'm Scottish," I said. In school it was the big thing to come from somewhere else, anywhere but America.

"No you're not, Kate," Julia said. I wished she'd call me Toad, but Toad had been forgotten on that long stretch of road. "We're New Yorkers." Julia flared her nostrils. "Born in Harlem. All of us."

"I am not Italian," Finny lashed out suddenly. His eyes widened, enormous eyes. I couldn't believe he wasn't wearing any clothes. We weren't allowed to go naked. Sofia started fighting with him, insisting he was Italian. I didn't see that it mattered where he was from. I thought maybe he was suffering.

"He wasn't planned," Timothy told us. "He was a mistake." Planned. *Planned*. That was another thing we asked each other in school: "Were you planned?" As if being planned meant being loved. It was clear to me Timothy liked to speak. There was nothing shy about him. He was all over the place—a wired energy. I preferred Finny, who was tiny and shy, younger than me.

"Let Finny be," Nicholas said. His eyes were sharp. Caroline took Finny into her arms and held him for a moment. His blue eyes caught mine and then he pulled away from her. Marks from a too-tight elastic banded his stomach with the promise of clothes. I loved him just then and wanted to tell Mom. I wanted to tell her that I loved Caroline too. I saw it then, our lives coming together. It would be easy to make this work. I looked up the bluff to see if Mom was coming. Instead came a procession of naked grown-ups, marching solemnly toward the other tub. Quiet, like ghosts. There were four of them, with pasty pinkish skin and dark patches of pubic hair. Heads bowed. In their hands they carried white candles, which they set around their tub as they sank gently into the water. The wicks flickered and hissed, the flames opaque in the steam.

Naked bodies. Everywhere naked bodies. Traipsing the grounds with their heads turned toward the sky in meditation. Sitting in groups, Indian style, deep in concentration, speaking of the process of processing emotions. Fat: stomachs bulging over penises. Fat: tubular breasts blending with bellies. Thin: all the private parts conspicuously revealed. Short and tall, old and shriveled: on the lawn doing calisthenics; in the baths and the pool; in the woods. Flat breasts and big breasts. Long penises and puckered penises. Big, dark nipples. Cherry nipples and nipples like sores. Hairy bodies and smooth bodies. Hair from beneath arms and between legs. Black hair and orange hair and blond hair, and one lady with blue. Unruly hair and trimmed hair and penises that flapped over large hanging sacks for the balls.

All over the place were signs, poking from the grass, dangling from fences and buildings and doors, warning kids. They didn't like kids at Esalen. KIDS DON'T RUN, KIDS NOT ALLOWED IN WORK-SHOP AREAS, KIDS STAY OUT OF GARDEN, KIDS NOT ALLOWED AT BATHS UNATTENDED, KIDS STAY OFF THE GRASS, KIDS BE QUIET, KIDS NOT AL-LOWED TO EAT IN THE LODGE.

At Esalen we were supposed to love a lot of things and out of love our new life would emerge. It didn't matter, therefore, if our car was gone, if we had no money, if Mom had had to borrow money from me. We were to love this new world, love it instantly and permanently. We were to love Anton as Mom loved him. Love his children, of course. Love Esalen, love the turquoise camper, you-name-it-love. Love, simple as that, as if the word meant *eat* or *breathe*. Love. The future was ours now, big and bright—a promise, a surprise.

We stayed at Esalen for just over a week, while Anton taught his workshops. As soon as he finished, though, we left, because he got in a fight with his supervisor, Helmut Kimp. It turned out they fought about jealousy and forgiveness and trust and love, love, love. Later we would all find that funny, since everyone was suppose to love one another so much at Esalen.

At first, though, Anton was busy with his "Romantic Love" seminar, so we barely saw him. When we did it was just briefly, and he seemed impatient, ordering us (and his kids) around organizing the camper so that all our luggage fit in properly, giving us all jobs. His big blue eyes weren't so flirtatious anymore. Rather they were determined, squinting, anxious to see that we did what he'd asked us to do. Then he was gone again. Even so it was clear that a lot was over. No more poker games or flirtatious stories about Texas meant to win us over. No more bills on our bedroom doors. Even our town, our pasts, had absolutely nothing to do with this new world—so utterly different, so out there, from what my sisters and I had known.

Mom told Jane, Julia and me not to worry about Anton's impatience. She said it only meant that he felt comfortable around us now, that he could be himself and treat us like family.

When Mom wasn't with Anton she was trying to help us settle in, being extra loving to Anton's children so that they'd fall in love with her. Only Caroline paid any attention to Mom. The others ignored her and I was glad, because it annoyed me, all the attention she gave them.

Then Mom disappeared. After Anton taught the "Romantic Love" seminar, he and Mom vanished into a seventy-two-hour session on "sensitivity training," and for almost three days we didn't see them. While they were gone we blended into the Furey family hierarchy.

They had an order: everyone watches out for themselves.

Our new home, the camper, was disgusting inside, even though everyone had "jobs" to take care of it. Jane was quick to point out that our "jobs" were so that Anton didn't have to do anything himself. The camper was dark, with a kitchenette on one side and a dining booth on the other. The faint smell of old milk lingered in the indoor/outdoor carpet and a curling yellow strip of flypaper dripped from the ceiling light. Mom had scrubbed out the camper, trying to clean it up the way she used to clean our house back at home, but the effort was useless and I felt sorry for her. Since there was no iron, the calico curtains looked worse clean than dirty. And the Fureys by nature were sloppy. Her cleaning meant nothing, so she gave up.

At night, beds appeared from everywhere—the walls, the dining booth, the ceiling. Bunks hung above the windows, and the cab seat was used as "a cot." That's how Sofia put it. She said the camper slept ten "uncomfortably," and I believed her. Anton and Mom had a bungalow on the Esalen grounds.

"It's my father's camper," Sofia said and looked at Jane, Julia and me. "He bought it with *our* money."

Good for you, I wanted to say. It was the ugliest place I'd ever slept in, uglier than the gas stations, and it was close inside and we kept knocking into each other, and Anton's kids, everyone but Caroline, loved to fart. The place stank. They lit each other's farts.

"You guys sure do fart a lot," I said. They didn't seem so sophisticated anymore.

In their world they wrestled and shot dart guns and listened incessantly to music. After a short time, even I knew the words to "Don't Let It Bring You Down" and "Old Man"—songs that Dad would not have liked: he called this kind of music "pimple music." In their world, they gave each other "dead legs" and "Hertz doughnuts," "hurts don'it," which were both punches. Finny and

Timothy pulled the wings off flies and then watched them try to fly. "Did you know that every time a fly lands it throws up?" Sofia asked us. "Watch out when you're eating and one lands on your food." Nicholas had a movie camera and filmed everything, getting the little kids to star in his features—that's the word he used.

Jane did her needlepoint or read, keeping to herself. From a cassette of theirs Julia learned by heart the words to "Aquarius," "Sodomy," "Air" and "Frank Mills." She sang the songs over and over until everyone told her to shut up.

It didn't take long for Julia to love this place. She was fascinated by all the nakedness and all the sex. She loved to watch naked masseurs massage naked bodies at the baths. She loved that there were so many children she could teach things to. On the chalkboard in the camper she drew pictures of vaginas and penises, diagramming them, and with a pointer pointing out the "labia majora" and "minora," the "clitoris," and other words I'd never heard of and didn't remember for long because I didn't pay much attention. Her drawing of the vagina looked more like a sailboat than anything else; that's what Timothy said and he laughed. And then we all laughed.

"You know what they do in workshops?" Sofia asked, interrupting the laughter. It was clear to me that Sofia didn't like that Julia had everyone's attention. "They get naked and paint each other's bodies with blue paint. All of them, even your mother."

For my part, I didn't like all the nakedness. I started wearing a lot of clothes. I even wore underwear beneath my bathing suit. The more I noticed naked people the more they seemed to multiply. Even the scarecrow in the garden was naked.

We came together and then separated into the "big kids" and the "little kids." The big kids were Nicholas, Caroline, Jane, Julia and Sofia. Jane and Caroline mothered us, making sure we ate. They cooked elaborate dinners with beef hash and hot dogs and beans and things Mom never let us eat at home. Julia spent her days falling in love with Nicholas and helping him with his movies. She said she wanted to feel like Mom; she wanted to know how Mom had felt falling in love with Anton.

The little kids were Timothy (nine), Kate (eight), and Finny (five). Timothy resisted being a "little kid" and tried hard to be a "big kid" and that was fine with me and Finny. We preferred it to be just us. For a while it was fun to have no one telling me what to do and even my sisters left me alone. I was independent now, like a grown-up.

"Put on clothes," I said to Finny. That was my first order. It wasn't only at the baths that he went naked; he never wore clothes and I couldn't play with him like that. "I can't have you following me if you're naked." And since he obeyed, I loved him, and together we explored.

Bands of shadow and sun striped the trees and we marched through the forest behind the camper to the giant buttresses to collect rocks. The first game I taught Finny was the game of following me. The second was finding rocks. I carried my prospector's pick and my chisel and my stout collecting bag. "Stout," that was the word Dad had used when he'd given it to me. I wanted to show Finny the fruitcake mélange of the Big Sur cliffs. I wanted to show him how geology was so active out here we could see it happening. I remembered my father pulling off the road with my sisters and me to dissect road cuts and outcrops, examining the lost geology of New Jersey. He'd explain that two mountain ranges, both as high as the Himalayas, had come and gone, but that now it was static and the only way to know what had occurred was to read it in the rocks. The West was a different story, young in contrast. In the West, plates were sliding under and alongside each other, sending up mountain ranges, causing geysers and springs to burst steaming to the surface like pimples, causing volcanoes to erupt and sea floors to disappear, and it was all happening now. The way Dad spoke, in geological time, it was as if you could see mountain ranges rising, feel the land folding in on itself—see the earth being made. Dad would put his hands out in front of him and slide them alongside and under each other to show us how plates worked. I did the same with Finny. I wanted to show Finny all of this. I wanted him to listen to me the way my sisters and I listened to our father. Just showing Finny about the rocks made my father feel nearby. I didn't know what I was saying or what I was doing with these tools, of course, but I acted as if I did.

We roamed. Esalen was beautiful, a brilliant green land with the ocean smashing on the rocky beach in front. There were lots of rocks in Big Sur. Serpentine; sandstone; schist. We found a lot of limestone inlaid with the fossils of conical shells—*Gastropoda conacea*. They were my favorite. Tiny shells trapped in permanence for so many years. Limestone of calcium carbonate. "Teeth are made of the same ingredients," I said to Finny and tapped my front tooth. "And so is the Empire State Building."

"Why do you wear such funny dresses?" he asked. He looked deep into me. He could stare for a long time. But I could stare even longer.

"What?" I snapped. I wore a black velvet dress. It was clean, with white linen piping. My legs were naked. I could feel a draft on my skin and in my hair.

"Why don't you wear shorts? Why those frilly dresses?"

"Why don't you cut your hair?" I asked, and he was quiet. His hair was tangled worse than mine. I thought the knots would never come out with a brush. It would have to all be cut off. I thought I would like to cut it all off.

Quartz. Quartzite. Radiolarian chert. There was so much radiolarian chert. A beautiful burgundy, red and beefy, laced with thin white calcite lines like gristle. Graywacke. Shale and slate. I pointed out everything I could to Finny. I could have spent forever exploring. I told Finny that I was going to be a geologist like my father when I grew up.

"It will be easier for you to understand about rocks when we get to the Grand Canyon," I said. "Their story is written out in the rocks there like words in a book. Rocks with beautiful names: Vishnu Schist, Coconino Sandstone, Muav Limestone, the Toroweap Formation and Bright Angel Shale." I sang the names to him as our father had to us.

"How do you know we're going there?" he asked.

"I just do," I said. "Like I know you're going to love me."

"No I'm not."

"You are too," I said. My eyes penetrated his. I could already tell that a little brother was the most wonderful thing in the world. I could tell he liked thinking I knew a lot of things, that it made him feel secure around me. I felt so grown-up and wise.

"You don't know what you're talking about. I'm tired of your games. They're stupid." He paused. "Your dad's gone, Kate."

"What?" I snapped. Slowly I lifted my head and looked down on him, piercing him again with my eyes until he had to look away. I told him never to say that again. From my pocket, I pulled my rock of gold and rolled it between my fingers. I told him my father gave it to me and that it meant he was with me always. Finny admired the rock, though I would not let him touch it. I held it there, the gold flakes sparkling in the sun, taunting him. But inside, I was tremendously sad.

I ignored Finny. It only took an hour; after an hour he was mine again and would play whatever I wanted. Something changed in me in that hour as I saw Finny come back around to my side. I realized that I had a lot of power, that his love and trust made me the possessor of something grand—I'd never felt this before with my sisters, in my old life. And that power made me both mean and more in love. Mean because I wanted to see how far I could push Finny, as if each concession of his to each push of mine meant he loved me all the more. And his love was imperative, with it I could save the family. His loving me meant that it wouldn't matter if Anton stopped loving Mom. I understood Julia for falling in love with Nicholas. I understood the trick, the key—why Mom wanted us to get on with Anton and his kids so well.

Sometimes Mom would ask my sisters and me to do little tasks for her, simple things she could often do more easily for herself— drying a pot when both the pot and towel were in her hands, digging a hole for a bulb in her garden when both the bulb and the hoe were in her lap. But she wanted us to do the favor anyway, because if we did it proved and confirmed our love for her.

I made Finny do a lot of things. I made Finny fall backward to me and each time I caught him I knew that he belonged to me a little more than the time before. I wondered if that was how Anton had felt when we'd fallen to him. I told Finny to be my slave for a day and do whatever I said. I promised I'd be his slave the next day. In the stout collector's bag I had him carry the rocks we found, I had him do my dinner job, I had him convert the table into my bed. I ordered him around in front of the others and though they warned him not to trust me, he agreed to it all. Fool, I thought, but I loved him.

"Bone's a bastard," Timothy said. "That's why he'd be so stupid as to be your slave." Alone in the camper. "He doesn't know he's a bastard yet, so don't say anything or Dad'll get real mad and you don't want to see Dad mad." He wore a floppy purple velvet hat. His eyes were wide. "He's illegitimate. He wasn't planned. A mistake." He wasn't planned, illegitimate like he shouldn't exist. Timothy and I stared at each other until our eyes watered and we had to turn away. "Dad had an affair and they had Bone. So his mom is different from ours. That's what bastard means. Mom adopted him, but he's still a bastard."

This was another way our two families merged, through each other's secrets. We traded them like baseball cards, trying to outdo one another with our stories, trying to prove that our respective lives were more complicated and therefore more exotic.

"His name is Finny," I said, trying to ignore Timothy. It was close inside the camper. Jane and Caroline had dinner going on the stove—beef hash and baked beans. Steam oozed from the bean pot. The lid rattled. A salad had already been brought to us from the Esalen kitchen. The lettuce had wilted around the edges. I pictured little Finny, naked. I wanted him now.

"Dad has lots of affairs. Your mother's an affair. Say something," Timothy insisted. Bastard, I thought, but I felt sorry for Timothy. I couldn't imagine losing my mother. It was bad enough to be without her for three days. I missed her, little things: her fingers braiding our hair. I thought about "sensitivity training" and wondered where she was now. Timothy looked tiny standing there, even though he was bigger than I. I wondered what he missed about his mother. I wanted to be nice to him, but couldn't.

Outside, the sky turned red through the trees and I could hear some of the others talking. "Mom's pregnant with your dad's baby and she's going to have it and they're going to get married," I said. It was a lie, of course, but she had been pregnant. She'd gone to New Orleans to have an abortion. Julia had said the doctors would stick a vacuum-cleaner hose inside of Mom and suck until it sucked the baby out. I had worried the vacuum would suck up more of her than that.

"She'll have a bastard then, and we'll have another bastard brother hanging around that Mom'll have to adopt and it'll be my brother and not yours, because you'll be gone and Mom'll be back."

My eyes stung with tears, but I did not cry. I would not cry. If I loved Finny that would never happen. If Julia loved Nicholas it wouldn't happen either. I repeated that to myself like a prayer. Sofia came in, opened the refrigerator and looked inside and then shut the door and then opened it again and took out an apple. Nicholas came in and popped open a beer and guzzled it. Caroline came in and poured herself a glass of wine. She leaned her head over the stove, holding back her long hair with one hand, lifting the bean-pot lid with the other, to check the beans. I would ask her about Finny. Julia raced in and out. I'd ask her about Mom. Finny came in and plopped down at the table. His blue eyes studied me. He was jealous when I spent time with Timothy.

My father had had an affair. That's what Mom said. Affair. I thought of the bulldog ants and sexuality oozing all over the place. I thought of all the naked people at Esalen, thought about them fucking. I'd never seen a person fuck, but I knew how they did it from the diagrams that Julia drew. I was glad Mom had had an abortion. I couldn't stand the idea of a brother or a sister of mine out there alone without Mom, my sisters or me. I thought of an escaped balloon drifting fast up to the sky. I didn't look at Timothy, but I could feel his eyes on me.

"Are you guys doing dinner jobs?" Sofia asked us. She was always asking about doing dinner jobs—overseeing who was doing what and doing a whole lot of nothing herself. "Like a smaller version of Anton," Jane would say.

"Come off it," Nicholas said to her. Sofia managed to make everyone turn against her, even her own brothers and sisters. Everyone was talking at once, flooding in and out. Sofia's fingers clamped a cigarette elegantly and she blew smoke rings. Finny flicked on the dull overhead light, shadows spread over everything. A moth orbited the bulb, crashing into it, falling, flying into it again. Finny tilted a plastic Baggie of marijuana and spilled a heap of it on the table and rolled bones for Anton.

"What's your dinner job, Kate?" Sofia asked.

"Give it a rest," Nicholas said, impatiently. He was protective of the little kids and for that I loved him.

"But they've got to understand what Dad's like," Sofia said.

"Sofia," Caroline said. I imagined Anton playing poker and remembered him at our house. And even though that was gone, I wasn't afraid of him. I looked around for Jane.

"Yeah, Kate," Finny said without looking up. He was mad at me because I hadn't been his slave and had laughed when he said it was my turn. "Sucker," I'd said—Timothy's word, he used *sucker* all the time.

We had adopted a cat once, I remembered. An orange cat with beautiful, thick long hair. We gave it a home so it wouldn't be killed. Dad shaved that cat because Mom had cut my hair very short. I had had really long hair and Dad had loved my hair and when he saw it cut off he shaved the cat. He actually hadn't shaved the whole cat, just a spot, but over time the story had grown.

"If you don't do a dinner job you'll get extra work," Finny said. He wanted me to react. It was clear by the way he held me with his eyes, and I almost did react just to make him feel powerful. I swore to myself I would never be mean to Finny again. I would protect him.

"Dad's good at giving extra work," Sofia said. The way his kids talked about him, Anton grew in my mind and I began to believe Jane really had seen something in him that Julia, Mom and I hadn't. A breeze came through the window and the whole camper smelled up with the smell of boiling beans. Timothy went outside, no longer interested in the bastard. I breathed in cigarette smoke. It smelled good. I wanted to talk to Mom. Then I wondered about home. I saw our empty house and wished I could crawl into my bed. I wondered how long we'd be gone. I thought about Toad and didn't feel very beautiful and the slate didn't seem very clean any longer.

"You guys don't have your car anymore, do you?" Sofia asked. She knew damn well we didn't have our car. I hated her. "What if you want to leave?" I saw our car on that long stretch of road, driven by the foreigners, I saw us—my sisters, Mother and I—standing on an island, isolated, here, unable to escape. We were absolutely powerless, with no money and no car, like beggars. I wanted my twenty dollars back, I had to have my twenty dollars.

"We trust you," I lied.

My rock fell out of my hand onto the table. I hadn't even realized that I was holding it. Sofia snatched it up and examined it. It flickered in the light.

"What's this?" she asked.

"It's gold," I said proudly and then wished I hadn't. I was afraid she wouldn't give it back. I didn't trust her.

Finny looked up and stared at it. "It's from her father, it's her father," Finny said. Ten tiny cigarettes were arranged in front of him in a perfectly ordered row on the linoleum table that would later become my bed.

"It's ugly," Sofia said and handed it back to me.

Mom came out of sensitivity training just the same as she went in. She wore the same stiff blue jeans, the same floral shirt. Her hair was pulled back in a red bandeau that matched her lipstick. The only thing different about her was that she talked a lot about living in the present and being here now. She and Anton were glad to be back with us. I studied them to see if they were in love. I had so many questions to ask her, there was so much I needed to know. I clung to her side, never wanting to let her go. "My silly-billy girl, what's wrong with you? Don't be such a worrywart." Anton gave us all wet kisses at the roots of our hair.

We went to lunch that day with Helmut Kimp and his wife, Heda. Helmut Kimp was fat, with a chin that looked as if it were being gradually reabsorbed into his neck. From his round face dangled lots of moles. I counted eleven, of different shapes and sizes. Some looked as if I could easily clip them off.

We all sat at a long table at an outside restaurant on a terrace overlooking the ocean. The restaurant was designed by Frank Lloyd Wright, something that Julia let us all know. The big kids sat at one end and the little kids with the grown-ups at the other. Wind chimes rang and water trickled over a fall. Tourists snapped pictures of the ocean. Japanese lanterns swayed in a light breeze.

Anton and Helmut drank beer and talked about the war and communists, and like a thunderstorm Nicholas and Anton were fighting. As Anton argued, his body seemed to inflate, making him enormous. I'd never seen him go like that before. Some of the big kids, including Jane, chimed in about Vietnam. Sofia rolled her eyes and said, "Anytime you want to get in a fight, bring up Vietnam or abortion." She smoked a cigarette that Anton kept telling her to put out.

But mostly Anton talked about love with Helmut, Heda and Mom. They had little fights, precursors to the big one to come. Mom flirted in her way with Helmut, cocking her head to the side and letting her curls fall in front of her eyes while encouraging him in everything he said—in his dreams. I couldn't hear what his dreams were, but I knew that Mom was encouraging them simply by the enthusiasm in her voice. She was always good at encouraging people in their dreams.

Anton tried to ignore Mom, turning to Heda Kimp, a blond with a high forehead and long hair that parted in the middle, fountaining around her face. Wrinkles fanned out from her eyes. She was older than Mom, but very pretty. Her shirt was black and painted with thin, lacy swirls of gold. Anton scribbled furiously on index cards, notes for his book. In his breast pocket he kept a wad of index cards and several pens. Mom had told Jane, Julia and me that Anton was very jealous. Once, back at home, he'd burned Mom's slides from our trip to Europe simply because Dad was pictured in them.

"The definition of romantic love is: I am you. You are me. In order to have this love we need sexual equality. You cannot have a marriage that remains romantic in a slave-master relationship," Anton said to Heda. Anton studied Mom, who was sitting close to Helmut. I wanted her to stop flirting with Helmut. I could tell Anton was getting mad. Anton went on: "Man and woman must be equal. Marriage cannot survive until we have equality of desire and options. Eve and I cannot survive unless she desires me with the same intensity that I desire her." Heda leaned in toward Anton, fascinated by what he said. "Or you and Helmut," he added. His lips were big and wet and I watched sunlight playing on them.

I looked around the table at all of us kids, and thought about us trying to love each other. Julia teased Timothy and Nicholas teased Julia. The three got up and shot some film. Caroline and Jane were deep in conversation. Sofia was giving advice to all of us. Finny and I talked to each other with our eyes. We all seemed comfortable, in the right place—blended, merged in our own world. Anton talked on about love.

Heda's accent was heavy. Lots of Zs. She laughed. She said she'd heard Anton had been a Jesuit and asked him why he left the society. Now they flirted. Anton sat back in his chair. He said there were other things in life and winked. His wink took you into him, into the inside of his world. "The Virgin tempted me," he said, slowly, slickly, and he told a story of falling in love with a statue of the Virgin when he was a novice at Grand Coteau in Louisiana. I knew this story. It was one of Mom's favorites. Heda laughed as he spoke. She was a flirt, but Mom didn't seem to mind. By the time Anton finished his story his accent had turned completely Texan.

"Isn't this beautiful," Mom whispered, looking around. The air was damp and cool. Cormorants and gulls dipped and dived, plunging toward the water. Nicholas, at the other end of the table, shot some film now of all of us. I wanted to ask Mom about the bastard.

Some gypsies floated by, reading palms, predicting futures. Anton paid one gypsy a hundred dollars, which he pulled from a wad in his wallet, to hear we were a solid family on the threshold of a rich and adventurous life. I saw that wad and was certain he had enough to give me my twenty dollars back.

The discussion moved on to chapter fifteen of Anton's book, which was on jealousy, and Anton was trying to convince Helmut that he was jealous.

"Jealousy is a natural part of humanity," Anton said.

"I'm not a jealous man," Helmut Kimp said. He pulled at the whiskers of his beard just below his lips and it seemed he was pulling strands of spit from his mouth. I wondered how such a beautiful woman could be married to such an ugly man.

"You are," Anton said. "You just don't know it. Have you ever been challenged?" And Anton winked at Heda and then at Mom.

"Sure. Yet I am not jealous." Helmut Kimp also had a thick accent, guttural, with heavy *U*s. "If you trust, there is no reason for jealousy."

"That's where you're wrong, Helmut," Anton said, his voice beginning to rise and his body began to swell again, as it had during the fight about Vietnam. "If you love someone deeply enough, you will be jealous." Finny's eyes squinted just like Anton's and then they rolled as if to say, "Here we go again." I thought about his mother. I bet he knew about her somewhere inside. But I didn't care about all of this. I was thinking about my twenty dollars, hoping Anton wouldn't swell when I asked him for it.

"Let's not turn jealousy into a virtue," Helmut said. Helmut looked around the table. He seemed to be noticing, as if for the first time, how many of us there were, taking us all in. A silence. I was afraid he was seeing something I couldn't see. "You've got a real tribe here, Anton. My lord, there are eight kids. What are you going to do with them all?"

"Teach them to appreciate the world. To love and to trust." Anton smiled and Helmut laughed.

"What's on my baby's mind?" Mom asked suddenly, noticing me. "Are you having fun? Isn't this wonderful? Does my little girl love me?" I hated when she asked what I was thinking. It was as if she could see inside my brain. I was afraid to lie because I was afraid she'd know I was lying.

"My twenty dollars," I said with fixed, determined eyes.

"Kate," she reprimanded, "you're not still thinking about that, are you? You've got to learn to be generous. Think of all we're doing for you. You should learn to contribute, Kate. You can't keep count of every penny."

"Do you forgive easily, Eve?" Helmut asked. I hated Mom. She hadn't been listening, too busy glaring at me, so she didn't know what to say. "Forgiveness," Helmut offered. "For example, do you forgive your husband?" He could tell Mom was blushing, feeling uncomfortable. She looked down at the table and then up at him—shy, like a child. He and Anton were now arguing about forgiveness and again they didn't agree. I could tell Anton liked to argue. He hadn't been like that at home. Dad hated people who argued for no real reason. He hated Brian Cain because at parties Brian Cain got drunk and argued just to argue.

"We're all friends. We can be honest. There are certain things that can't be forgiven," Helmut said.

"That's bullshit," Anton said vehemently. He sat forward in his chair, determined to prove his point. "Forgiveness is the beauty of Christianity." Finny gave me another look. I saw his mother standing alone in a field.

"Would you forgive Eve if she were unfaithful?" Helmut asked, trying to provoke Anton further.

"He left me in a very difficult situation," Mom cut in quickly, to turn the conversation away from Helmut's question. I didn't care if Anton were jealous or if Helmut were provoking him; I was worried about what Mom would say next. I shut my eyes and tried to stop listening, knowing what would come with the chance to talk about Dad leaving. The way she'd describe it, I'd see her standing alone in the world. The world empty of everything. Helmut's hand gently touched Mom's shoulder. Then I heard Mom say she forgave Dad, and at first I was happy and then I hated her even more because I knew she was telling an absolute lie.

"Insane!" I heard someone scream through the night. It was Helmut's voice. I sat up in bed, waking abruptly, wondering at first where I was. "You're too fucked up to be doing therapy!" This was Anton's voice, coming in through the camper window. I couldn't see anything at first, it was so dark. All us kids had been asleep. Two-thirty, three in the morning. The night was lit by the thin light of the full moon. Helmut had led a midnight workshop on a hike to the Tessajara hot springs, and Mom had gone along. They'd probably just returned.

Anton's voice was screaming something unintelligible, a monstrous voice. Then Helmut's voice again. "You always need to be the leader! You're afraid of the world. It's a good thing you have your tribe of kids to lead around. You can rule your own kingdom, Anton! You can preach about love and jealousy and forgiveness. What about forgiveness, Anton!"

"Insane!" Anton screamed again.

I lay with Julia on a single bunk. Her feet were at my head. My feet at her head. The sheets were gritty. I rubbed my eyes. She turned around to be close to me and wrapped her arm around my waist. Out the window I could see Mom in her jeans and floral shirt coming from the cottages. She clutched her bag and shoes and other clothes close to her chest, scampering toward the camper. "Get going, Eve," Anton said, appearing behind her. Large. "We're leaving this place." We sat up in our beds, half-bodies, vague and indistinguishable. Julia felt warm. Anton and Mom got in the front of the camper. The doors slammed, and the engine started with a jerk and a cough.

"Admit it, Helmut. Just admit it. You're not above it all. Just admit it. You're as weak as the rest of us," Anton screamed back toward the cottages. And then we roared away, up the long steep drive out of Esalen. The refrigerator door sprang open and the milk and a bottle of Coke toppled out, spilling over the floor. Bubbles of soda sighed, swelling and then settling. Dishes rattled in the sink and in the cupboard. We were gone.

The intercom connecting the cab to the camper was on in the front so we could hear what they were saying. Anton asked Mom why she'd taken so long to get back from the hike.

"Where were you?" he snapped.

"Don't be ridiculous. You knew where I was," she answered. "Where were you?" Their voices crackled with speaker static. "You've been drinking," I heard Mom say. I heard the name *Heda* and then they were screaming, loud piercing screams. I heard the words *kill Helmut* and I was afraid for Mom. I thought of Brian Cain coming to our house to kill our father. The camper jerked to a stop and Mom jumped out, Anton right after her. All I could hear now was the high pitch of their voices. The summer moon hung in the sky full and bright like a surprise. The distant lights of a plane became confused with planets and for a moment I thought it was a slow falling star.

We were parked on the edge of the highway at the top of a towering bluff. I could hear the ocean and their shouting and I tried to remember things. Anything. Dinner with my mother and my father at the same table. But I couldn't. A hundred million years had gone by. All the sense I'd tried to make of things made no sense at all. I thought about the ice-skating rinks with the incisions that skate blades make and I thought about chalkboards messed up with numerals. I couldn't keep track anymore. There was so much I didn't know. Inside I felt dirty, rotten actually. I thought about my sisters and I trying so hard to fit in. I didn't understand anything of how I felt. I thought, love or no love, we belong to Anton now. I wondered what it would mean if he were afraid of the world. I wondered a lot of things: if my sisters and I would become hippies; if we'd go to Erehwon in Dallas. What would happen to Dad, our home, our lives. Suddenly I felt very awake and this new life felt for the first time very real.

"You can't always know what's going to happen," Mom would say whenever one of us worried now. "That would be no fun. That wouldn't be being alive. Live in the present, be here now."

But I didn't care about all that. I wished we had our car, so we could get away. I thought about my father—I saw him walking down our driveway to get the mail, and he kept walking, walking away.

"Dad thinks your mom was sleeping with Helmut," Sofia said into the dark. "That's crazy," she added. I loved her just then, since she was standing up for Mom.

Then there was silence. Mom and Anton were back up front. The camper swayed and picked up speed and moved more deeply into night.

"It's a good thing we're out of there," Anton said, his voice warm and tender now. "They don't like children and they're all Buddhists."

"What's a Buddhist?" I whispered.

"Someone good," Jane said from the bunk above.

PLANS

With my father we always had had plans. When we traveled we had typed itineraries with the names and addresses of the hotels we would be staying in, their phone numbers and the time of our dinner reservation. Every night we ate at six with washed hands and clean faces. Jane, Julia and I in our matching Liberty print dresses. My mother and father with their nip of bourbon. After a trip to Scotland, the summer before my father left, he prided himself on the successful outcome of all of our plans: three months and not one plan fouled up. He didn't include the fight with Mom. Our days ticked by, marked by meals and sights and the relief that spread over my father's face as each day passed without incident.

Beneath an oak tree at the edge of the Culbin Forest on the banks of the Findhorn, they fought. Mom wanted to lie in the sun and pass the afternoon in leisure. He wanted to move on, make our dinner reservation. It was a clear blue day spiked with the rumbling of the river's strong current. Mom lay long, with her dress pushed up her thighs and the sleeves rolled to her shoulders. Dark glasses covered her eyes. Dad stood over her impatiently. A breeze lifted his curly black hair. Panic electrified his face. He was terrified of falling, of falling off course.

"Why can't we be spontaneous just this once?" my mother asked. "There's no need to be so rigid about everything. My father wasn't like this. He knew how to live . . . "

While Dad shoved the remains of our lunch back into the wicker basket, he screamed at Jane, Julia and me. About Mom's laziness, her self-centeredness, her childishness. Each condemnation a slap on our faces, until we shattered into tears. But Mom didn't respond anymore, and that made him madder. She stood up, straightened her dress and disappeared into the forest.

"Your mother's a child," Dad screamed. "She had to ruin a perfect day. She's no older than any of you."

Mom stayed away until our dinner reservation had long passed and stars overwhelmed the sky. We drove around in our black Peugeot searching for her. The glare of the headlights made black skeletons of the trees. Dad's hands were cold and unsoothing on our scalps.

For two days they spoke to each other through us, slipping slowly into polite nods and respectful exchanges. It took five days for things to get back to normal.

With Dad, Mom didn't realize that husbands weren't like children, that they didn't have to need and love you always. That they could go away.

UNION

Our real life together with the Fureys began on the road, after we left Esalen. Anton wanted a following. Mom wanted a family. They both wanted a utopia. A traveling utopia, that's what Julia said. I liked the word. Utopia. I was like my father in that way, I could repeat words over and over just for their sound. *U toe pee a.* Anton wanted to teach us about the world—about love and trust and forgiveness and generosity—and Mom wanted us to learn.

Road stretched on for miles. Nothing and then a town rising in a hurry of corrugated metal and cement. A boom town, advertising airplane parts and GOOD EATS restaurants in big block letters and a whole lot of stucco forming row upon row of identical houses. Windblown towns with plastic clinging like withered flowers to the dried and prickly branches of Joshua trees. Then the town disintegrated into land. Orange, yellow, a dappling of fiery red, platinum, depending on where the sun hung. Peach. Clean whites exploded into reds smothered in the rippling beige of sand. Then burst endless, clear blue. Mountains emerged haphazardly, shooting up to snow-covered peaks, flowing down gracefully into canyons, swallowed up by the brown expanse of land. At dusk and dawn an orange haze settled on the earth.

"Isn't this beautiful," Mom's voice sang through the intercom. "I just feel like stopping all the time and screaming, 'Isn't this beautiful!' " I could see her head through the cab glass, bouncing up and down. We were alone out there. She had said that was a good sign. It meant we were smarter and better than the rest. "Just think of your schoolfriends," Mom would say. "Going to camp, renting the same house as always on Fire Island, doing all those ordinary things. You're a lucky little girl, being with all these kids, seeing all these things." And for a short while I'd inflate, believing her, believing we were extraordinary. It was our own private world, and though there was nothing out there it seemed like there was a lot that was ours.

"Don't you all think it's magnificent?" Mom asked.

"You know, there're Hell's Angels in these parts," Sofia said, flicking off the intercom and bracing herself against the sink. The rest of us were lying all over the place, bumping into each other. It was crowded in the back of the camper. Sofia's curly hair was tied back with a large pink bow. "They'll get us at night." She lifted her eyes. "They come in packs on motorcycles and chop off women's breasts and fry them up like eggs. They like big breasts like Eve's."

After Esalen we searched the Mojave Desert for undiscovered ghost towns and isolated hot springs and a place to celebrate Finny's sixth birthday. Somewhere special, so that Anton could tell Finny he was adopted, and give the rest of us our first lesson on forgiveness.

We traveled from place to place on the whim of Anton's curiosity and on ideas picked up from strangers. Anton had a vast imagination and a knack for meeting strangers with fascinating ideas. Mom sat up front encouraging Anton's imagination, in love with all the possibility that spread out before us. The eight of us in the back made bets, guessing where we'd end up next.

Panamint Springs. The Chocolate Mountains and Mono Lake.

In San Francisco the big kids saw *Hair* and the little kids saw a Chinese film in which all the good people died. We were mad, though, about missing *Hair*. We'd wanted to see the naked people dancing onstage. Rancho Mirage to Funeral Creek and Dead Man Creek. Convict Lake. Oasis. Anton and Mom liked going places just for their names. Devils Playground. Tecopa.

"She had a splendid bosom and a nice wide behind," Anton said after meeting a Russian in the tiny town of Tecopa, a landmark because of its hot springs. Anton stood on the dirt road that cut through town. His accent intensified and his words drew out long. I looked around for where a Russian would be. I saw the Gila bar with its rickety porch and the Casa del Sol mobile-home park, a blue stucco structure concealing the baths, and not a soul in sight except us standing around Anton.

In every town it was the same. We emptied from the camper, spreading over the town, and the people seemed to disappear. Maybe they were afraid because we looked so strange. All scruffy, some of us in long dresses, some in raggedy tuxedo tails, halter tops and bell-bottoms, bare feet and polyester plaid. Some of us played stretch, throwing a jackknife between our feet. Nicholas carried his guitar and his movie camera. Timothy carried a .45 caliber pistol from the First World War that had belonged to his grandfather. Our hair was unbrushed. Layers of dried sweat slicked our skin. Everyone disappeared and the town was ours.

We took baths and washed up in the hot springs, scrubbing ourselves in the steamy water, and there was nothing in the world that felt so good as being wet and chilled and clean in that heat. Until I was told to shut up, I explained to anyone who would listen about the geology of the West and the formation of hot springs.

Dust swirled at our feet and heat drummed into our scalps. "There's a town she told me about not too far from here where they don't mind if children play the slot machines. Just over the state line in Nevada." Anton's cowboy hat shaded his face and he pulled his pants up by the belt loops. "She says there's a vineyard with an active winery and tastings. Even kids can taste. And in the hills above, a ghost town. Says it's the best in the area. Tonopah, Nye. Said she even saw a ghost." Anton gave us a wink and pinched Mom's behind.

Mom gazed at him lovingly, and then at us, Jane, Julia and me, her daughters. The gentle closing and opening of her eyes said, love him.

At first I wanted an itinerary, something to hold on to like a cane. I didn't believe that we would find ghost towns without knowing where to look. I didn't trust, Anton included. Mom promised it would all work out, smiling down on me with that smile full of hope. "The Big Sur fight was just a little misunderstanding," she said. "Anton loves us and is giving us a lot." Even the gap between her teeth was somehow promising, encouraging me to believe. Her curly golden hair blew away from her face. She said she would explain about Finny. She knew how much I loved Finny. I was a good sister to him now, protecting him always, never mean. I showered affection all over him. We were together everywhere, trying to figure out if our paths had ever crossed before. He was my one true love, my first love, and I wasn't ever going to let anything bad happen to him.

"Be here now, Kate," Mom would remind me. I still wanted to pinpoint on maps where we were going, but Anton didn't like plans. Plans left no room for spontaneity. Often we didn't eat dinner before ten.

Anton gave us five dollars apiece to buy birthday presents for Finny. We rode off on the Hondas to the nearest town. Anton had the idea of getting Finny a pet iguana, but he hadn't found one by the time Finny's birthday came around, so he gave Finny a piece of white paper with an IOU written on it. I bought a chunk of turquoise from an Indian—a nugget to hold on to like I held on to my rock of gold.

In the evenings we played football. Tackle, not touch. It was a big deal if Anton chose you for his team. It meant he thought you were good. On his palm he drew imaginary strategies which I always got backward. Julia was always chosen to be on his team. She had to be the best at everything. She even claimed she could shoot her pee farther than the boys and would engage them in pissing competitions, lining them up at the edge of a field. Their pants down, her dress hiked up, hips thrust forward. And she would win. She'd never have done this around Dad. But things were different now. I thought maybe things were better.

At dusk the whole world turned red and the few cottonwoods that were out there changed from green to brown to black. We left the road for unmarked lanes, and parked at the edge of someone's field. Mom and Anton propped up an orange tent that claimed the land as ours. We'd play a game of football and then Anton would open a bottle of wine and have a smoke. The rest of us would do our jobs. The girls did the cooking, except for Julia, acting more like a boy. Anton didn't think it was right that the girls did all the cooking. He was a feminist, he said. He believed that girls should be more like boys. But when we cooked we ate earlier than if the boys did it. Mom set up the aluminum card table and draped it with a cloth. It was the one moment all day when I knew what to expect.

We cooked baked beans and hot dogs, adding brown sugar to the beans. "It makes them more gourmet," Sofia said. When she was nice, you felt special. It could be a smile or a touch or a simple comment that included you with her against the rest and you'd want her to be on your side all the time. We made Chicken Surprise, which meant you put whatever you could find into it, and hash browns and hamburgers and grilled chicken marinated in mayonnaise and mayonnaise brownies. There was nothing quite like the smile you'd get from Anton when you cooked something he liked.

Sometimes after dinner we would play poker or sometimes Anton would gather us around to scare us with a ghost story, having fun with us. Once Mom jumped out with a stocking over her head and a dagger poised in her hand.

Anton organized us with scrawled lists indicating who had to do what when. His name was never on any of the lists, which Jane pointed out. He taped the lists to the cupboards in the camper. From the cassette player Anton's classical music would blare. Evenings we weren't allowed to listen to anything else.

"Why don't you ever help out?" Jane asked Anton one night after dinner. "Why isn't your name ever on those lists you write up?" We all sat at the table. I took a deep breath. I wished she hadn't said that. Everything had been going along just fine. Our faces were illuminated orange by candlelight, our bodies lost to the dark. It was quiet out there and the night sky was bright and thick with stars. An airplane flew overhead.

"Don't tell me what to do, babe," Anton said calmly. He took a sip of Jack Daniel's, holding Jane with his eyes. "I've been driving all day." Silence.

"Driving us to where?" Jane asked.

"Jane, babe, be happy with where you are." The muscles at the corner of his mouth tightened and his eyes squinted.

"You tell us what to do all the time," Jane persisted, "yet you never do anything yourself." Jane knew how to provoke him. She knew how to argue.

Mom sighed. Her thumbnail ran over her lips. "What about dessert?" she suggested.

"Looky here, babe," Anton said, shifting forward in his seat, "do your dinner job and don't let me hear about it. I'm warning you." He gulped some more Jack Daniel's. The music blared— Beethoven, Mozart, I didn't know which. I could feel Anton getting bigger. Even his sideburns became more severe. Jane's braids hung long, pulling her face down. Her big brown eyes opened wide.

"Warning me? I think you're just lazy," she spit the words out, shoving her chair back from the table with a stack of dishes in her arms. "All you do is smoke dope and drink and it makes you lazy."

Anton stood up quickly, raising his hand to strike, and a surge bolted through me. His chair fell back and he kicked it out of the way, moving toward Jane. Julia jumped up and blocked him, while Jane walked quickly to the camper. She was too proud to run. "What are you going to do? Hit me?" she asked, turning to face him. He loomed above her with his hand rising again and I thought he would actually do it. I tried to get up, but Finny whispered, "Don't," laying his big hand on my thigh—protecting me now.

"Cut it out, Dad," Caroline yelled, and Julia screamed and grabbed his arm. "Stop it," she said, her eyes piercing him. He tried to knock her out of the way.

"Anton?" Mom asked. She sounded small, tentative. Yet she stood up and went toward Julia. "What are you thinking of?"

Anton froze. He couldn't look at Mom. Finally, Caroline and Julia took the plates away from Jane and they all went into the camper. Then Nicholas went in and the four of them talked—the big kids. I could hear Jane crying and I could see the silhouette of Julia comforting her.

"Looky here, babe," Anton said, loud, into the camper. "I'm warning you. This once. I'm not going to put up with this." Then he disappeared into the night. All we could see of him was the amber tip of his joint.

I told myself, he tried to be patient. There was so much to organize with all these kids. But even so, I wished we had our car. We started eating and talking again, cleaning up. Sofia spoke gently to Mom, explaining. Finny stayed by my side. I could feel he wanted to explain too. After a fight we'd all feel a little closer, more like a family.

"Anton has a lot on his mind," Mom said later that evening, apologizing, trying to make everything all right. "With Finny's birthday approaching. He's adopted, you know." She held us, Jane, Julia and me, with her eyes. Her look pleaded with us, Forgive him. She explained about Finny and I hated her for using him as an excuse for Anton's behavior, for forgiving Anton so easily. I thought of cats again, ones from the 4-H club and the pound. Skinny and sad with droopy eyes, the corners of which were filled with crusty dried tears. When my sisters had wanted to torment me they had said that I had been adopted. I realized we didn't torment each other so much anymore.

"I'm sorry, babe." I heard Anton apologizing to Jane in the night. The rest of us were trying to fall asleep in the camper. "It's been a hard time. You're not mad at me are you? You forgive me, I know you do. Right, babe?"

Finny. Big hands and those magnificent eyes. Naked and tiny, he's holding the bag of marijuana. It's an enormous bag and he looks kind of silly holding on to it; he's carrying it around like a security blanket. Anton has to remind him not to carry it around in public. But for the most part there is no public, it's just us, and those vast stretches of desert with nowhere to hide, and that overwhelming sun. I just stare, making sure nothing happens to him. Finny, too, can concentrate for hours. Sometimes I can feel his eyes on me like I feel the sun on my skin, burning into me—as if he's trying to figure out what it is that we share.

Sure-boned and flat-footed, Finny is. Flat-footed like me. Peasant feet, that's what Mom says, Dad's feet. Anything that's bad about us belongs to Dad. Jane's weak chin and brown eyes. Julia's stubby fingers. But Julia's nose, that slightly upturned, aristocratic nose, belongs to Mom and so do Jane's long legs and slender knees and so do my cheekbones and my green eyes and long, curling lashes. My crooked teeth and dark hair are Dad's.

I study Finny to see what his mother's given him, to imagine what she looks like. Thick curly hair, a strong jaw, high cheekbones, olive skin. His hipbones poke through his skin and there's a birthmark there, a blotch of brown like a stain that could easily be wiped away. I love everything about him. I think about the baby Mom almost had with Anton and I think about Timothy saying that baby would be his brother and not mine and I wonder if Finny has any sisters he doesn't know about.

"What are you looking at?" Finny asks, glancing at me from the corner of his eye.

Mornings before the heat. Anton would go off on the Honda 70 to get a paper, if a town were near enough, and some sort of Danish for a surprise. Before breakfast Anton would say grace and read a short prayer. "Eating is one act that we all must do." His face serene and gentle. Eyes contemplative, hands folded in prayer. "Food is a surprise which we often don't think about." Then he'd say the prayer. Mornings, fights of the night before would be forgotten.

In the beginning, I didn't care about all the prayers and blessings and I didn't really listen. Anton had a red book and in it he'd written his favorite prayers and blessings and with it in his hands he stood up at the head of the table. His mouth was dry and sticky when he spoke. His kids bowed their heads, so we bowed our heads too and everyone held hands. Finny's were sweaty and cold.

Oh my God I am heartily sorry for having offended thee. I detest all my sins because I dread the loss of heaven and the pains of hell but most of all because I love thee oh my God who art all pure and deserving of all my love.

Mom smelled in the morning, a kind of old smell like bad breath except it came from her skin. You could see through her nightgown, her big breasts like eggplants drooping heavily down her chest. She loved that Anton was religious. She said Dad wasn't religious. She said he'd never had a sacred thought. But it did something for her, made her feel more moral, good, incredibly good. I didn't bow my head. I watched her, her eyes gently shut, and I could feel she was far away and then I bowed my head and gently shut my eyes too and listened to Anton's voice, a part of me trying to go there, wherever, with Mom.

In small towns like Tecopa or big towns like Barstow, Anton met strangers. He and Mom wandered off, leaving us to stretch our legs and drink our sodas. They met a tattooed Indian riding a Clydesdale horse. They met a young bald woman with silver barrettes sewn into her scalp. They met a cowboy driving a platinum Cadillac with a pair of bullhorns straddling the hood. And from these strangers they learned of county fairs with rodeos and fiddling contests and chili-eating contests, racing armadillos and tobacco-spitting contests. They learned of craters made from meteors and craters formed from sunken volcanoes in which ran creeks of gold. They heard of sites filled with dinosaur bones and sites with the remains of early man, of sand dunes from which blasted hot springs, and he and Mom wanted to find it all.

"Ask and you shall receive," he would say, with that wink that invited you into his world.

"He's a phony," Jane said to me in the baby blue and smelly bathroom of some isolated service station where we were washing up. Her long braids frayed like ropes and I thought, she's at it again, and I knew before long there'd be another fight. Her entire body was wet and soapy. "A nobody, gathering us around to feel like a somebody. He's a monster. Helmut was right." She scrubbed with brown paper towels. At that moment I didn't agree with her. It took very little for me to love. Momentarily I let my twenty dollars go. I forgot about plans and destinations; in the end the places would always be there just as he had promised: the ghost town, the craters and the dinosaur bones.

We saw a man break the world record for spitting tobacco—thirty-six feet, one inch. In Pahrump we got drunk on the best desert wine and won lots of quarters that were as good as the promised gold. I forgot about Finny. I forgot about home. Everything—the road, the sky, the Joshua trees—would hang in suspense, waiting for us to discover our discoveries. It was all there, everything.

The first stranger of Anton's that we met was James. James was an English hitchhiker and he led us to an ancient inland sea and bird sanctuary with over three hundred species: red-winged blackbirds and song sparrows, common yellowthroats and killdeer, snowy egrets and the black-masked loggerhead shrike. He had binoculars and monoculars and bird books, and it wasn't long before we were settled there with the orange tent erect. Anton was a Jesuit and a giver and he never left anyone in need. Through James, Anton tried to teach us generosity.

"Where's he gonna fit in?" Sofia asked, leaning out the back door. Sun flooded into the camper. She wore her halter top and short shorts and a pair of platform sandals. One of her arms linked the outside ladder and she dangled out the door with a smile. Her eyes inspected the stranger, absorbing him, while Anton helped him in with his pack, asking him questions to make him feel welcome and comfortable. "We're crowded enough as it is back here with Eve's kids."

"Don't start, babe," Anton said.

I held the gold rock tight in my fist and thought of Dad. He would never ever pick up someone we didn't know, a hitchhiker. My nostrils flared.

James was quiet at first, sitting on the floor with his tired body folded over his knees. Then he started asking questions, trying to get to know us. Sofia did most of the talking. "We're not all family," she said, "so don't get the wrong idea." Then she distinguished us, first by family, the Fureys and the Coopers, then by groups: the big kids and little kids. "Anton is our dad and he's a doctor. You can call him Dr. Anton. Eve is their mother and she's just like Doris Day."

"Grace Kelly," I said to Sofia, studying the ends of my hair. I'd picked that habit up from Sofia. She could look at the ends of her hair for hours. I didn't see what was so fascinating about it, but I pretended just the same. Dad had once said Mom was as beautiful as Marilyn Monroe, but Mom hadn't liked that. She'd said it wasn't nice to be like Marilyn Monroe and had suggested Grace Kelly instead.

"Doris Day," Sofia said. "She has no sex appeal and she's not elegant." The others ignored us. For the most part, everyone except for me ignored Sofia.

James wore faded jeans and a T-shirt with holes. His hair was long, brown and curly, and his skin tanned. He was thin, medium-tall, with high cheekbones. Around his neck hung chunks of turquoise, and silver bands ringed his fingers. He had pale blue eyes flecked with yellow. His accent was smooth, with a twist of sweetness. He came from both London and Scotland and was in America trying to discover what it was he wanted to do with his life. He wanted to be a poet. Recently he'd been robbed and was waiting for a wire transfer to come through. I thought he was cute. He smelled of smoke and of outside, wonderful and clean.

"Furey?" James said. "Like Michael Furey from "The Dead"?"

"That's right," Caroline answered. No one else knew what they were talking about.

"And Cooper," Julia said. "Like James Fenimore Cooper."

James looked around at us hanging all over the place. Finny sat at the table and rolled Anton's joints. "Out of sight," James said and relaxed his back into the counter and straightened out his legs, getting comfortable. It didn't take him long to be absorbed by us. We all fell in love with him. We all wanted an English accent. He taught us words like *bloody* and *suss* and *chap* and *brilliant*. He didn't take sides, Fureys or Coopers, because he knew us as one family, as if we'd always been this way. By Finny's birthday, two days later, James was like a ninth child and just as much a part of the family as any of us, with a dinner job and his name scrawled on Anton's lists, with no plans to leave.

In a field of juniper bushes at the edge of the ancient sea, we collected around Anton like a congregation around its preacher. Family meeting. We had family meetings all the time to discuss stuff: where we were headed; what us kids thought about Anton and Mom as a couple; how we felt about God; what food we should buy for the week; you name it, we had a family meeting about it.

Breakfast just finished, plates were heaped on the aluminum table. One hundred degrees in the shade, but dry and light as down. Near our feet little balls of cacti clung to rocks like sea urchins. In the distance the White Mountains and the jagged Sierra Nevada rose purple to snow-covered peaks. Their reflection shimmered on the lake. It was an eerie lake, like nothing I had ever seen, with thousands of white towers emerging from the water and from the banks, knobby and fragile like enormous sand-dripped castles. I wanted some of those rocks.

Brine flies droned steadily, feasting on brine shrimp, and the sur-face of the lake was thick black. The flies lifted and settled in waves.

Anton read a few prayers about nothing becoming something, about the generosity of Christianity, about saints and sins and heaven and love. Divine love. And I tried to pay attention to all he was saying but couldn't. I didn't care. No one paid attention but Caroline and Jane, who both prayed with Anton. Caroline re-minded me of the Virgin, the way she folded her hands in prayer. Timothy spit spitballs at our feet and Sofia polished her nails. Julia stood near me. The sound of Anton's words soothed, and I thought of his soft hand patting my head. Nicholas filmed the scene, paus-ing now and again to listen to Anton. Nicholas looked pale and sick, as if he could throw up at any second. He'd had too much to drink the night before.

Finny's presents were a colorful heap on the table, with the IOU taped to one of the boxes. Anton's glasses rested on the end of his nose and he studied the pages of his book earnestly, squinting. He seemed gentle and almost beautiful. He wore a long white cotton tunic with an embroidered yoke. He was comforting and the shirt billowed away from his body. I looked at his hands. I looked at Finny, standing in the group impatiently, kicking the dust; I won-dered if he knew what was coming.

"The beauty of Christianity," Anton said, "is forgiveness. To learn that Christ loves you and forgives you is to be saved." Anton spoke on about forgiveness and generosity. Forgiveness. I didn't know anything much about religion, but it seemed both grand yet nearby in him. The wind fluttered the napkins on the picnic table. The moon was still in the sky, thin and transparent, from the night before, and that worried me. I thought it should be somewhere else.

When Anton finished preaching, Mom led Finny away to the camper with a handful of dishes. Jane pulled me close to her. I knew this kind of thing would make Jane sad. I hoped she wouldn't cry. Sometimes it was as if all the pain in the world went through Jane.

"I'm including the Coopers and James in this because we're all family here." James stood there awkwardly and uncomfortably, smoking a cigarette he'd rolled himself. I worried he wouldn't like us anymore, knowing so much about us. Anton stared at the ground. "No need to keep anything from anybody. Today I'm going to tell Finny about his mother. As my kids already know, he has a different mother. This won't be easy for him, so I want you all to be supportive." He spoke with a penitent voice. He talked about mistakes and about how good things come from mistakes. He said Jesus had been a mistake, which I really didn't understand and it confused me when I thought about it so I didn't for very long. It seemed like it was painful for Anton to talk. His eyes couldn't meet ours and his head jerked a bit. "I was selfish," he said. "Too stupidly Catholic to believe in divorce then." He fingered his chin and held back tears. He waited until they passed to speak. "Selfish. I wouldn't let his mother have him." I was sorry for Anton. I thought he might cry, but instead he read a prayer.

When Mom and Finny came back, Anton took Finny for a walk. As they walked away across that brown parched land, they became smaller and smaller, two specks in the distance, the tufa towers rising all around. I had a hollow feeling in the pit of my stomach, watching Finny's long hair. His snarled curls. His plaid pants hung low on his hips. The cuffs dragged in the dirt. His enormous hand clasped Anton's. I held my rock and thought about my father, the day that he left. I thought about us being here and then I thought about the moon and the men landing on the moon and I looked up at it and then looked around and I imagined this was how the moon would be and I knew Finny was about to lose a lot. His world was about to alter permanently, half of it draining out of him to evaporate in this lonely landscape. I stood there watching as he receded into space, wanting to scream for him to stop, as if I could save him. Sand blew into my sandals, between my toes.

"Finny's a bastard," Timothy spat into my ear. "I told you so. He's a bastard, bastard, bastard." A smile spread wide through his lips. Timothy loved to hear himself speak, the sounds of his words, and he pecked them at me. Mom's baby came to mind and made me sad and then the idea vanished. Timothy's boxy hair shimmered and his big teeth glistened, long like a lady's polished fingernails. He coughed out *bastard*. Shooting it out: bastard. Chills rushed through me. "He's a bastard. Bastard. Bastard."

Finny started wetting the bed all the time and the camper smelled up with pee. Timothy wouldn't let him alone about it and Finny got his own bed, which made everyone else mad. Anton wrapped his mattress in special plastic that made a crinkling sound every time Finny turned in his sleep.

For the most part I was on his side, until he stole my rock. We were in the parking lot of a diner, stopped for lunch in one of those makeshift towns.

"There are hundreds of rocks out there," Sofia said, gesturing out toward the land, "that are much prettier than that ugly one of yours. And what about all those rocks you've collected that are all over the camper?"

"You stay out of this," I screamed. Finny held the rock up in his fingers for me to see and smiled.

"Give it back," I said. "I gave you a rock. That one's mine."

"Not anymore. It's mine now," he claimed. His blue eyes glistened, such a weird blue. "I don't like the one you gave me."

It was dusty on the pavement and very hot. A light wind blew scraps of paper around in circles. Mom and Anton approached us.

"Mom," I pleaded. "Tell Finny to give me back my rock."

"Work it out yourself, babe," Anton said. And then Mom smiled as if we were cute animals playing.

"Settle it between the two of you," Mom said, as they went into the restaurant. We fought for several more minutes, rolling on the asphalt. He was stronger than I and I hated him. In fact, I'd never loved him. My dress ripped. I scraped my knees. I could feel them bleeding.

"You can have it, it's only a dumb rock," I said, finally. My knees stung. "At least I can get another one. At least I know where both my parents are. I know where my father is," I screamed, standing up and wiping my dress smooth. "I know where my mother is."

The restaurant was all chrome, blond, shining in the relentless sun. Inside was air-conditioned. The sweat dried on my skin, making it brittle. I shivered in the cold. Foot-high cakes swarming with jimmies rotated in a glass carousel. Wedges had been cut away and the insides were a beautiful fluffy white, laced with berry jam. The cashier smiled at me through a heavily madeup face.

An extra-long table had been put together for us in the center of the diner and everyone sat around it. Finny pushed in next to Anton. Red plastic water glasses stood by all our plates and in the center of the table were baskets heaped with rolls. I was hungry. I took a deep breath. I looked at Mom. She was asking the waitress lots of questions about where she was from and if she knew any wonderful out-of-the-way spots that we should visit. Black grime wedged under Mom's fingernails. She wore a T-shirt with a caption reading STAMP OUT SEXISM in bold letters above a picture of a little girl in jeans stomping on *Dick and Jane* books. Mom's breasts bulged through her too-small bra. The waitress spoke back enthusiastically. Finny had my rock in his hand. I could see the little flakes of gold sparkling through his fist.

"Two-dollar limit," Anton said sternly.

On the menu there were only hamburgers for two dollars. I didn't eat hamburgers. I didn't like chopped-up things. I didn't eat tuna fish, it was like eating cat food. Mom had always felt that way too. Never before did we eat chopped-up things. There was a basket of fried chicken and french fries for $3.35.

"I want the fried chicken," I said.

"You heard me, babe. Two-dollar limit." His voice had a keen edge to it. He was the biggest man in the world. I had never known anyone so big. I didn't love him anymore. I didn't love anyone anymore.

"I don't eat hamburgers," I snapped.

"Looky here, babe, there're other things on the menu. How about a grilled cheese?" Anton offered. "Or a bowl of soup?"

"I want the chicken," I said. My nose stung. My eyes were wide.

"Kate, you're gonna listen to me." His face pulsed. The veins running up his temples swelled, becoming thick like worms.

"I won't eat then," I answered.

"If you're gonna behave like that, fine."

Mom chewed on ice. Her expression said, "It would have been so much easier if you had just given Finny the rock." This was how we blended. We had to give each other everything and not look back and not get upset. Give, give, give until our identities melted together. No privacy. No locked doors, not even while peeing. There should be nothing to hide if we loved each other. If one of us wanted to be alone it meant something was wrong, that that person wasn't having fun. "You aren't having fun?" Mom would ask, her world momentarily ruined until you reassured her and she was happy again. That smile full of hope plastered on her lips.

I sat on my hands while they ate, rocking my body, and started thinking about my twenty dollars. If I had my twenty dollars I could buy my own lunch, but then I thought that, if I had it, I wouldn't spend it on lunch. I'd use it to get home. I'd go on a bus. I'd ask Mom for the money again as soon as we were alone, and then in the next big town I'd run away and if she didn't give it to me I'd steal it. Jane snuck me a french fry. It was cold and limp, but it tasted good. I thought, I could get Jane to go away with me.

Sounds of the restaurant slowly filled in the silence. Plates clattering, small families in window seats talking, songs on the radio, the sizzling of food on the grill. A fly. Anton told James about his book, and they talked about love and poetry and Anton told him poetry was a noble profession to pursue. He said he wished he had the means to be James's patron. Anton was making the newcomer welcome. He didn't feel a need to do that with us anymore. I hated him. Then Anton told James proudly that he was Irish and asked a lot of questions about Scotland, if it were true that mushrooms grew there freely on the moors. James said they did grow and that you could pick them yourself right out of the goat shit and this excited Anton and even Mom chimed in, trying to smooth over the fight, iron it right out of that afternoon. Then James, fascinated, asked a lot of questions about us and how we came together. Mom told him everything about Anton, from his being a Jesuit, to a poker player, to a Gestalt therapist, and as she spoke James fell in love with her, with her enthusiasm. I could see it. "Is this a typical American family?" he asked Mom with a smile, and she laughed. "It's becoming more and more so," she answered brightly. I didn't care about Anton or this family anymore. My plan was warming me up inside, making me feel big again.

Everyone talked—pass the salt, the pepper, the water, oops something spilled—fixing their food just so. A chaos of voices. Mayonnaise oozed from James's sandwich, dripping off a piece of lettuce. Anton told Sofia not to smoke, but she smoked anyway. I wondered if James were paying for himself or if he too, now one of us, were part of the two-dollar limit. I snatched a roll.

"I thought you weren't going to eat," Finny said.

"Shut up."

"Looky, babes, I won't have anymore fighting." Anton spoke to both of us now. "I'm going to send you to the camper if you don't behave." His mouth made an unsucking sound when he spoke, the way it did when he smoked too much. Finny rolled my rock in his fingertips quickly, flashing it for me to see.

"Bastard. BASTARD," I shouted. I was shivering, breathing quickly, frozen for a second while the word vibrated through me, but then I saw Anton rise with a red and swollen face. In a second I had locked myself in the bathroom. I sat in there on the sink and stared at my face, my big green eyes flecked with spots of brown. My long hair tangled. My dress filthy. At first I was afraid that Anton would come in, afraid he'd rip open the door. But he didn't come. Nobody came. And then that made me mad. I thought about the rock and then about Finny. When I fought with friends at home, Mom would pull me aside and gently whisper, "*La noblesse oblige*" and send me back with a pat. I hated Finny and didn't want to oblige. I wanted my rock back. It was *my* rock, from my father. I had to have that rock. I scrubbed my arms and legs vigorously. I combed my hair with my fingers and twirled it into a knot. I rinsed my face. I wanted to be clean. I wanted to get away.

On the phone outside the bathroom I called my father collect. He answered and accepted the charges before I had a chance to change my mind.

"Kate, baby, where are you?" I didn't speak right away. I wanted only to hear his voice. "Are you there, honey. Kate? Katy?" His voice was just the same. Somehow I expected it to be different since everything else was different. The receiver chilled my hand. I pictured him at his desk in his apartment in New York. It was a tiny apartment filled with rocks and maps, but even so he had beds for all of us. Beds that folded away into each other, "Like a matrioshka doll," he'd say. I wanted to crawl between the cold sheets of one of those beds and fall asleep.

"Dad," I said finally. The hem of my dress tickled my ankles.

"Where are you, baby? What's wrong, sweetheart? Is something wrong? I'm so glad to hear your voice." My nose twitched and my palms sweated. There was so much to explain.

"It's fine." I pressed the receiver into my lips and wrapped the silver cord around me. "I'm in a diner in California." My heart jerked but I breathed more slowly. "I just wondered if you'd come get me? I want to come home." I spoke very matter-of-factly, actually believing that it would be so simple. I'd just wait for him there in the diner. He'd show up in his little white VW. I'd get in, close the door and together we'd go home, where things would be just as they used to be, before all this. I was impatient, I wanted to get there right away.

"Of course I will. Baby, I miss you. I miss my little girl so much. I need to speak to your mother." His voice was urgent now. "Put Eve on, Kate."

"It's his fault, Kate. He didn't give me anything, Kate. He left us, Kate." Mom's voice scratched through my mind. A woman squeezed past me to get to the toilet. Her body knocked into mine.

"What town are you in? Tell me the name of the town?" he said.

Then Mom appeared and I killed the line. Dad's voice receded,

sucked back across America through all that wire, just like a mea-
suring tape snapping into its metal casing. Mom looked at me,
wondering. I flushed, prepared to lie, but she let it go. It wasn't
easy. Her hands clutched her hips, her lips quivered, but she did let
it go. I was just tiny standing there. She knew that I wasn't going
anywhere. Anton appeared behind her and his arm slid around her
waist and he smiled and inside me filled and then emptied and I felt
dirty even though I was clean.

"Don't be mad at me, babe," he pleaded gently. His eyes asked
forgiveness and we stared at each other for a minute and I was
hoping he'd give me my rock, but he didn't. Then I hoped he'd give
me fried chicken or, better, my twenty dollars, but he didn't.

"How about a little football game?" he asked.

HUNDRED-DOLLAR DAYS

Jane lined us up in a row. First Jane then Julia then Kate. Jane's hands were cold and she was giddy. She listened. Her brown eyes widened. Julia giggled and I mimicked Julia and giggled too. Nervous, anxious laughter. "Shsh. He's coming," Jane said. We were in the foyer of our house, looking out the window behind the door. There was a nook near the window for coats and boots, and the three of us could fit into it if we squooshed. Sun streamed through the window, blinding the outside.

The car door slammed. Julia hugged Jane's waist and I hugged Julia's waist, leaning forward into each other squinting; as Dad came closer through the white light, we could see him. A briefcase in his hand and a few newspapers. It was as if he were in a cloud or a dream, and I giggled again. We waited behind the door, ready to surprise him. We waited for this moment every day and every day we surprised him.

The door opened and we leaped on him. Inside me felt dizzy, opening and closing. Julia always managed to be the first to kiss him, her arms clinging around his neck. Inside his briefcase he always had a surprise for us. Once he had a sweet-gum sapling he'd found by the train tracks. He'd planted it in our backyard for Mom.

Then Dad started to work at home.

The school bus let us off. Every day we wore matching outfits that Mom had made on the sewing machine in the basement. Julia would decide which outfit we'd wear and would lay it on our beds in the mornings. Jane and I always agreed. We didn't care so much about those things. Jane took the mail from the red mailbox and we walked up the driveway. Each day Dad was in a new spot. Sometimes he was behind the door in the nook. Sometimes he hid among the trees lining the driveway and he'd creep around in there, making noises, trying to scare us. We always knew it was him, but we pretended to be scared anyway. Sometimes he was so impatient he'd just be standing there at the end of the driveway, waiting for the doors to open and for us to burst off the yellow school bus.

Then that too was over.

Allison was the first friend from my old school whose mother stopped allowing her to come over to my house to play. She was a blond girl with light blue eyes. They weren't jewels, kind of dull, but they were blue and she was blond and that nose was angled just right. Her teeth were straight and she had a Chihuahua named Spinky. I wanted one of those dogs. Her barrettes were gold filigree. She loved the word *filigree*, and I thought the word was beautiful too like the swirling design that it made. Filigree pretty. Allison was filigree pretty, with all her delicate lines and birdlike ankles. Her thin blond hair.

"I can't come over," Allison said. "I've got piano lessons." I stood in the kitchen, the phone cord wrapped around me. It was a long cord that you could wrap and wrap and wrap around you. I was wrapped up like a mummy. My fingertips turned white. She had piano lessons yesterday. My mouth twitched and hung open long, the way it did when I was denied something that I wanted, feeling stupid for asking.

"You must want to be an expert," I said. "How about after?"

She was quiet a moment. Sun came through the window, making me hot. It was one of those hot fall days. I'd worn wool to school when I should have worn cotton. I was always getting the weather wrong. Julia wasn't deciding our clothes anymore. I'd been uncomfortable and red all day.

"Lessons," she finally said. More lessons. Ballet and dance and swimming and skating. You-name-it lessons. Her voice was annoyed. I used to hate spending the night at her house. She had five sisters and three of them slept in one room. Not because they couldn't afford to have their own rooms but because they preferred it that way. The older two were at boarding school. I slept in Allison's trundle and we talked until late, the four of us. Allison and I were the youngest. Just after we'd drifted off the fighting would begin. Allison's father had a mean voice and he was large with deep eyes and a thick mop of black hair and Allison's mother was beautiful, very tall with black hair too and blue eyes and she'd hold me. In her arms I never felt like leaving. They were long, slender, warm arms that wrapped me up like the telephone cord and made me feel protected. We'd hear things fall and the older sisters would talk loudly and tell a story and Allison would laugh and the mysterious sounds would be vaguely hidden.

One morning Allison's mother had a patch over her eye, a gauzy patch, and the edges were surrounded with Vaseline so that her skin shone, but some of it had turned brown and crusty like pus. Even so that other blue eye beamed and her hair curled perfectly, pushed back with a wide bandeau.

Clara was next. She was blond too. Then Dolly. Dolly had been my best friend. We had best friendships like boyfriends. Breaking up with miserable tears, declaring new best friendships, avoiding the ones we'd outgrown. "Who's your best friend now?" we would ask each other. "Did you know that Allison dumped Clara and now Allison is best friends with Dolly who had been best friends with Kate."

A bird flew against the kitchen window and fell onto the bricks outside. The kitchen floor was cold. "Mom thinks you treat me like a priest," Dolly said. Dolly was Catholic. I was confused. "You tell me too many things," she said. I wondered when Jane and Julia would be getting home. "She thinks you're troubled and need too much right now." I remembered her house. It was always messy and her father was never home, which I liked. The fathers frightened me.

I spoke with Wendy's mom directly. I called her house and asked for Mrs. Baird and I asked Mrs. Baird if Wendy could come over. Wendy wasn't ever a best friend. She'd been Clara's best friend once, but as far as I knew they'd broken up.

"Hello, Kate," Mrs. Baird said. She had an English accent. She made us chocolate sandwiches the one time I'd had a play date at her house. Slices of white bread spread with chocolate icing. "Wendy's schedule is tight these days with the new school year under way. You must be busy too, with your new school? Now I'm planning a party for Wendy's birthday in November. I hope you'll be able to make it."

"Hello, Mrs. Conquest." "May I speak with Mrs. Tiller." "Dolly, is your mother home?" Hello, Mrs. Davenport. Mrs. Campbell. Mrs. Fritz and Mrs. Fitzpatrick. Mrs. Love.

I had a friend at my new school who loved me very much and so I tortured her. She loved me because I was the only other child in our class who had lost her father. Monica DeMore lost her father when she was five years old. He disappeared and that was it. One morning early, while she and her mother still slept, he left and they never heard from him again. He sold something door to door, encyclopedias or Bibles. It didn't matter. We wouldn't have been friends if things had been different. After her father left, she and her mother dressed entirely in white and bought a white car. They moved into one quarter of a duplex near the train tracks. The back of the house looked out over a graveyard.

Monica had pale, translucent skin and stringy orangish hair that fell in clumps as if she had just five thick strands. You could see through it to the pink of her scalp. Her eyes were suspicious, little red slits like a lizard's, that watched. Nasty eyes searching others, roaming them to see what it was that they'd taken from her, as if anything they had had been stolen directly from her. Beneath the diamond-shaped slide on the vast field that was our school playground, she searched me with those lizard eyes as I told her about hundred-dollar days.

"Dad gives us a hundred bucks for our birthdays and we can spend it on whatever we want as long as we spend it with him." I made it sound like he'd been doing this forever, but hundred-dollar days only began after he left.

"He must really love you," she said. I looked at her until she had to look away. I loved watching her eyes quiver. I loved hearing her wavering soft voice, laced with a rasp of wonder. Cautious. Afraid to let me know too much, yet still revealing everything. It did something for me, her jealousy, her pain. It made me feel like I really had a lot.

"Yeah, I guess," I shrugged my shoulders and pulled up my socks. "And the hundred doesn't include lunch or any of the extras, like a show or a carriage ride. That's why I go to New York. There're more extras. Julia goes to the racetrack to gamble. A different one each year. But there's not much else to do at the racetrack." I didn't mention Jane, who refused the hundred-dollar days, who sent Dad's presents bounding back to him.

"I'd go to the racetrack," Monica declared. "I'd rather double the money than spend it." Little blue veins shone through her translucent skin. She thought she'd said something smart and that made me mad. Especially because Julia had won.

"No, you would not go to the racetrack," I said. "Because you'd lose. Besides, in New York I collect rocks and minerals and paraphernalia for my collection." I loved that word, so lusciously big and sophisticated, rolling off my tongue. "We go to these tiny shops in basements and they're jam-packed with gems and fossils and rare rocks. I've got a soft blue kimberlite, the rock in which diamonds form. Hundreds of ancient fossils, and a nugget of gold.

I've got all the tools for collecting more rocks and minerals and just this year Dad bought me a rock tumbler."

"What would you want with a bunch of rocks?" she asked.

I gave her a look. That question annoyed me. "Make a million dollars is what. Some day I'll know so much I'll be able to prospect for gold and diamonds and I'll be worth a lot, a whole lot." Then I looked into the sky, searching it, pretending to calculate while Monica studied me. Her fingers played with the holes in her tights. It was cold, late autumn. Only the silver beech still had leaves. They would hold on all winter, turning yellow, until spring, when new leaves would push them off. "Last year Dad took me all the way to South Africa to look for gold. We traveled 6,800 feet down in the ground in an elevator to get a nugget of the rock that gold comes from." That was a lie, of course. I wished I had my bit of gold with me so that I could show it to her. I decided then that I would carry it with me always. "All the gold we saw down there, it was worth millions of dollars."

"A hundred-dollar day," she said, her eyes far away in the trees.

"You should get your mom to give you one," I said, flexing my toes inside my shoes.

One of the hardest things about living in the camper was changing clothes. I changed a lot. I changed at least three times a day. In part because the temperature was always changing. In part because it was just something I liked to do. But I learned to master putting on a new dress without revealing any of my body, slipping one arm out, the other in. Lifting one dress off, the other on.

"I'm going to strip you," Nicholas said, catching me practice. He stood in the doorway of the camper, sunlight flooding in behind him. A beer can rested in his hand. His eyes were red circles, blood-shot, hidden behind wisps of thin blond hair. He was always drinking beer. "In the middle of the night while you're sleeping." Of the big kids, he was the biggest, and he scared me the most. He had said there were so many of us, odds were one of us would die, soon.

GETTING AWAY WITH THINGS

Anton taught us to love and we all tried to learn. When we were all in love, times were great, and after a fight there was always a lot of love to go round—everyone always trying to make everyone else feel better. I was in love with Finny, but since he betrayed me with the rock I gave him the silent treatment and started to love Timothy. I knew it would irritate Finny. Love became a sort of currency with which you could negotiate—the more love you had, the better off you were. We tried to outdo each other with love. Julia was in love with Nicholas and at night they'd sneak out of the camper to wander off by themselves. Jane and Caroline were in love and together they loved James who loved them. He taught them to identify birds and arbitrated for Jane when she and Anton fought. James and Mom loved each other. They'd spend long hours talking about poetry, memorizing and reciting poems to each other. But best of all was when Jane was in love with Anton. When Jane was in love with Anton she'd tease him about his clothes—the lime green Bermudas, the tunics and shirts exploding with colors, the striped shirts and checked pants. "Oh, come on, babe, do I have to teach you a sense of style too?" he'd say, smiling at her with that pouty flirtatious grin.

Mom was in love with Anton and Anton would never let her out of his sight. Sofia and Nicholas were beginning to love Mom. Caroline already loved Mom. She helped Mom learn the rosary, which Anton had taken to chanting in the evenings before football. We were limber, falling freely, and our world was opening up. Wide. And even Jane was happy. We fell freely backward to each other. Human pillars, we fell and fell and fell.

The thing about us was that when we all got on we didn't need anybody else. The world was ours. Or the desert, at least. Some of the most fun we had was getting away with things. Some of the most fun we had was washing up. We washed up in hot springs and when we couldn't find a hot spring we washed up in hotels. Early, but just after the customer from the night before had left. A roadside hotel. The long kind, flat against the sky, beneath a neon sign. The customer would have left the key in the lock, the way you're suppose to, and we'd pull into the parking lot, cautiously and through the intercom Anton would tell us the numbers of the rooms that had keys dangling from the doors. We smelled. Dirty. The nine of us lying all over one another. Our clothes wrinkled. Quick like thieves we flashed from the camper to the rooms, showering before the maids got there. My insides raced. Even Jane liked this and momentarily we were complete and perfect and I couldn't stop smiling.

Anton loved to get away with things. Mom stood by his side, smiling and proud. We'd roll into town on an empty tank. We could go down lanes marked "private" and not get in trouble. We could go down roads with big orange warning signs about the bridge being out and the bridge wouldn't be out, or if it were out Anton would find a way around it. We visited parks that were closed, but the rangers let us in. Anton believed. He had faith and even the police couldn't catch us. If they tried, he'd outrun them or lose them, or if they did pull us over they wouldn't ticket him.

"Finny, babe," Anton said through the intercom. "Put the dope away, babe. No one look out the windows." We'd seem suspicious if we looked out the windows. He'd taught us that already. The flashing lights swirled over the road and the sirens hollered. Timothy kept squealing that we'd get arrested. "We're gonna get arrested," he'd say, his eyes and toothy mouth opening wide. "Arrested." The camper rolled to a halt. All of us a little nervous. "Bloody hell," Julia said, trying to sound like James. Nicholas held his guitar and James switched off the cassette player. Each time the same. Sofia put on lipstick. She said she had always wanted to fall in love with a policeman. Caroline said a prayer. Jane stopped stitching her needlepoint.

The policeman walked stiffly in blue, metal clinking. Mirrored glasses. Finny rolled up the bag of dope and slipped it in the Wheaties box. I worried about the roaches in the cab ashtray. "Roaches." I liked that word. It was one of those words that using made me feel big.

"Well, officer, I'm a, I'm a little embarrassed about all of this," Anton said, stuttering. His drawl thickened. The policeman asked for his license and registration. Anton had two licenses—one from Texas, the other from New Jersey—so that if he did get ticketed he could divide them evenly between states. Through the intercom you could hear Anton fumbling for his wallet. Inside the wallet there was a J-87 badge. Deputy Commissioner of Parking: Texas State Department of Transportation. It had belonged to his father-in-law—the oil heir—and was an honorary badge the state gave to rich people who "contributed" to the construction of roads.

"Pardon me, Commissioner. I apologize for the inconvenience, Commissioner." The policeman tipped his hat and bowed away. Anton told him to have a nice day.

Sometimes Mom would take a turn. She'd lean across Anton and smile up at the officer and embarrass him. "Officer, it's just, it's just . . . I apologize. You see it's my fault. It's my period and I I . . ." Embarrassed, he'd back away.

Sofia would start painting her toenails again and Julia would flirt with Nicholas again and Finny would dig into the Wheaties for the dope again. The sky was blue, blue and wide with absolutely no clouds.

We rode the minibikes into town sometimes to do the shopping. A couple of us kids on a bike and we zoomed off as fast as we could.

Anton gave us some money and stickers that read, THIS AD INSULTS WOMEN and we were supposed to sneak them onto boxes that showed women in a compromising way. Women sweeping or ironing or cooking or wearing aprons or doing the laundry. He was trying to teach us things, claimed that was his job. "We're his acolytes," Julia said dreamily, lifting her left eyebrow. Mostly we didn't care about all that. Mostly we just wanted to ride.

It was vast out there, with nowhere, absolutely, to hide. And though the bikes were little they could move pretty fast. I liked riding the 50 by myself. You could see us spinning doughnuts and you could see us doing wheelies. Sometimes we rode as fast as we could to nowhere, just out, away, zooming over the bumps and leaping into the air. We were riding over sand that used to be a sea. A few patient clouds mocked the blue sky. Air rushed over me and I shut my eyes, feeling the speed. A wake of dust kicked up behind and the soothing sound of the motor sang in my ears.

We raced. I was racing Timothy when I fell, chasing him actually, through a field of flowering Joshua trees. The trees flowered red, white and blue and we camped near them just because of that. Anton said it was unusual for them to be flowering this time of year and Mom said we were blessed. We had hiked through that field so that we could see all the trees. Hiked haphazardly, without a plan, all of us spreading out into the landscape until we'd gotten ourselves good and lost. Anton loved to get lost. He'd get lost just to get lost and find his way out. Mom had said we were blessed on that hike when a storm rolled in and the rains came down. We were standing there, all over the place, between the trees. The sky turned yellow and the air began to smell, first like an herbal bath, then like mildew and sewers, and as the light turned yellow all the various plants took on the most magnificent colors. Their own colors, but intensified, no longer muted by the sun and heat. Radiant reds and greens and yellows and browns and it was as if we were inside a prism. We had absolutely no idea where we were. "To be alive," James said. " 'To live, to err, to fall, to triumph, to recreate life out of life!' "

"Joyce," Anton answered. "I always believed that line myself. But add, 'to be lost.' "

I was riding the Honda when I hit a creosote bush full throttle and my pubic bone smashed into the handlebars and the minibike somersaulted. We landed together in the sand with the hot engine singeing my shin. All around tall grasses. Brown. With a wonderful straw smell.

It didn't take long before everyone knew about my bruise, a big, deep purple bruise on my private part, punctuated with tiny spots of black. It was so ugly I told Mom, because I worried something more serious was wrong with me. I worried I wouldn't be able to have babies and thought maybe I should go to a doctor to check it out. I suggested we go home.

"Don't be a silly-billy girl," Mom said. "Worrying about babies. You're eight, Kate." She smiled down on me, pushing her curls behind her ears.

Then Timothy started teasing me about my bruise and Nicholas too and Sofia and even Jane and Julia thought the bruise was funny, so after a while I began to think it was funny too, except that it hurt. And since everyone knew, I complained.

"Do you want me to have a look, babe?" Anton asked. He squatted down in front of me and held my hand. We were in the camper. Outside the sun was setting and the sky was all fuchsia.

"I think it would be a good idea if he checked it, Kate," Mom said. "Since it makes you such a worrywart." I felt special that he wanted to check it. I thought checking my bruise was the kind of thing a father would do and I wanted Anton to love me like that.

Anton put a blanket on the table and lifted me onto it and told me to lie back. Mom stood beside him, pressing her thumbnail into her lip and smirked at me for being so silly. I kind of did feel silly for worrying about babies.

Some of the others came in and out. The screen door banged. Mostly they stayed outside, doing their own thing. I felt kind of sick and feverish. No one had ever seen my private part before except when I was a baby and I couldn't remember that. I wished I were wearing better underwear. I took it off. The elastic was frayed and holey. It had been nice underwear, white with a band of fringy lace. Mom used to say that elegant people wore only white underwear. She said we should always have on clean, fresh underwear in case something happened to us, like a car accident or a plane crash, and some stranger had to look at it. I imagined the four of us dead and strangers lifting up our dresses daintily, inspecting our underwear. Mom didn't say stuff like that anymore.

Anton's hand was cold on my stomach. I couldn't look him in the eye while he inspected the bruise. I drooled. I could feel the drool wet on my cheek and I wiped it away and the back of my palm was shiny with it. It wasn't that easy showing Anton my private part. But he spoke gently, like a father, so I did as he said. Relaxed, took deep breaths. Mom started fussing around in the kitchen, preparing things for dinner.

I flinched. I didn't want to feel anything. I was afraid it would hurt. But it didn't. Instead came a chilling, whispery sensation. Like I was cracking. Unfamiliar. Mom opened the refrigerator and something toppled out. "Fuck," she said. Anton's head was really close, inspecting. I thought of Julia, who loved to inspect. Then I thought about her pictures on the chalkboard and remembered her pointing to the clitoris and the labia, left and right. I almost started laughing, thinking about her pictures. I really hoped something serious would be wrong. My eyes opened wide and my stomach tightened. I wanted to laugh. It seemed like forever was passing.

"Relax, babe," he said. I heard Jane yelling at Julia. They were fighting about something or other and I wished I were out there to fight with them, or better, to mediate. Inside it was really hot. I wished Mom were holding my hand the way she used to when I'd have to have a shot at the doctor's office.

"It's a pretty big bruise," he said. A million knots formed in my stomach. "Relax, Kate," Anton said again, his voice almost impatient. Goose bumps rose all over me. Suddenly I had this awful feeling crushing through me. I was staring into the camper ceiling. It was dirty, filthy. I wondered if he loved me. I was afraid he didn't love me. Mom had promised he did. I thought of the way he loved Julia and how she always flirted with him. I wished I could flirt with him.

"Does she look okay?" Mom asked.

Someone came to the screen and asked for something. "How's the bruise, Kate?" Sofia's voice.

"She'll be fine," Anton said. "You feel a little better, babe?"

And he stood up and kissed my forehead. "How about a little game of football?" he asked.

Family prayer and rosary.

"We'll do three Our Fathers, ten Hail Marys, and one Glory Be. The idea," Anton says, "is to chant as the Muslims do and while chanting reflect on whatever you think. Though the idea is to train yourself to think about God."

Hail Mary, full of grace, the Lord is with thee. Ten times. Those are the only words I can remember. The others I mouth, but there is something soothing in the repetition. I want to learn the words by heart. I love saying them. I want this chant to last forever.

"If you don't know Hail Mary or Our Father it doesn't matter, follow in spirit."

After one decade Anton stops and tells one of the joyous mysteries, the Annunciation, and tells the story of God deciding to become man and of God telling Mary by sending the angel. "There doesn't seem to be anything more joyous than God making himself man to man in the body of a woman." Anton's head remains bowed. He asks Julia to read Psalm 4, which she does. "Some of the psalms are didactic and repetitive, but this one I particularly like."

During the psalm I can't think about God. I think of Anton checking my bruise and of how even so the bruise still hurts and then I remember how it had felt, shivery and good, when he'd touched it. I feel dirty. I think about all of us loving each other, about times being good, but how now, even so, I want to go home.

Then dinner. Green beans and shepherd's pie. Angel food cake with brownie-mix icing. That was my idea and everyone loves it. Everyone is noisy setting the table. Fighting over this and that, the same as every evening. Everyone afraid there won't be enough to go round. There always is. Anton taps his glass to say grace. We quiet down and join hands. Listen. When he's finished we each say our own blessing to thank Anton. We thank him for providing the food, for driving, for being generous. Caroline thanks him for bringing our families together and then she thanks Mom too for loving her as a daughter. I'm in love with Caroline. She's soft and quiet and warm and just the way she speaks to you or touches you makes you want to be good, like her. Jane's turn. "Thanks for teaching us to argue." She smiles. Everyone laughs, relieved. James keeps his hands folded and his eyes closed and he thanks Anton for saving him when he was destitute and for giving him a place to live and he thanks Mom as well for loving him as a mother would. He's decided to stay on and live with us. My mind empties and all I can think about is Anton checking my bruise and that whispery sensation I had had. Thinking that makes me feel dirty inside like I'm black and rotten in there. Mom said she thinks of her insides as clean and white like a potato, but I know mine aren't like that. I felt them moving, sloshing around, excited and hurting. Now I can't think of anything to say except that I want to go home. I look at Julia, who encourages me with a nod. Anton's prayer book is opened in front of him.

"Kate, say a blessing," Mom urges. "Ka-te, it's your tu-rn." To the others she says, "She's just shy."

"I'm not shy," I murmur, then add: "I love Anton." My voice is so soft I have to repeat it. But that's not what I want to say.

I saw Dad and our big white house receding into a past, left there alone like a dream, a memory, getting smaller, smaller, fading as we moved forward. His life stuck there, unchanging, so unlike ours, so utterly separate. As if time stopped for him when we weren't there.

I began to believe in the ordinary. Believed in it so absolutely.

When I would want to crawl beneath the cool sheets of my bed back at home. My knees ached. I was tired. It was tiring being extraordinary. It was tiring loving all these people. "They're just growing pains, your knee-aches," Mom would say. "Knee-aches?" Anton would say and smile at me as if I'd just invented something ridiculous yet grand. I became shy around Anton, afraid he'd want to check my bruise again. He'd smile at me with that pouty, flirtatious grin, sensing my new shyness, trying to knit me back into him.

He bought me things. An orange book called *Poisonous Dwellers of the Desert* with a scorpion on the cover poised to strike—he knew how much I liked to identify things. A BB gun because he wanted me to be tough and to trust, more like a boy. It was a beautiful shiny black gun that looked real. I identified gila monsters and learned to shoot straight at a pyramid of beer cans Anton had set up for me. He stood behind me in his robe, his arms wrapped around me to help me aim. One by one I shot all the cans down, and as I did Mom clapped and shouted, "Brava, brava." I learned to twirl the gun on my fingers like John Wayne and Clint Eastwood. I belted the leather holster around my hips and wore the gun proudly.

But even so, despite the gifts, the gun, I wanted my old life back. It sat out there on the horizon like a poker hand that was just within my grasp of winning. I saw our white house on that horizon and my father walking down the driveway to get the mail and the newspaper. Ordinary and simple like before.

We were finally headed for the Grand Canyon, because none of us had ever been there. Anton held a family meeting and the issue was decided. "I told you so," I said to Finny and winked proudly. I could see in his eyes and by the way he looked at me that he held me in awe.

"You don't know anything," he said, but I ignored him. If we went back to my father he wouldn't be my little brother anymore and none of this would matter.

For a long time it had made me sad, the idea of Dad at the Grand

Canyon waiting for Julia and me to arrive while we were at home studying the multiplication tables, and I had wanted to go there as if Dad would still be there—his life frozen, waiting for ours to catch up with his. But I didn't care about all that now either. I wanted to go home.

I didn't have any crazy ideas about going home by myself. I was going to go with my sisters and Mom, back to our house. I was tired. Exhausted. Inside I started getting anxious, feeling if I didn't act soon it would be lost. I started drawing calendars, marking off the days. I made lists of the things I needed to do in order to get us home. One way or another I was going to do it. I knew it would take some planning and time, but I was resourceful. That's what Mom had always said about me. We'd take a bus or a plane. I'd get us there. I thought about my twenty dollars all the time now, knowing that if I had it I could multiply it. I remembered poker. I had an inscrutable face, could have it if I wanted it. And if that didn't work, I was going to call my father and get him to come. But he'd have to promise to take Mom too. I felt good inside. Grand, actually. I liked having a plan. With a plan I knew what would happen next.

I wrote my father letters, preparing him. The first letter was mailed from Lee Vining. I dropped it in a blue postbox. Weeds curled up its legs and it stood alone at the end of a parking lot by the edge of the road. There wasn't much in that town, a strip of stores, a few hotels flashing VACANT signs and miles of dry, brittle terrain. A yellow-shirted boy raced by on his bicycle with a baseball bat poking from his knapsack. My legs were sore. My knees ached. I imagined he was riding home.

The red earth reddened in the early evening light as if about to crack, and the air turned cold. The moon was a wafer, blending with a few wispy clouds. I dropped the letter in the box and listened to it clap against the bottom. I had told Dad where we were, had described the tufa towers of Mono Lake because I thought he'd like to know. I described all the rocks of the different terrains we'd visited. I told him about the fruitcake mélange of the Big Sur cliffs. I told him where we were headed, hoping he would come. Then I thought about the letter being picked up by a postman and taken to somewhere, to another postman and then to another, passing through all those hands, until eventually it made its way, dirty, to my father sitting at his desk. By then we'd be long gone from here.

I thought of how on my father's office walls, over the maps and charts, he'd hang the notes and letters we'd write to him. "I love you"s scribbled down on scraps of paper, singing to him, keeping us present.

I wrote my father from several towns along the way, really believing he would come after us. I imagined him following the trace of my letters, scattered across America in the pits of those mailboxes, collecting them like bread crumbs until he caught up with us. His little white car dawning on the horizon, slipping in the oily mirage of road, catching up with the camper. I saw him standing by his car at the Grand Canyon, excited, preparing in his way to give us a lecture about the land. Waiting, with an itinerary for our trip home in his hands.

Even if Dad had tried to come after us, he never would have found us. One moment you thought you were going one place and the next thing you'd be somewhere entirely different. I had written Dad that we were headed for the Grand Canyon, but just when we thought we were going there we ended up in Malibu. I still saw Dad everywhere, sneaking over the horizon in the white VW, coming around that bend in the road, appearing late at our campsite a little tired, smelling of sweat, that dry, dusty sweat—the way you sweat out here. Jane would forgive him and Julia would hug him and Mom would wrap her arms around his neck and kiss him on the lips. We'd put our stuff together and kiss everyone good-bye and get in the car and drive away.

We went to Malibu because we needed another car. There were too many of us for the camper and when we picked up strangers we were absolutely uncomfortable and we were picking them up all the time now. We picked up some Ursuline nuns whose car had broken down. Lively ladies who flirted and teased with Anton in a way I didn't think God, or those working for Him, were allowed to do. We picked up some proper girls who were trying to be hippies. But they left quickly because they found us strange. Anton got it in his head to postpone the Grand Canyon and go to Malibu to borrow a car from Mark Bitar, an old patient who hated children. We'd be doing Mark Bitar a favor if we borrowed his car and drove it back across the country. Mark Bitar was a bicoastal millionaire and wanted a car in the East, so the plan was good for everyone. I didn't care what the reasons were, I was glad we'd finally have another car.

Mark Bitar's house was a long, flat modern one overlooking the ocean, with lots of windows and mirrors and green carpeting. Candles lit the house and the soothing sound of waves and of the wind in the palm trees came through Japanese doors. The living room had high ceilings and an indoor swimming pool surrounded by a rim of steps on which rested wooden candelabras carved with naked figures having sex. A thin layer of mist drifted just above the pool. In the corners stood peach-cushioned massage tables and from the ceiling hung ferns. The Japanese doors led outside to another pool and beyond it was the ocean.

We descended on that house like we descended on any town, making it momentarily ours. It was after midnight when we arrived, and all of us clomped in, dropping our stuff here and there. We carried sleeping bags and pillows and found places to sleep anywhere. We were tired and hungry. My knees ached. I wondered if Mark Bitar knew we were here.

I fell asleep easily in a beanbag chair, although I felt a little uncomfortable sleeping in the house of someone I hadn't met. I worried they'd wake up in the middle of the night and see us sprawled all over the place and it made things worse that he hated children.

"Do you know," Sofia said in the dark, "this is the worst place we could be when the big one happens, the big earthquake. It's expected, you know."

"Shut up," Timothy said.

"Like the Hell's Angels?" Nicholas teased.

"The land'll just break away and we'll all fold into the ocean and disappear." I knew better than that, but I was too tired to explain.

"You've multiplied," Katherine said to Anton, as she came out to greet us in the morning. Everyone was eating and some of the kids were already swimming or down by the beach. Katherine was Mark Bitar's girlfriend, although she was twenty years older. Sofia had said that since Mark Bitar hated children, he had an old girlfriend so he wouldn't have to have children. Katherine was beautiful, with lots of blond hair piled on her head and soothing brown eyes. She dressed entirely in pale blue. "Every time I see you you've multiplied." Anton laughed and they flirted for a moment and she asked about his book and he asked about her work. She devoted her life to religion and traveled everywhere learning about all the different religions. She had her own bedroom, separate from Mark's, and there was one gigantic waterbed and an enormous bathtub in front of a window that opened onto a tiny courtyard in which stood statues of religious figures that she said came from all over the world. The only one I recognized was the Virgin.

It wasn't long before the orange tent was erected on the front lawn and all the contents of the camper were strewn over the asphalt driveway. Anton and Mom wanted to clean the camper out before we got going again, which was a good thing because it smelled. We spent a few days vacuuming and scrubbing, rearranging our luggage, throwing away garbage. The rocks that I'd collected in Big Sur and Mono Lake had spilled all over the place and Anton told me I either had to keep them orderly or throw them away. Sofia threw them out, but I didn't notice until later, and by then I didn't care.

Anton put Mom in charge of the cleaning and we were supposed to do what she said, but Anton's children didn't pay attention to her. Mom got mad at them, but then Anton got mad at her for getting mad at them. In the end he had to take charge. "I can't be responsible for everything," he said. Jane told Mom that it wasn't fair that Anton could boss her kids around, but that she had no authority over his. "Ja-ne," Mom said, drawing out the name to mean, "Let it rest. Everything's wonderful." But I agreed with Jane.

Mark Bitar was a tall man with a thin red beard and large brown eyes fringed with stubby eyelashes. He wore white patent-leather shoes that clicked on the asphalt and a pair of hip-hugger jeans that were so tight I could see the outline of his penis. He laughed a lot and Sofia said that he'd spent time in a Swedish Hospitality Institute in Connecticut. "A funny farm, you know." He made silly jokes and laughed at them and somehow the funny farm made sense. I hated people who laughed at their own jokes. I thought about a story my father had told me about a tall man, so tall his head touched a live electrical wire, the kind up with the telephone wires, and he got electrocuted and died.

In the afternoons, Mark and Anton did therapy in the study and we had to be quiet. Sometimes we'd hear Mark cry. Mostly we heard nothing. I hoped he was discussing why he hated children.

The kids were scattered all over the place, trying to stay out of the way. Mark Bitar and Katherine were hosting a party for Anton. Jane and Caroline were in the kitchen making dinner for us. It was night. A green night. The music was loud. Incense burned. People filled the house. Anton flirted with Katherine, telling her about the dolphin therapist, John Lilly, who spent his life studying the thought patterns of dolphins because he believed we could learn from their placidity and love of sex and life. The outdoor pool was heated up and steam lifted off it. Katherine kept asking for more stories. I saw the silhouette of their arms and hands, fingers pinched together. Nicholas and James were in the pool with the adults. James and Mom and an older man with a deep, drawn-out English/American accent that sounded strange, discussed poetry, quoting poems to each other. They drank champagne. Mom's eyes were wide and remote. Her nose red. Her arms crossed over her breasts. I could tell she didn't feel comfortable being naked in front of them. The man with the funny accent said he'd heard about their blow-up at Esalen, said he wanted to hear her version.

"Oh, Lord," Mom said. "Anton was just being ridiculously jealous over nothing."

"Marvelous," the man kept saying. He put his hand on Mom's shoulder, rubbed a little. "Absolutely marvelous." And then they continued to talk about poetry.

Bottles of champagne popped open and people milled about the buffet under a blue-and-white striped awning. Oysters and clams. "They're alive," Sofia warned and she squirted lemon on them so that I could see them flinch. I didn't eat them. People dropped their clothes everywhere. I worried that they'd all get mixed up and nobody would find the right ones. Then I laughed at myself for worrying. Then I hoped the clothes would get lost and everyone would have to go home naked. I didn't want to see any of the naked bodies. I hoped they'd all stay in the steam. I thought about my bruise. Anton asked me all the time if it was better. At first I was honest. Now I lied, still afraid he'd want to look at it again.

On the buffet next to the oysters and clams a heap of tiny mushrooms rested on a silver platter. "They have to be eaten in groups of seven," Mark Bitar explained, pinching together a bunch of seven and popping them in his mouth. He totally ignored us kids. "For a good high try forty-nine. Seven groups of seven."

"Were they really naked onstage?" I asked Jane in the kitchen. Her face was red. She was making creamed chipped beef. It had been a long time since we'd had any of that. Caroline cut up parsley. I thought Jane looked beautiful, though her big brown eyes were tired. I felt sorry for her. "You mean in *Hair*. Yes, Kate," she said, annoyed. She'd told me they were naked a hundred times already. And so had Nicholas and Caroline and Sofia and Julia.

Anton fed seven mushrooms to Katherine. Mom held seven in the palm of her hand, eating them one by one, standing alone now in the shallow end of the pool. Her big breasts hung like weights from her chest. I watched her and kept thinking about maggots, as if she were slipping maggots between her lips. Mark had said the mushrooms grew in shit and that in the shit there were little white maggots.

Someone walked around playing a flute. He was followed by another man playing the harmonica. Timothy splashed in a cannon ball into the outdoor pool to make Mark mad. I was so tired.

Everyone was lost in the mist, drifting in it. A woman in a long dress stretched her arm over her back and unzipped her dress and it slithered to the ground and she stood naked with no underclothes. Just high heels. "Dina. Marvelous Dina," the older man said. Anton drifted over to Dina and they hugged naked, and started talking about his book. I thought of Dad showing up now in his little white VW and I almost started laughing. The candles hissed, sparks flitted. Dad would be mad.

"My father's coming to get us," I said to Finny as he marched by.

"No he isn't."

"Fuck off." I paused, thinking of something mean. "When he does you won't be my little brother anymore."

"Kate." Mom floated up to me and wrapped herself in a robe. "Anton's promised shooting stars." She clutched my arm and dragged me down to the beach. The ocean was glassy, iridescent, running over our feet. Shells rippled on the sand. Water soaked the hems of my dresses, making them heavy with sand. They smacked against my ankles, chafing the skin.

With her heel Mom dug a hole in the sand. Then she shoved her fingers down her throat and threw up. She wobbled, clinging to me. Spit drooled from her lips as she heaved. The chewed-up mushrooms followed. I held her steady, wiping away the throw-up with the back of my hand. I wanted Jane here. She'd know what to do. I tried to act grown-up like Jane.

"I'm going to get Jane," I whispered.

"No. No," she said. "Absolutely no. I can't bear another fight." I felt older than Mom, and that scared me. "Just my little Katy." Houses lined the beach, lit and glowing, in perfect order, warm inside. I could see figures walking around. I didn't want anyone to see us. Mom threw up again, heaving. From the beach Mark Bitar's house looked like all the others. "Look at that moon. Just look at how bright it is. It's a million-kilowatt moon." She wiped her lips with the back of her hand and together we lay down. Her hands crept up my warm stomach. "You're my baby. This flesh belongs to me," she said, squeezing my chest.

"Stop it," I said. I worried about what would happen to her with those maggots and mushrooms inside her, worried she hadn't gotten them all out. I thought about a dog we once had named Bark. A stupid name, but we loved it then. Bark ate two of her puppies that had died during birth and Mom had to make Bark throw up so that she didn't get sick. Mom explained that dogs did that. It was just what they did. They ate their dead puppies.

Mom's hands felt awkward and uncomfortable, massaging me. "You're drunk," I said, sounding like Jane. I wanted to get away from her. I thought about my letters in the pits of all those mailboxes. When Dad came I thought he probably wouldn't want to take Mom and that made me sad. And then that thought kept stabbing me like when you do something horrible and embarrassing and keep remembering it. I'd make him take her. He'd have to take her. He loved her. I knew he loved her.

"What are the mushrooms going to do to you?"

"Don't be like Jane," Mom said. Then she was quiet for a moment. I thought about a long time ago when I'd come home from the hospital and Dad had come back to our house. I wondered what would have happened if I'd have opened the door. I moved her hand from my chest. Sometimes I thought they'd be together if I had done that; Mom could have told him how much she loved him.

"But Katy, I created you. You're my Katy." She held my hand and stretched our arms out toward the sky. Her skin was dry. "Such a silly-billy girl. Why in the world are you wearing two dresses?" Then she laughed uncontrollably, and nibbled on my ear. She felt the holster around my waist. "You like the gun?" she said, as if my wearing it meant so much more than it actually did.

"When are we going home?" I asked. But she wouldn't answer. She just held me there, rocking me. It seemed like a long time. Our ears pressed into the sand. I could hear things in the sand: Mom's unsteady heartbeat, pulsing in my ear as if the earth were breathing. After a while I thought she almost fell asleep.

"Go get Anton, Kate," she said suddenly, jerking up. "He was supposed to come right out here. I think he's gotten himself lost. Come on, honey, go find him. Maybe he's in the tent." I thought about Katherine. I thought about Dina. Mom's nails bit my arm gently and she nudged me in the direction of the house. "Ask him for your twenty dollars. He'll give it to you, sweetheart. I spoke to him about it. Go get your twenty dollars."

Anton was alone in the tent. Its zipper peeled open with a loud metallic sound. He lay on top of the sleeping bag, illuminated by a dim flashlight suspended on a cord above him. His skin was an awful jaundice yellow and his face pasty and pale. His lips were white and a smile spread over them.

"Who is it," he asked.

"Kate," I said. "Kate."

"Not so loud, babe," he said. "Shsh. I'm listening."

"To what," I whispered. A thin line of red ribbed his eyes and his lashes were wet. He didn't speak. I wanted my sisters. His breathing slowed. The tent was close inside. My dresses felt tight from being wet. A jar of Vaseline glistened next to his head. Mom's underpants and bras were folded into neat piles in a corner. I thought about our laundry back at home. How it smelled of lemony soap, folded perfectly and you couldn't tell whose pile was whose. Outside, wind chimes chimed.

"For gila monsters, babe. Shsh." His accent was slick and sticky. He put his hand on my thigh and I noticed his wallet bulging out of his pocket, on the verge of falling. It was a fat wallet. I thought about the hundred-dollar bill he had paid the gypsy with. I could tell the wallet held a lot of money.

"There aren't any out here," I said, adjusting myself close to the wallet, gently touching it so it would fall. I lay down on my side next to him and opened it. Many hundred-dollar bills lay between the leather. Crisp and glorious, new money. My eyes widened and I swallowed.

"The tent's breathing, babe. Can you see it? Looky there." His voice startled me but his eyes were still closed. His finger pointed to the canvas. I wondered if Julia had ever been alone with Anton. "Can you see that?" I couldn't see anything. Then he faded again. My fingers touched the money and I watched his shut eyes. I thought if I just had a little bit of that money, it could be useful. I could buy things, get us away if we had to. I would have taken less if there'd been a smaller bill, but there were only hundreds.

"I had a dream about a baby," Anton said. Gently I moved my hands and laid them by my side. I was getting impatient. My blood rippled and I felt high, eager. I wanted to get that money. "I was being chased through a house. Running, and all the rooms kept opening up on more rooms like a Chinese box until I got to a bathroom." His words came slowly, spaced by long pauses. "And you know what I saw? A baby, a little pink bald baby, sitting on the toilet seat. As I approached it the toilet flushed and sucked the baby down with one big *whooossh*." He made a long-drawn-out *whooshing* sound. His lips curled out into a wet, red "o," but still his eyes stayed shut. My fingers slid back to the wallet. "All that was left was one pudgy leg, poking from the bowl." I lifted the bill, quickly, noiselessly, and tucked it into the pocket of my dress. My cheeks flushed. The soles of my feet turned hot. My ankles stung, chafed from the wet sand.

"Did you try and save it?" I asked. "I mean did you try to pull its leg out?" I sat up and kissed him on the forehead and he kissed me back, a dry sticky kiss. My heart pounded against my ribs.

"Lie here with me a minute, babe." His arm straddled my belly, pulling me to his chest, against his hairy stomach. "You're wearing your gun, babe. You're a smart girl, babe." He was quiet. Then, "We're going to the fantastic."

"Right," I teased.

"Shsh." He put his index finger to his lip. "You'll see in a minute." His stomach pushed into my back with each deep breath. One of my hands rested on my pocket, protecting my hundred-dollar bill. I was tiny in his arms. I thought about a picture of me with my cat, the cat that Dad had shaved. The picture hung in our study back at home. A black-and-white snapshot. The cat was folded over my arm, limp, as I crushed it against my chest.

"How's your bruise, babe?"

POWDERED MILK AND
MARGARINE

I had stolen before, back at home, before California.

I stole chicken from Camille Cain, my father's lover. She made the best chicken—all white meat, with a peach glaze—and she made lots of it, a whole cookie sheet, so that they could have it for leftovers. One meal for three days.

Camille was a practical woman. She had ledgers with her budgets written in them, and all her food she got for free by collecting coupons. It was a science, with entire notebooks divided into categories and filled with colorful coupons. She knew which supermarkets were having double-coupon days and would drive fifty miles to those offering triple-coupon days. Her cellar contained a small market of food, shelves for canned goods and an extra freezer for meat and frozen vegetables and breads. Everything alphabetical. A whole world of food that was dictated by special values and not by taste or desire. She used powdered milk and margarine instead of whole milk and butter simply because there were coupons. Cheaper. For free. Money saved. My father loved her. She devoted hours to teaching Julia and me about coupons, showing us her ledger and her calculations. She liked mothering us;

she had no children of her own. Sometimes Julia and I worried she'd want to have children with Dad.

"More children?" Mom would say to us. "Don't kid yourselves. Children take time. He doesn't have time."

We tried hard to learn about the coupons. We wanted to save coupons at home and get all our food free too. But Mom thought it was cheap to collect coupons and do all that saving and work for food you wouldn't ordinarily eat.

Sometimes, on weekends, Dad took Julia and me to Camille's house, a small place in the woods two towns away from ours. Jane refused to come. The house smelled of pine, and a little brook rippled outside the window. I always loved going to Camille's. There were rules. You knew what to expect: dinner at six sharp served with a meat, a starch, a vegetable, a salad, rolls—always rolls—and dessert. You didn't get dessert if you didn't eat all your vegetables and meat. If there was a vegetable that you hated you had to try at least three bites to make sure. But she rarely cooked something that we hated. Hamburger Helper and baby green peas; the baked chicken with a sweet golden crust and string beans. I always ate a lot when I visited them and sometimes I'd catch her watching me, but then she'd turn her head quickly as if she hadn't been staring at all.

The chicken was nestled in foil at the bottom of my overnight bag when she found it, four pieces, one for each of us. Camille's long ginger hair curled down her shoulders. She had beautiful shiny hair, which sometimes she let me braid. I was trying to grow mine to be just like hers. Her brown eyes sparkled with understanding and pity, holding me. I bowed my head watching the floor, smelling the chicken. She wore loose white cotton underwear and a T-shirt of Dad's. No bra. Her nipples pegged through the thin cotton. Her thighs jiggled, jellylike and large, but she wasn't self-conscious like Mom, who was always wrapped in a robe.

"Did you like the chicken, ducky?" she asked. I nodded. "Let's give you some more to take home." She held the nest of chicken in her hand. The pieces were beautiful in the tinfoil, with the peach glaze glistening on the crust. Pubic hair crept from her underwear, scaring me. I scratched my ankle with my other foot. She plucked more chicken from the refrigerator with tongs, lots of it, and wrapped it in tinfoil and repacked it neatly, first in plastic, then in paper, so grease wouldn't leak into my bag. "Would you like to take anything else home?" I thought of the basement filled with food, but said nothing.

"Throw it away, Kate," Mom said, standing in our kitchen in her nightgown. Her eyes were tired, her hair messy. She'd been sleeping. "I won't take chicken from Camille Cain." I dropped the chicken in the wastebasket and listened to it thunk through all the lighter garbage to the bottom.

The next time we went to Camille's, Mom sent us with a gallon of whole milk and a pound of sweet butter. She had clipped articles about margarine and powdered milk stunting the growth of growing children. We were to tell Camille to use the whole milk and butter in her cooking. Camille looked down on us with her hands on her hips, her hair pulled back in a net. "Now, duckies, that's ridiculous." She shook her head and rolled her eyes and continued to stir the new batch of powdered milk with a long wooden spoon. "Your mother really is something else." I liked the powdered milk, actually, although without the water. I liked spooning it into the palm of my hand and licking it off like Pixie Stick dust.

I noticed Dad using the whole milk on his cereal in the morning. We were up first. The house was quiet. Before, we always got up early together, at six, when the light was muted and you couldn't tell what kind of day it would be. I loved watching him use the milk and butter as if it were somehow a gesture toward our mother, a bond connecting them still.

"Do you like the milk?" I asked. My legs dangled from the chair, the tips of my toes barely touching the floor. The kitchen was chilly. Camille kept the heat low.

He looked at me with quizzical eyes, then looked at the spoonful of cereal and milk he was about to put in his mouth and smiled and said, "I love the milk." I smiled back at him.

In bed that night I nudged Julia awake. My lips pressed into her curls and my arms wrapped around her stomach. She rolled around to me, her body twisting in her nightgown, warm and a little sticky, though it was cold.

"What, Kitty?" she whispered. Our noses touched and she stared at me. Her eyes glowed like a cat's in the dark. She smelled sweet, of vanilla.

"Julia," I said. I wanted to tell her about the milk, but was afraid she wouldn't understand.

"I wanted you to be awake with me," I said.

"I'm awake with you," she said. She pressed her lips into mine and we touched tongues. She loved touching my tongue and I loved doing what she told me. It tasted warm and of nothing. She gave me nickels when I let her touch my tongue.

"Julia," I said again, "did you know that Dad likes the whole milk? Did you know that?"

"And the butter," Julia said and my eyes opened wide. "Did you see him glob it on his toast?" Inside me raced. I knew I'd have a hard time sleeping.

Outside it was a thick black night and through the trees you could see the universe, all lit up bright and hopeful. Anything seemed possible.

In the room down the hall, footsteps and then the gentle creaking of bedsprings could be heard.

"They're fucking," Julia said. "Mom didn't like to fuck."

DWAYNE: OUR SECOND
STRANGER

Finny quit speaking and we picked up Dwayne. It was no big deal, Finny's silence. In fact, since he never really spoke a lot anyway, no one seemed to notice much but me, and I only noticed because I spoke for him. I was tired of giving Finny the silent treatment. He needed me now and I liked to be needed. I liked speaking for him. It made me feel older.

Dwayne was our next stranger and he led us to the Desert Princess, where we stayed for many days because Julia got sick. He wore saffron robes, and was standing at a telephone booth. His hair was platinum and so were his eyebrows and eyelashes, making him look ethereal and religious. He wore cowboy boots with dust caught in the thin designs of the leather. He said he was a messenger from a mystical god, sent to lead people back to their selves. Dangling from his neck was the picture of a hairy-faced man in an amulet of nuts. We picked him up at a filling station on one of those junk-food strips, just as we left Los Angeles.

All it took was a dime. Anton loaned this man a dime and within minutes we were offering him a ride because his girlfriend had abandoned him. Plastic banners fluttered above car dealerships and dry cleaners, drive-thru restaurants and pool & patio stores. Palm trees shot high, their heads polka-dotting the sky. Garbage spilled from Dumpsters and an afternoon heat settled down on us like a thick wool shawl. The camper and Mark Bitar's beautiful silver Eldorado filled up with gas. Music blasted on the car radio and Sofia smoked a cigarette. Nicholas popped open beers. The others milled about, giving each other piggyback rides, fighting over who'd get to sit in the front. The convertible top was down. The smell of fried food made me hungry.

"My parents are at a spa. The Desert Princess. I suppose I could go there," Dwayne said, looking out at the road, his head jerking around nervously as if he feared something. He had fast eyes. He stared back at us, contemplating us, then out to the road again. His sharp Adam's apple poked through his pale, freckled neck. He began to cry. "She just dropped me and took off in the car." He had a southern accent.

I studied him along with Finny, who clung to my dress. He was glad I'd taken him back and that too made me feel good. The robes shivered over Dwayne's long, thin body and it didn't look as if he were wearing underwear or as if the robes had pockets, and I wondered where he kept his money.

"Don't do anything," Mom said earnestly to Dwayne, with her thumbnail pressing against her lip. "Don't call or write or anything. That'll bring her back. I know the type, dramatic, but don't play into it. Just you wait and see. She'll come back." Mom talked like a fortune-teller and Dwayne's eyes stuck on her. They were big and blue and he believed in her and Mom could tell and she could tell too that Anton was listening to her and he was proud of her, offering advice and generosity to a stranger as he so often did. "No one wants a burden. A burden's just a trap." Pink lipstick brightened her lips and a matching bandeau pushed her hair away from her face. She wore blue-jean cutoffs and the STAMP OUT SEXISM T-shirt.

Anton took off his cowboy hat and wiped his head with a hand-kerchief, made a phlegmy sound and spit. He offered Dwayne the ride. Thousands of tiny bits of glass and metal sparkled up from the pavement. It was easier for Anton to add a stranger than to cope with the problem at hand—Finny's silence—the way it was easier for Mom to believe more in other people's dreams than in her own.

"That'd be mighty nice of you, sir, but are you goin' that way?" He jittered some more, looking over his shoulder, then he reached down and lifted a small canvas bag from beneath his robes, swung it over his shoulder and started to cry again. "Is that all your family?" he asked, pointing at me and Finny and beyond us to the others at the Eldorado. "It's a beautiful family."

Mom wrapped her arm around him and that annoyed me. "Of course we'll take you," Mom said and raised her eyes to Anton for approval. Within a few days he'd be adopted.

"It's out of our way," I blurted. I knew because I had bought a map. "We're going to the Grand Canyon," I said. I'd scavenged money off the camper floor to buy the map. I wasn't going to break my hundred. It was my first map since the drive across the country and just holding it made me feel safe. I knew in which towns we could get a bus at any time. I knew how much the ride would cost for the four of us. I had been resourceful. I didn't need much more money. I held the map wide and it flapped in the breeze. Finny tugged on my dress, trying to quiet me, but we'd been headed to the Grand Canyon for weeks and now I just wanted to get there. Sometimes I still imagined Dad waiting for us, and if he weren't I knew that we could definitely get our bus from the canyon, and it'd be cheaper from there than from here.

"Kate, babe," Anton reprimanded. But I didn't care about him anymore. I was grown-up. With the hundred dollars burning through the pocket of my lower dress to my thigh, I was strong. Money made me strong, tough, tucked there in the fabric of my dress like a passport. I knew what it could do, what it could buy. I had cut the sleeves off the shoulders of my dresses and had torn away the white eyelet pinafore. My hair blew in the light north wind and I was beautiful. I could feel it, my cheeks slightly sunburned. My toes glittered a bright red polish of Sofia's. I glared at Dwayne and fingered my gun.

But Anton was a giver and he tried to teach us kids to be givers too. Generosity and forgiveness were the beauties of Christianity. And by evening I knew Dwayne would have his name scrawled on the list of dinner jobs and a space to put himself on the camper floor.

"Utopia," Julia whispered. "He's joining our utopia. U toe pee a. Another acolyte." We laughed. Even that laugh with her made me feel sophisticated. I wanted to tell her that I could take care of her.

Anton helped Dwayne into the back of the camper and we left that filling station and Los Angeles. The kids rode in the Eldorado with James driving and Julia and Nicholas by his side, flirting. An afternoon sun coppered our faces and the wind whistled in our ears. Now we had the convertible, no one wanted to ride in the camper anymore. It trotted in front of us, winding into the mountains and descending again into the desert on that long straight road. I thought of Dwayne alone in there and wondered if I'd have to love him too.

"How long do you think this one will be around?" Sofia whispered. "The longest we ever had someone was a year." Strands of her hair blew into my mouth and her breath was hot in my ear. "For that matter, how long do you think you guys'll be around?"

Not that much longer, I'd wanted to say. But I could tell, I knew she loved us. I loved her.

Dwayne called himself Consciousness of Breath, said that was his religious name, and asked us to believe. He'd been to India, where he'd lived in an ashram like Anton's wife. He was twenty-one, and didn't want to go to war, an idea we all thought would make Anton mad, but it didn't. He believed in the concept of the war and the concept of the right to life, but respected individual choice and told Dwayne he'd support him in any way he could.

At camp that night, after a game of football, when the desert came alive and snakes could be heard snaking through the sand and a million trillion stars lit up the sky, Dwayne led us in meditation which then became a dance. "We're trying to regain ourselves," Dwayne said. "Meditation is about throwing yourself back into your body." The eleven of us sat in a circle with straight backs and I wanted to laugh. Anton thought it would be enlightening for us to see another religion. He thought it would help his kids understand their mother. "Neurosis is rooted in the body. At some point in our childhood we decide that in order to survive, to get the love needed to exist, it is necessary to stop being ourselves and be what our parents and society want us to be and so we become fakes. We forget reality and stop feeling, tensing our bodies to suppress our needs." We sat with our palms up for several minutes and then with our palms down. Anton lit a joint, puffed on it and passed it around. One by one we took a puff. I watched Julia and Sofia when their turn came, watched them pull in a breath, hold it inside for a moment and then exhale. I tried hard not to cough. My eyes teared and my lungs burned. Slowly I let the smoke out and then my lips tasted of it, bitter. My head went dizzy. And then we smoked another.

For a while we were silent until Anton interrupted the silence to talk to Dwayne about Catholicism, which led into a conversation about his book on love and I didn't pay attention except that I heard Dwayne say that Catholics were the most opinionated people in the world and I thought that would make Anton mad, but it didn't.

"Palms up," Dwayne said. "Gets rid of the bad energy. Palms down welcomes new energy." He began to hum and asked us to hum too. "Hmmmmmmmmmmmmm. Hmmmmmmmmmm. Hmmmmmmmmm." Our voices were loud and echoed in the basin, against the mesas and the mountains, and I was embarrassed that someone might hear and think we were doing something strange. But it seemed we were in the middle of nowhere with no one else around and when I thought about that I became sad and listened again to the humming, which soon turned to screaming. It did something for us, screaming. I screamed until my throat became sore. Finny clung to my side. Dwayne rose to dance, lifting Mom who lifted Anton who lifted Julia who lifted Nicholas who lifted Sofia who lifted Jane who lifted James who lifted Timothy who lifted me who lifted Finny. We danced, jumping, spinning, twirling falling. Shouting. Screaming. Falling backward to each other. I went crazy with the screaming, trying to make Finny scream too, but Finny wouldn't scream.

"You're in your childhoods," Dwayne screamed. "Be yourselves."

"This is idiotic," Caroline said suddenly. Silence. We looked at her. She was shaking. She'd had too much to drink. It was the only time she spoke out. Her cheeks would flush as if burned by the sun and she could be either loving or hateful. Her hair was down and her eyes sparkled fiercely in the dark. She wore jeans and a sweatshirt and the sleeves were pushed up above her elbows.

"Why is this 'idiotic'?" Dwayne asked. His tone mocking the word *idiotic*. I didn't like him. I agreed with Caroline. His face held this weird laughing expression, but he wasn't laughing. He reminded me of a clown, a creepy clown. His platinum hair glowed in the dark.

"Go to hell," she said.

"Caroline, babe," Anton said, "you've had too much to drink, babe." He was always gentle with Caroline and treated her cautiously as if he were afraid of her. He never seemed big around her and that made me jealous.

"It's. It's just . . . " she stuttered and wiped her head. She said she didn't know and then cried and apologized and Anton held her in his arms and stroked her hair and she rested her head against his chest. "It's all right, babe." His big hand patted her back and Mom came near and said something comforting, pouring love all over Caroline.

"I'm acting stupid," Caroline said softly.

"You're not," James said, approaching her. Jane approached too and they comforted Caroline.

"This must be difficult for all of you," James said and he stared at us, an intense and puzzled gaze, as if for the first time. Dwayne gave James a quizzical look and I could tell he was jealous of James for knowing us so well. But that look of James's momentarily scared me because I thought he could see something we couldn't. For a moment his look reminded me of the look that Helmut had given us at Esalen so many weeks before and I became scared that he'd start to hate us the way Helmut had.

"I feel . . . It's no big deal," Caroline said, stumbling over her words. She put her face in her palms and took a deep breath. "I just started thinking about Mom—that's all." There was something sacred about her words, somehow like prayers, like the way she said the rosary. Soothing. And something beautiful and good in her sadness. I thought Anton would get mad when she mentioned her mother. Whenever I brought up Dad, Mom got mad, but Anton didn't. He held Caroline closer and her crying turned to muffled laughter and Dwayne looked on stupidly and I hated him because he, who actually knew nothing, already acted as if he knew everything. Anton said some tender words about their mother and about how wonderful she was, and the way he talked it sounded like he was still in love with her. I looked at Mom to see if she was annoyed, but she wasn't. Then Caroline started dancing with Anton and we all started dancing and the moment passed.

I thought about the day my father left, how it had taken me a long time to understand, to get it, as if I were an idiot, and my sisters refused to keep explaining it. I asked anyway over and over what had happened, while my sisters and mother cried into pillows. I kept thinking he'd come back—walk through the door in his dirty white shorts as he had after every tennis game that had come before. Brian Cain would vanish from the day like a bad dream. The moon was in the sky, a fingernail, and I watched it. I liked the moon better than the sun because it was constantly changing and always surprising you, up there when you expected it least. I wondered what it was like for the Fureys when the nun decided to go to India.

We danced until too tired to dance anymore and then we ran. I ran deep into the darkness of the field, running with night splashing against my arms and my dresses brushing my legs and little Finny trying to keep up with me. I wanted to cry about Dad and have Mom hug me the way Anton had hugged Caroline. Better, I wanted Anton to hug me the way he'd hugged his daughter. Better still, I wanted Dad to come and explain why he had left us.

Running, I became dizzy with excitement. Finny followed and then I stopped, breathless, and he caught up to me. I grabbed my BB gun from its holster and spun it on my finger.

"What's wrong, Finny? Speak, Finny," I shouted and pointed the gun at his face. His big blue eyes looked into me and he laughed, laughed hysterically at me. "Leave him be," Mom had said. "He'll get over it if you leave him be," she'd promised. He laughed and so I put the gun away. He wasn't afraid of me, he never had been.

At the edge of darkness the camper stood lit up bright, home. The Eldorado with its roof up was elegant. I could see Mom and Anton disappearing into their tent. The others spread out. James played the harmonica and Nicholas strummed the guitar and Julia sang a Neil Young song. Everyone orbited in his own space. A heaviness pressed into my eyes. Inside me clenched up like a fist, and my mouth made that unsticking sound the same as Anton's so often did. Everything seemed so incredibly complicated when I thought, so I tried hard not to think. Finny's warm lips kissed my neck and I held on to him, pulling him close to me.

Many things made me feel lucky. I'd make lists about what was good out here. School. It was September. I didn't mention school. I hoped they'd forget. I hated school. All over the roads there were school buses and older people. Bright yellow school buses and older people traveling in their silver caravans. At monuments and gas stations and roadside attractions there'd be only old people. It was as if the road were suddenly surrendered to a different set and now we didn't belong anymore.

Thousands of school buses, it seemed, a little different from the school buses we had back at home, a brighter yellow and somehow softer, older, rounded edges, with the stop signs that dropped like flags from the driver's window, the white-roof tops, and the bright red brake lights that light up all over the back and the sides. In the mornings they chugged over those roads, their red lights flashing and the doors opening to suck up clusters of children. Afternoons the red lights flashed again and the clusters of little children coughed from the bus, running up their long drives to a trailer home or some small house that rested on cinder blocks. One blond girl with stringy long hair—a pink cardigan over her shoulder and a book bag almost her same size ran up the drive, running to get home. It was a hundred degrees at least, but still she had that sweater over her shoulder and still she ran. I imagined a snack waiting for her up there in her home, a place surrounded by trees to protect it from the wind. I imagined a mother in pink slippers with dinner planned for a few hours later, early, before the light faded. I thought about school and felt lucky. I wondered if our school bus still stopped at the foot of our driveway every morning. It occurred to me that our fat driver probably thought Dad was picking us up and I imagined he thought that Jane and Julia were getting along with Dad now because they weren't there every day as they used to be.

At a service station one of the older people had asked why we weren't in school. She had beautiful blue hair spun like cotton candy and just as stiff from spray. She said we must be in private school to be out traveling this time of year. "We're in free school," I replied. "Erehwon. Nowhere spelled backward. We go to Erewhon in Dallas." I trumpeted the phrase as Anton's kids so often did. Mom had said that Anton was going to try to enroll us in Erewhon so that we'd be enrolled in school. "In free school you teach yourself. You decide what you want to learn and when you want to go." The old lady had smiled. She wore a T-shirt that read WE SUPPORT OUR TROOPS.

"What are you thinking about, Kate?" Mom asked. "What's on your giant brain?" She rustled my hair and smiled down on me. All around was an ocean of space and wind. Nowhere to hide.

"School buses," I said.

"Now that's odd. What about school buses?"

"About Felicity James." She came to mind suddenly and I said her name. When I was five, Felicity was hit by a school bus and sent thirty feet into the air. Her neck snapped when she landed on the pavement and she died instantly. She was an English girl and was in America for one year because her father was doing research. At school we had traded sandwiches, her butter for my tuna fish. The thinnest white bread spread with sweet butter and nothing else. She had a pretty English accent and missed her front teeth and I had thought the beauty of her accent came from the missing teeth and had wanted to lose my front teeth so that I'd have the accent too. The bus hit her in the fall, just after the time changed and when the mornings suddenly became dark.

"Oh, Kate, why were you thinking about Felicity James?"

Our camp was different by morning. The world was no longer ours. Instead, we shared it with a small white home on the other side of the road. In the doorway a woman stood, small in the distance. I couldn't make out her face, if she were young or old, mad or indifferent that we were there. She watched us wake up, come from the tent and the camper, prepare breakfast, stretch in the cool bright morning. Mom set the table. Sofia cooked eggs and sausage and Bisquick biscuits at the stove in the camper. Chickens clucked in the woman's brown yard. A barbed-wire fence marked off a square of land that I figured was hers. She fingered her ear and a breeze blew her hair away from her face. I wondered what she made of us, if she'd heard us chant and scream in the night. Four pairs of black pantyhose hung on a clothesline stretching from a window to a lone tree. The legs danced. Junk cluttered her yard. Dwayne waved and Anton tipped his hat and Finny stared hard. We all sat down to breakfast. She continued to stand there with her fingers on her ear. Anton took off his cowboy hat and placed it in his chair. He cleared his throat and blessed the food and welcomed Dwayne and then read a version of a prayer from St. Ignatius Loyola. He was calm and generous when he prayed, hands folded at his front, head bowed to the ground. His shirt inflated with wind.

> Teach us good Lord to serve you as you deserve,
> to give and not to count the cost, to fight and not
> to heed the wounds, to work and not to seek for rest,
>   to labor and not to ask for any reward except
> that of knowing we have thy will.

Foot-high twisters swirled over the golden fields and tumble-weeds rolled, some catching in the wire fence, and everyone was silent, listening to Anton. When he finished he said that it was a beautiful prayer because it was the essence of pure love and that the difference between truth and idea was practice. We ate. The eggs were wet and good. A few buzzards circled in the sky. I looked at Dwayne drooling our honey on the biscuits, at his comfortable position in the chair like someone long away finally home. Then I looked at James, who sipped steaming coffee and whose blue eyes were tired from just waking up. I wasn't sure why I felt generous toward him and not toward Dwayne. I wanted to understand more about God.

The woman still watched. I wanted to explain us to her because I knew for sure that she had us all wrong.

James had been with us one and a half months already and he was as good as a brother and son by now, with no intention of leaving. Mom and Anton would have been upset if James had wanted to leave. They would have felt betrayed, as if he were leaving to spite them. And in the beginning, that's the way it was with Dwayne. It didn't matter that none of us kids liked him. He annoyed us actually and had this awful habit of referring to things by their initials. It didn't matter that his parents weren't at the "D P," that they had never been to the "D P," that they never intended to come. As far as we knew he had no parents, but he did have a reservation, for which we were grateful when Julia got sick.

DESERT PRINCESS

I loved tourist bureaus for the same reason I loved gas stations. They were little huts of comfort in the middle of a nowhere town on some wide dusty street, offering bathrooms and information and little treats—colored suckers, fishbowls of them, and I always fisted a lot, shoving them into the pocket of my dress to save for later when dinnertime had passed and we hadn't yet eaten. Those huts were cold inside, well air-conditioned. The smell of coffee was strong and a fat woman with thick eyelashes always smoked a cigarette with a long ash teetering on the cigarette's amber end. You knew what to expect inside those huts: menus and flyers from resorts and newspapers with calendars of events: festival of the fiddlers and square-dance jamborinas. Postcards for free. Pamphlets and leaflets, maps and brochures advertising Indian reservations and the sale of jewelry crafted by the Havasu, the Hopi, the Hualapai, advertising the recent erection of the London Bridge, balloon rides over the desert at dusk, teepee tours. I collected all that information, heaps of it, so that I knew what was out there on those deserted roads, what we were driving through when it seemed we were driving through nothing.

At one tourist bureau I spotted a leaflet written by the FBI warning vacationers, a blood-red leaflet with bold white lettering:

THE BECKONING THUMB CAN BE A LURE TO DISASTER IN DISGUISE. THIS VACATION SEASON, COUNTLESS CITIZENS WILL BE INVITED TO PLAY A FATEFUL GAME OF CHANCE WITH HITCHHIKERS—WITH LIFE AND DEATH THE POSSIBLE STAKES.

The back page listed several murders by hitchhikers. One driver had his throat slit, one was raped and then hanged, one was buried alive.

I didn't trust Dwayne, but I almost loved him for having led us to the Desert Princess. It was the most beautiful hotel I had ever seen, rising in pyramids from a grove of coconut palms and green lawns that rippled out to the soft beige of dunes. Torches lined the drive and peacocks strutted across the lawn. There were eleven pools and seven restaurants with all-you-can-eat buffets. Mud baths and hot springs. Water, so much water, cascaded from fountains and sprinklers sprayed mists over the grounds. Small boats sailed on a network of canals, ferrying guests between buildings.

I was embarrassed by the camper, and even by the Eldorado, so hidden with dust. And by us, dirty, smelly, hair unbrushed. Dwayne in his orange robes. My hands were sticky. I looked at the hotel and had the urge to be clean. In the fountain in front of the lobby a marble Venus balanced on one foot, spurting water from her mouth and I leaned beneath her quickly and rubbed my hands in the water and splashed my face. The water was cold, dissolving the stickiness. A lot of change sparkled up at me, big change quarters and half-dollars and I bet there were silver dollars in there as well and I was tempted to steal lots of it, but I only got a quarter.

At the desk the receptionist thumbed through a book, licking her finger before turning each page. She was trying to find Dwayne's and his parents' reservation. It was fall. The busy season had begun. She studied Dwayne and then us, littering the lobby.

"Dwayne Dyer the Third?" she asked, chin high, finding Dwayne's reservation. "Dwayne Dyer the Third, that's you?" She didn't seem convinced. Nicholas stepped forward and verified that Dwayne was in fact Dwayne Dyer the Third.

"The Third," Nicholas stressed, placing his hand on Dwayne's shoulder. He repeated "the Third" a few times, making fun of the name. Nicholas was always teasing everyone. I bet Dwayne Dyer the Third wasn't really his name. The woman looked at Nicholas, who wore his raggedy tuxedo tails, and then at Dwayne. A golden name tag sat erect above her left breast, pinned into her golden gown. Her name was Candice and Dwayne kept calling her Candice and that annoyed Candice. Her lips puckered and wrinkles fanned out around her mouth from puckering too much. "I'm afraid your parents are not here," Candice said, her mouth smiling slightly, relieved. She wanted to get rid of us. "Could you have the wrong hotel?" That was stupid because there hadn't been another hotel in miles. She studied us some more, trying to control us with her eyes. James was making cigarettes and Timothy kept shouting, "Can you dig it? Can you dig it?" He'd just learned that expression and loved it. Jane had stayed outside in the shade to read. She read all the time now, crouched over novels. I couldn't read novels. I tried, but I couldn't absorb the words. I couldn't concentrate. There was too much else to think about.

Guests walked through the lobby. Women in bikinis toppled on heels. Coconut oil glistened on their skin and the air smelled sweet, like you could drink it. Little bells rang and the low murmur of money wafted through the open doors: heels clicking on marble, the thrumming of water, forks and knives and the *chin-chin* of clinking glasses from the poolside café. I wanted to stay here. Valets unloaded cars and carted suitcases on trolleys into elevators, off to plush rooms I could imagine. I wanted to be taken care of. I looked at Mom and she didn't look at all beautiful. Her eyes were tired, a little sad, and that made me sad. She needed to rest. Anton studied a menu.

"I sure don't know what could've happened to them," Dwayne

said, with his head bowed to the floor. "How could they do this to me?" He buried his face in his hands. I thought he might cry. Then I thought about the FBI leaflet and touched my pocket to make sure my hundred was still there. I could just tell he was lying.

"How 'bout a little drink?" Anton suggested, ignoring Candice. He slid his fingers through Mom's hair. She smiled a tired smile at him. He kissed her on the forehead. "You're tired, babe. We'll take a minute to decide what to do." I knew by now that a "little" drink would lead to a "little" snack and then a "little" dinner. I thought about the two-dollar limit for a moment, but I'd given up figuring out how Anton spent money. It seemed we always had it, some-how, when we needed it. He either went to a bank and cashed a check or ran into an old patient and did therapy.

Just then Julia got sick.

Her face turned pale and her eyes rolled to the back of her head, leaving the sockets white. She had been saying she didn't feel well all day, but nobody had really paid attention. Her body trembled and she clutched her head as if to steady herself. "I feel awful," she said to Mom, who studied her. Julia could make anything she did look beautiful. Her body shivered and goose bumps rose on her skin. "I can't see right," she said. "Everything's funny. I can't hear right." Tears came to her eyes and then she started heaving, vom-iting first putrid green then air, heaving until she couldn't anymore. Anton scooped her into his arms and Mom smothered her with kisses, not knowing what else to do. I was scared for Julia.

"She's faking it," Sofia said. She already had her bathing suit on. She knew her father. She knew that one way or another we'd be staying here awhile. "She just wants Dad's attention."

But I thought Julia might die. I'd read in *Poisonous Dwellers of the Desert* about insects that crawl in one ear and out the other, eating your brain on the way. I thought of the amoebas from the sulfur baths, which reminded me of what Nicholas had said, about one of us dying soon.

"Is there a doctor here?" Anton asked Candice, who was horrified by the disturbance. People were looking at us. James had come over, crouched down to see if there were anything he could do to help out. Anton smoothed back Julia's curls with his big hands, wiping the vomit from the corner of her mouth with his handkerchief. She cried hard now, complaining that she couldn't see right. "Can we get some rooms?" Anton asked, impatiently. His face puffed, swelling. For a second I worried about Candice. He plucked several hundreds from his wallet and thrust them at Candice who said that there was Mr. Dyer's room, but that it wouldn't be suitable for all of us. She refused the money saying she'd have to speak to the management because otherwise the hotel was "*complet.*" She liked that word. *Complet.* She said it a couple times. The bills dripped limply between Anton's fingers. His eyes caught mine and I blushed. I wondered if he knew about my hundred. I kept looking at him, my face twitching, afraid if I looked away he'd really know. But he wasn't looking at me. He was spotting Cynthia Banks, a San Franciscan millionaire he knew from Esalen. A tiny woman with an enormous stomach and bleached blond hair, bronzed skin and blue-shadowed eyes that were very, very round. She wore lots of gold and she got us the rooms we needed.

Julia's room had a terrace overlooking the pool and the dunes. Diaphanous curtains danced through the sliding glass doors and the refrigerator was filled with snacks and drinks and the scent of bougainvillea flooded the air. Cynthia Banks arranged for a doctor, who gave Julia an enormous shot of Tylenol. He said she'd be feeling better in a few days. For now she needed rest.

Anton took Dwayne's room and two other rooms and told the management that the rest of us would stay in the camper at a campsite. But none of us did. After all that traveling it was so nice to have a bed, even if three or four of us shared one.

That was one thing about Anton, why it was hard not to love him: just when it seemed you'd be stranded—on a deserted road without gas, without food, with a hitchhiker, in the arms of the police—things changed, leaving you wide awake, feeling grand like you'd won something, the world.

The sheets were cold and starched and pulled tightly over the bed; slipping between them with Sofia and Jane made me feel like I was back at home again in my bed with the sheets pulled taut and tucked with hospital folds. But it had been a long time since any of that.

Outside Mom and Anton and Nicholas and James and Cynthia Banks and Dwayne Dyer the Third sat by the pool, chatting, becoming fast friends over a bottle of special wine. I heard Mom's gentle laugh and Anton's deep voice, Texan tonight, telling stories about his childhood, and Cynthia Banks's hyena giggles. "Oo-la-la" and "simply divine" was her reaction to everything Anton said and Mom gently encouraged him. I could just picture her, smiling, nodding. Anton tried to talk to Nicholas and James about Vietnam, but James said he didn't think that was a good idea. Dwayne talked about gimmicks and money-making theories, which interested Anton and "oo-la-la" rose above their conversation and everything was "simply divine" and I was glad. I was grateful to Cynthia Banks and wanted them all to get along.

The mint from my pillow dissolved in my mouth and I heard my mother's beautiful whisper, which soothed me like her lullabies had when I was still tiny.

"How long do you think we'll stay here?" I asked.

"As long as we can keep Julia sick," Sofia replied.

"How can we do that?"

"Shsh," Jane said, almost asleep.

"I'll come up with a way," Sofia said. And I believed that she would. I loved Sofia then as much as I loved Julia and Jane. I was happy about that and wanted to tell Mom. Sofia lay between us. Her warm skin, dry, touched mine. "How long do you want to stay here?" she asked and ran her fingers through my hair. My legs were sore and tired. My knees ached. I wanted her to run her fingers over my legs.

"A hundred million years," I said. I felt as if everything in the world was exactly as it should be.

James and Dwayne added two more to the eight of us, making ten. "Treat them like brothers," Mom said. Ten brothers and sisters; I said it to some of the old people who liked to talk. "I have ten sisters and brothers." That amazed look swept over their faces like when I said my father was a Gestalt therapist and had been a Jesuit priest. He actually had never been a priest. His novice master had suggested he leave the society before he'd become a priest because of his visions of the Virgin and his affair with the nun. But *priest* sounded better, like more. *Ten* sounded better than three, as if just the number could protect you. I was like Mom in that way. I believed in more.

"All these children from one marriage?" an old lady asked. They were busybodies, the old ladies around the pool. They watched us. There was always somebody watching us.

"My mother was married before," I said. "But my first father died. He died in a gold mine in South Africa. He was a geologist, you see, and he went 6,800 feet down into the ground in an elevator and the elevator malfunctioned and fell. The cords snapped. A free fall," I said. My eyes were wide and teary. They beamed down on me with sympathy. I loved telling stories. I loved all that attention. "A utopia," I'd say.

I tried to remember my father and I couldn't. I couldn't see his face. I saw only a blot of white nothing, as when you look into the sun and you're momentarily blinded. I saw our old blue VW bus being lifted by a crane from the belly of an ocean liner. My sisters and I watched it, amazed at how vulnerable it was up there suspended in the air in the claws of the crane.

I remembered a picnic one day in the spring, one of the times I had had pneumonia. My sisters and parents rode bicycles and I was in the blue VW with the Irish au pair and she was driving me to the hospital to have an X-ray. I watched them out of the rear window, receding. The picnic basket was on Mom's bike and she wore checked slacks and had a sweater over her shoulders. A yellow wool sweater with pearly white buttons and leather patches over the sleeves and her curled hair was back in a bandeau. All her weight was on one foot while the other rested on a pedal and she waved as we drove away, getting smaller and smaller until she vanished. Dad was there too, but I hadn't been looking at him. I thought memory was like a murky photograph and if I'd been looking at Dad he'd be in my picture now instead of Mom.

By midweek Cynthia Banks was part of the family, paying for treats here and there in exchange for therapy with Anton. She was a big fan of his and had taken several of his workshops over the years at Esalen. Anton told her she didn't have to pay, but she insisted. "You've got all these children and I've got all this money," she'd say and laugh her hyena laugh. Her purse was a crocodile purse with a big golden clasp that clicked as she opened it, pulling out bills as if they were tissues, with those fattened fingers of hers.

I liked Cynthia Banks. With Cynthia Banks as a friend the hotel respected us and I marched around pretending I was a little princess. I sent my dresses to the cleaners and wore my nightgown as if it were a dress. It was frilly, of thin cotton, cooler than the velvet and sexier. I loved the way air blew right through it to my legs. They wouldn't let me wear my gun, though. Guns, no matter what kind, weren't permitted in the hotel. So I wore just the holster in order to have a place to keep my cash. In the boutiques I figured out that I could charge to my room just by signing and I was charging up a storm. I'd already bought a bikini, a towel, several T-shirts and one crocheted shawl and a pair of clip-on earrings that turned my lobes black. Then I figured out that I could return the items I charged and get a cash refund so I had lots of money, loads of it. All I had to do was make sure I never went back to the same salesperson. I wanted to steal another hundred. I was happy here now, but I knew what money could do for us and if we ever got stuck out in the desert again I wanted to be prepared to get us home.

Finny came with me to charge, but I didn't worry he'd say any-thing, since he still wasn't speaking.

At the pool in the late afternoons we sipped Virgin Marys, and almost every night, early, before the buffets were picked over, Finny and I had dinner, eating all we could eat of the all-you-can-eat buffets—mountains of shrimp cocktail followed by tastes of four or five desserts. I liked the way the waiter bowed down to us, his face lit by the flickering candle on our table. A gentle smile slid across his lips, smiling at us like we were somebody, like all the other people eating calmly at their tables.

Cynthia and Anton did therapy in the hot springs beneath the stars, late, after we'd gone to bed. Mom was proud of Anton, of his reputation. "She was beaten by her husband, you know," Mom told Jane, Julia and me in confidence. Sympathy flooded her eyes. "She needs therapy." Her thumbnail pressed her lips.

"You don't have to put up with this," Jane said. Jane had stopped speaking to Anton again and lately she'd been talking about running away.

"Be generous," Mom responded. Julia lay in a huge bed with many pillows. Mom walked around the room opening windows and the doors to the terrace. Julia's mints stood in a stack by her bedside table. I stole them.

"Everything hurts," she said, her eyes closed. It made her dizzy to keep them open and it really hurt when she rolled them. She couldn't take penicillin because it didn't work for her. When she was four she'd had rheumatic fever and had had to take so much penicillin that she was immune to it. Her curls had gone flat when she'd had the disease and Mom had worried they'd be lost forever. So the doctor here had had to use Tylenol, but that didn't seem to be working. Julia looked ugly and pale and her curly hair was flat and greasy. Mom put her palm on Julia's head. Her temperature had been up to 104.2 degrees.

"Do you think you'll die?" I asked.

"Kate," Julia sighed, but I could tell it made her laugh. She knew I didn't think she'd die. Mom and Jane said "Ka-te" too. I liked it being just the four of us. I felt I could be more like my old self.

"He's sleeping with her," Jane said.

"Jane, that's really gross," I said. It made me feel dirty just think-ing about it. I looked at Mom to see her reaction. She was silent, running that thumbnail over her lip.

"We can leave," Jane suggested. Her hair still hung in those dopey braids. I wanted her to shut up. For once things seemed to be going so well.

Dwayne and I had a thing.

"You need a G, Kate," Dwayne said.

He understood I liked money.

"What's a G?" I asked.

"A gimmick, an ingenious angle," he said. "Like a square egg. A G always sells." Light played on his white eyelashes, turning them a glittery platinum. Dwayne liked me because I was the only one who'd listen to him. He told me lots of stories about his girlfriend, who'd left him for a man she'd met while they were on a religious retreat. I suspected his religion had more to do with her, since he didn't wear the orange robes anymore, but wore black jeans and a black shirt instead. "Basically people are stupid and will buy any-thing as long as it's equally stupid."

I looked into the pool. It was a blue I'd never seen before, and placid. The sun bit into my back. I could see the reflection of Nicholas, who was drunk again. The day before, he'd thrown up in the flowers and Anton had gotten mad at him. Not because he was drunk, but because he'd driven the car without asking. Nicholas didn't care about his features anymore. Mostly now he just cared about a drink.

"A G is something that'll sell just because it's neat, like a spe-cially designed straw you can plug into an orange to suck up the juice. No bother squeezing. No sticky fingers." He flashed his hands to demonstrate. "You need to invent a product that people don't need but think they do, and that's cheap enough for them to buy on a whim." I thought about what he said.

There were people all around, some mothers with very young children, but mostly older women, who waded in the water slowly, pink caps covering their white hair. The older women were all a bit fat, and Sofia said that was because they'd stopped getting their periods and that when that happened you got fat. She'd fallen in love with an English doctor who was there at a doctors' convention. Sofia had brought him around to meet Anton and Mom and Anton had gotten him stoned and they'd talked for a long time on the patio. The English doctor had taken to Mom, and now they spent afternoons chatting by the pool—evenings too, when Anton was busy with therapy. He checked in often on Julia for Mom. The English doctor was tall and devastatingly handsome. That's how Julia put it, "devastatingly." He had thick dark hair with dashes of gray, and bright, light brown eyes. His face was tanned and a little weathered. His jaw strong. He practiced in third-world countries, trying to help the poor and starving. Sofia hated that the doctor liked spending time with Mom. "Your mom's going to stop getting her period soon and she'll swell up like a balloon."

"My grandfather invented the football helmet, but he didn't think it was a gimmick because he didn't even patent it," I said to Dwayne. That's what my grandmother had said to explain why we hadn't made any money off the invention. Granpy had not actually invented the football helmet, but a safer version of it. He was a sports doctor and wanted to come up with something that would better protect his players. But he could have patented his invention anyway and we'd all always wished he had, because then we'd be millionaires.

"How about you do me a favor?" Dwayne asked. He didn't care about the football helmet. "I'll pay you. It'll be our little G. You see, K, I need a car to run an S M, a secret mission, for a G I've got going. I'll pay you a fee and all you have to do is get the keys to the E and keep Dr. A busy while I'm on my M."

"Why don't you just ask Dr. A yourself?" I said. That's what all the big kids called him behind his back, Doctor Anton.

"Now Dr. A's a trip. You know that, don't you? He's a real character with all that Jesuit shit and sex stuff and his book on love. All the same, he's also a cool dude. A real generous man. Saved me, he did. A real G M. But you see, K, I'm trying to give you an opportunity to earn a little dough, bread, moola."

"What'd he save you from?" I asked. I suspected something. I suspected Dwayne had done something terrible. "Did you murder somebody?"

"Yeah, I murdered somebody. Now how about this little G?"

"Ask Dr. A," I said.

"You're not too smart, are you, K?" I hated it when people said I wasn't smart.

"How much are you going to pay me?" I asked.

"How about if I give you fifteen a mission?" he said. He had a wiry energy and he moved a lot, as if he'd been switched on, and he had a laugh that would have scared me if I didn't think he was pathetic and if he hadn't had that white, white hair and those blue eyes that looked red.

"Twenty," I said.

"Fifteen."

"Ask Anton."

I rented Dwayne the Eldorado. He took the keys and drove off to the desert for an hour or so in the afternoons and while he was gone I kept Anton busy. Or rather made sure he didn't need the car. Once he asked for Dwayne and I had to come up with a lie. I said he'd met a waitress and was flirting with her. He actually had met a waitress and sometimes he took her with him. He said they went to the desert to meditate. I didn't care what they did out there as long as I got my twenty dollars. I stole the keys from Anton, a massive set with at least thirty keys and a miniature ivory cobra poised to strike. I wondered what all those keys opened as I searched for the one to the Eldorado, why he had to carry them about when we only had a few locks to open. The hot air blew. Dwayne stood on the asphalt, dressed in black. His white eyelashes and lids made his face shine. His skin so pale, albinolike. All around the chrome of the cars danced and glittered in the sun. Dwayne's waitress was young-seeming, wearing a red-checked bikini top and hip-huggers. Her flesh was pinkish and soft. She was shy around me, not saying anything. I liked that she hid her face in Dwayne's arm, away from my eyes, so I kept staring at her.

I snatched the keys for four days, eighty dollars, and Dwayne and the girl would drive off on their mission while I went to the pool and splashed around with Finny and kept an eye on Anton.

I'd sneak back as they'd return. They'd be red and sweaty from the drive and the heat. Little beads of sweat dripped from Dwayne's nose and his shirt had patterns of wetness on the back like plastic does when you wrap it over a hot pie. Their eyes were big and glistening, scary, as if sizzling.

I thought that girl was stupid to buy his gimmick, but Dwayne said people were stupid for the most part.

That's how we passed our days and I felt grand. I was making a lot of money in this new life of mine.

It turned out that Julia was sicker than we had thought, which made me happy because it meant we'd be staying longer. She had a Mexican disease you pick up from drinking bad water and it seemed strange to me, since we hadn't been to Mexico. But the English doctor said the disease was carried in by those strong southern winds that blow in each day at four. A thick hot wind that came with the precision of a clock and blew us all to sleep, no matter where we were.

"You've got to take antibiotics," Sofia said to Timothy, Finny and me. "The doctor said. It's preventative so the disease doesn't jump onto you." She looked hard at us, chomping on her gum. She chewed gum all the time now instead of eating. It was a diet and she was losing weight. I liked the idea, but all that chewing made my jaw sore and I got hungry from the sugar and started eating even more.

In her hand she had a teaspoon filled with white powder from a capsule. She shoved the spoon in each of our mouths. The powder tasted bitter and made us cough and we wanted water to wash it down, but she said no. "It's like cough syrup. It's got to stay on your throat in order to work."

It was just the same with the White Blotter, the little triangle that

Dwayne stuck on our tongues. It had to dissolve in your mouth. It was just like a tiny piece of paper, coming apart thread by thread on our tongues. The ten of us kids walked out to the dunes beyond the hotel and the sun disappeared in the west, coloring the sky with purples and oranges, turning the mountains and mesas white like glaciers and then black and James sang rugby songs, trying to teach us the words.

> The Mayor of Bayswater
> He had a pretty daughter
> And the hairs on her dicky-di-do
> Hung down to her knees . . .

The sand sifted between my toes and I could feel each grain on my skin. The sky so sprinkled over with stars now. "More stars," I yelled. I stood up and spun around and fell back into the sand. I itched. I thought about the Joshua trees and getting lost in the field of Joshua trees that afternoon, which seemed so long ago. Sofia had hated the landscape and that had made Mom mad because Mom had loved it and we all needed to believe in the same thing in order to be strong and united. All the while that storm blew in from the west, getting us soaked, and Anton loved being lost, preaching to us out there beneath the Joshua trees, about the beauty of faith—of being able to appreciate uncertainty. Now I worried about the buffet being picked through and wanted to get back before all the shrimp had been eaten. Then I forgot about that. "We're gonna figure everything out, man," Dwayne said, coming up with a new theory. "And when we do, when we figure out how the whole goddamn universe came together, they'll be no room left for God and God'll laugh and step in with that big old hand of his and wipe us out."

> "One black one, one white
> And one with a bit of shite on
> And one with a little light on
> To show us the way . . . "

"Is that your fucking poetry, man?" Nicholas said to James.

> "It took a coal miner
> To find her vagina. . . . "

"Yeah, it's my fucking poetry." James mimicked an American accent and flashed a smile.

"Where'd you get this shit?" Nicholas asked Dwayne. Dwayne shot me a look that said, "Don't speak." I had no idea where he got it and then I did. I thought about him in the Eldorado with the girl and then that left my head and I forgot what I'd been thinking and momentarily that scared me. Then came an image of Mom saying we were blessed to be in the desert in a rainstorm in a field of Joshua trees and I believed her. "Are you having fun? Are you having fun? Are you having fun?" Her voice pecked at me. I was glad Mom wasn't here. "I hate the rain," Sofia had said, practically spitting it at Mom. "G's gonna come down and extinguish us, obliterate us," Dwayne shouted, trying to act like Jesus, standing tall. "And the whole evolutionary thing'll have to start all over again, from microcosm to man, and he'll laugh at how the next group evolves and dies." "Are you having fun? Are you having fun? Are you having fun?"

James played the harmonica and Nicholas told Dwayne to shut up. Then so did James and so did Caroline, who sat quietly off by herself, looking at the stars. I looked at them again to be like her and felt scared again. It scared me to look at the universe.

> "And the hairs on her dicky-di-do
> Hung down to her knees
>
> She married an Eye-talian
> With balls like a fucking stallion . . . "

"Stop," Jane screeched. "Make it stop." She clutched her head and stood up, shaking. Caroline drifted over to her and held her.

"I warned you," Dwayne said, doing magic tricks now. Quarters came from his nose and his ears. His face was big and awful-looking with those shiny white lashes. Sticks of incense poked from the sand and the big moon made the night glow. And then his face became Cynthia's and then Anton's. Finny clung to my side, passive, staring at the sky. Sand pricked my scalp.

"I do believe there're more stars than grains of sand," I whispered. Jane yelled. Caroline held her. I couldn't listen to Jane or look at her. Her hair was long and wild, out of braids. She frightened me. I cupped my ears with the palms of my hands and squinted my eyes. Dwayne told her again that he'd warned her. She'd eaten more than he'd recommended. Jane had said she'd wanted to disappear. I was afraid she would. We'll disintegrate, but everything else will remain the same, Julia had said on that long stretch of road. I thought of the postcard with the nuclear bomb mushrooming into the sky, and laughed. Finny nudged me and I fell to the sand. Nicholas strummed the guitar and sang a song about water. Water over and over. I only ate a quarter. That little tiny triangle. Jane had taken a whole square to be like the boys. She wanted to disappear. Everyone talked at once and their voices clogged my ears. It was as if I were beneath water. "Paralyzed from the waist down," Sofia said with delight. "Because she passed out in a bathtub with those tight, tight jeans on. You know, the kind you have to lie down to put on. And the water made them shrink on her and that cut off her circulation. Paralyzed."

"I have another theory," Dwayne said. I couldn't keep the sounds straight. "About black holes and God." I sang the rugby song and laughed and drizzled sand on Finny's stomach and then I kissed him on the mouth with my tongue. It was awful. His tongue was hard like wood.

"Make it stop. It's so weird." Jane was crying. "Protect me. Somebody. Help." She slapped her face, breaking away from Caroline. James went to her and held her, brushing her hair down. He told her to breathe slowly, to concentrate. "It'll be all right," he said. "We're here. No one will leave you alone." Jane was shaking, clinging to him. "We won't go away." Now I wanted Mom, but she and Anton and Cynthia were away at a friend of Cynthia's—an artist who had a studio in the desert and Cynthia wanted Anton to see his work. I stuck my arms out, reaching in front for something I couldn't see. Finny tried to follow but I knocked him down. "Scram," I said. Something made me mean and it felt good. GRAND. The hotel was far away, lit up like Oz. I kept walking, feeling like I'd never get there. The more I walked the more it receded.

And though there had been thousands of Joshua trees in that field they seemed isolated, standing in their own space. Alone. I had wondered if their roots touched underground.

I called collect from the lobby in a private booth with a Princess phone. It took a long time for the operator to come on. She was on the moon and when she finally came down she didn't understand me. I kept explaining myself until she said, "Miss, I have understood that your name is Katherine and I have understood which number it is that you are trying to dial. It's busy now." Her voice was a machine, shooting out words—each word a distinct hard block that crumbled after it had been spoken.

"Can't you make an emergency breakthrough?" Sofia had told me about those so I knew how to make them. She'd tried an emergency breakthrough to Poona, India, to her mother. But they had no phones at the ashram. I thought about the nun. The nun should be with her children and husband. Dad should be with his children and wife. My head spun. I started to laugh.

"Well, is this an emergency?"

"Yes!" Currents ran through my body in waves. I sweated.

"You should have said so first, Miss."

I waited, tangling the cord around my head. It was a short, straight cord. Green velvet upholstered the walls. The light buzzed overhead in a small chandelier dripping crystals, loud, distracting me. In that buzz I could hear Jane screaming still, her voice echoing in my ear, begging for us to make it stop.

"Ducky?" I heard Camille's voice and I got a jolt. I had never heard her answer the telephone before. I didn't say anything. "Ducky, are you there? Your father wants to know where you are, Ducky." I thought about ducks. Mom and Dad had given us ducks for Easter once. One for each of us. They had done that kind of thing. One year they gave us lambs. For a little while we'd had a real farm at our house. We ate the lambs the next Easter. Thinking of that made me want to laugh. But I held it in. I saw those ducks and wondered why she called me Ducky. But her voice was warm and friendly and she didn't know for sure if I were on the line. "Operator? Operator?" Camille asked. I was hoping Dad would take the phone away from her. "Well, Kate. I know you're there and I wish that you would speak. We're concerned about you girls." *We,* that *we* of Camille's slapped me. "School has started. When are you coming home? Your father's very upset." She spoke fast. I saw my father in his little white VW, his head bent over the steering wheel. Part of me wanted to speak out to her, thought she could be warm like her voice, envelop me, feed me chicken and rice. I thought of Mom in bed and of the messy room we'd left behind. I wanted to go back and open the door to that room and let my father in. The air was close in the booth. "What about school? What about school?" I heard it over and over in my head. Erehwon backward . . . I'd wanted to say.

Camille's voice became Mrs. Jackson's, my new teacher in my new school. When my father left I switched from private to public. Mrs. Jackson took me into the teacher's office and sat me down in a chair that stood very high and my feet couldn't touch the ground and she asked if I were all right and I thought she meant would I adjust to the school. I nodded. She looked at me with those big warm eyes of hers, but there was something in them that I didn't trust. The way they held me, taking me in, as if my nodding weren't enough for her, as if she wanted me to break open so she could see what was inside. On my feet I wore Julia's Jack Purcells and they were too big and I was embarrassed because Mrs. Jackson kept looking at them and I knew that she could tell they weren't mine.

But I hadn't been able to find my shoes so I had had to wear Julia's. I was relieved that I was at a new school where nobody knew me. Mrs. Jackson's voice turned back to Camille's and I heard the operator on the line telling Camille that we were at the Desert Princess.

"Ducky, your father's away on business but he very much wants to know where you'll be in the next week. He very much wants to speak to you." She paused and sighed. I hated that she was in his apartment. "He misses you, Kate. He wants to help you, Kate." Then again she repeated that he missed me. "He has your letters. I don't know if he'll be able to come and get you but he . . . " she stuttered. A knot clogged the back of my throat and my eyes started to water and then to burn. "Well . . . ," That "well," came quick and sharp like a bullet. I saw her as a soldier standing in front of Dad. "He certainly wants you to come home, with school having started, and he could wire you the . . . " Very gently and quietly, as she was saying something else that I couldn't make out because she was a million miles away from me, on another planet, I put my finger on the lever that disconnected the line and pushed it down, cutting her off. I held it down for what seemed a long time, as if I were stomping on a fly extra long to make sure it was dead.

"Nope. Na. Na," Anton stuttered. "Na. Na." His lips were dry, the way they got after smoking too much. He needed a drink. One was in his hand. An umbrella blossomed over the table, shading his face. A waterfall thrummed into the pool. Beneath the waterfall was a bar and a band of Spanish musicians played on a platform that hung suspended over the pool. Cynthia sat to his right. Mom to his left. We were having a family meeting so that Anton could speak to Dwayne and Nicholas and James about the night before. Jane was all right now, in bed with Julia. Anton couldn't get the words out, it was as if he weren't convinced by them. "Iiii just . . ." Pause. "DDDDon't think it's a good idea giving stuff to the little kids. Iiit might be too much to handle." He cleared his throat and spit. He thought good and hard. "If you're gonna do that stuff with the little kids, an adult should be there." Experience was at the root of enlightenment and travel was the most important form of education, this was what he taught us, to be here now, to live in the moment. He ate an hors d'oeuvre and licked his fingers. The world was a treasure box and the more we opened it up, the more we would open up. All around were old people, slowly slipping into the water, cutting it first with their hands.

Mom was mad. None of that eager enthusiasm lit her pretty face. She was mad at everybody for what had happened. Mad at Nicholas and James, but especially at Dwayne. There was something in Mom's eyes, a strength, there for a moment, then gone. "You've gone too far, Dwayne," she said. Dwayne's head was bowed. I thought he'd try to cry, but he didn't. Without lifting his head, he shot me a look that said, If you breathe a word you're dead.

Mom wore her bathing suit with the enormous daisies and for a second I remembered the day the men landed on the moon and that made me sad so I stopped thinking about it. Her skin was tanned. Eyes rested. There were too many people. "I want Dwayne to leave," she said, staring Dwayne in the eye, but speaking to Anton. "I want at least some rules," she said. Then she asked Anton for his support in asking Dwayne to leave. She asked him to give extra work to Nicholas and James for allowing this to happen. "They should know better," she said.

Anton stuttered, asking the boys what they'd learned from this experience. Nicholas and James tried to apologize to Mom, but she wasn't listening. I thought she didn't love them anymore.

"We lost sight," Nicholas said. I could tell both he and James were sorry from the expression on their faces.

"I feel fantastically stupid," James said. He slicked his hair back with his hand and tried to talk to Mom. "It's hard to understand where to stop sometimes, where the limits are."

"I just can't handle it anymore," Mom said. "It's just too much." But Anton couldn't ask Dwayne to leave and he wouldn't give extra work to Nicholas and James. "I have to think about this," Mom said. She scraped her chair back across the concrete patio and stood up. In her face there was that strength that hadn't been there for a very long time, but even so I thought she might cry. She walked away, furious, giving Anton the silent treatment. I was sorry for Anton. In that moment he seemed so powerless, watching Mom walk away.

Then I thought about Dad. It occurred to me that he knew where we were because Camille had asked the operator. I imagined if Camille told him, he would come. He would want to come. I pictured him showing up, and the five of us, Mom, Julia, Jane, Kate and Dad, getting into his white VW and leaving and nothing about the silent treatment or the night before would matter; it would pass. Would be like the end. Of a movie, a TV show, or a dream, when you leave one world to go back into your own again.

EVE

Mom knew who she was.

She'd been educated. Four years of college. They taught you how to be a wife. A diamond before you graduated. Her mother taught her how to be a wife. "An extra river water from Tiffany's," my grandmother would say—whatever that meant. "A penny saved is a penny earned." Mom could throw a brilliant tea or cocktail. Her china served twelve. Her father laughed at her idea for secretarial school. Ha ha ha. "Secretarial school?" Big brown eyes beaming. Stern voice. "A blue blue Bostonian. Eleven generations Lynn," as my grandmother liked to say. The Battle of Bunker Hill was fought on Breed's Pasture, my grandfather's forebears' pasture. The Buster Brown boy all grown up. A doctor now, who had invented the safer football helmet. He loved his Evie. Her golden curls the color of sand. Her delicate hands. The silent type, he just looked at her, smoking his pipe, telling her with that look she'd have no need for secretarial school. Babies. That kind of thing.

Mom knew who she was. She knew French. Spoke it to anyone who'd listen, waiters in French restaurants. Dad took her to France in 1961 and they collected menus from all the three-star restaurants they ate in. At home she framed them and hung them on the walls around the house. Above a small table in the kitchen, a nook to look like a bistro. Little checks on the menus marked off what they'd eaten for dinner at the Hôtel de la Poste Chevillot. Escargot de Bourgogne, la douzaine; Filet de Boeuf aux Truffes; Soufflé aux Fraises, 2 personnes, Spécialité; Vosne-Romanée–Les Malconsorts 1957. Mom would chant the words to us later, like a song. At the time she and Dad would leave Jane and Julia, babies then, in the back of their rented car while they feasted and drank. "They'll be all right," Dad said and nudged Mom, encouraging her, and together they laughed and feasted. Dad loved her. Her golden curls and the gap between her teeth. He loved her enthusiasm and endless optimism, her sense and passion for adventure.

Mom loved black Chiclets and burnt toast. She loved to suck on ice. She loved poetry and had had ambitions to be a writer. She loved Emily Dickinson and Virginia Woolf. She loved to collect names from tombstones in an abandoned graveyard hidden in the woods behind our house—Jay Bo Lackey and JoJo Lipp. She loved to talk to strangers and strangers loved to talk to her. She got things from them, little secrets about their lives that somehow taught her about her own. She loved raw meat, and she loved to drink coffee with heated milk before getting out of bed in the morning. She loved to sink her arms into her garden to find the roots of weeds and she loved to tug and tug until she tugged them all out. Her home was immaculately clean. The brass chandelier shone and even our underwear was always ironed. In the basement she kept a sewing machine and bolts of Florence Eiseman and Liberty print fabrics, out of which she made us matching dresses.

She knew how to have babies, even though her mother had told her she wouldn't be able to because of the split vertebra. As a child her mother kept her out of gym, away from all physical exercise because of this split vertebra. "Eve will never be able to have babies," my grandmother told my father when he picked my sixteen-year-old mother up for their first date. But Mom knew how to have babies and would have had five if the last two hadn't miscarried.

Every other year a baby—Jane, Julia, Kate. Kennedy was her hero. She was in the grocery store checkout line when he was shot. Mom believed that her insides were pure and white like the insides of a potato, that they didn't slosh around. She knew she'd been born a blue baby and she knew my grandmother had whacked her to life. A registered RN, she sat up, having just delivered, and grabbed her daughter from the doctor by the leg, held her upside down and whacked until she coughed and cried and then she named her Eve. Eve because Eve had fallen. Eve because Eve was, literally, life and living. Eve because eve preceded something big and she'd been very late. Eve because Eve was evil and my grandmother had wanted a boy.

When Dad left, Mom left. She went to bed and didn't get up until she met Anton, who offered her the world. At thirty-two, she'd been fired—from our father, from herself. She sank her diamond in a blue glass bottle filled with water and left it there. Several months later she sold it for a thousand dollars. Severance.

LOVE AND SEXUAL EQUALITY

The back of his hand came down like a paddle and smashed into her face. His fingertips in her hair. His enormous turquoise ring in her eye. I could see the ring. The silver setting and the black hairs of his knuckles and the tightly pulled skin. His fist in her cheekbone. The back of his palm in her jaw.

Anton knew who Mom was. Anton knew who Mom could be. It was she who had the potential to fill in his other half, to make them, as one being, whole. To pour her self into him, his self into her. The thought scared me. I saw Mom becoming Anton. I saw Anton becoming Mom. Fused together and both lost. Gone.

No one had ever known her before, the way Anton knew her, that's what Mom said. He believed in her endless optimism and her relentless sense of adventure. "Residual omnipotence," were the words he used to describe Mom's driving forces. Her ability to believe that she could make anything happen—sleep in gas stations all across America to get to Anton, with three kids and forty dollars in her pocket—that she could stop time, change the course of the stars. Make a new family out of old and damaged families, a new family that would be bigger and better than the ones that came before. Anton loved her, cherished her. He thought her mind was wonderful, magical. He loved to hear her talk about Virginia Woolf, to recite Emily Dickinson. He believed there wasn't anything she couldn't do. She could be a writer, if that's what she wanted. She could be a gardener, a painter, a comedian. Anything. A clown. A secretary. It was she who was by his side, helping him discover his discoveries: the tobacco-spitting contest, fiddling jamborinas and racing armadillos. The craters left by volcanoes in which ran creeks of gold. "The thing about Anton," Mom would say, "is that we really have fun together."

Anton believed that the ideal love could only happen when man and woman achieved perfect equality. When their passion, desire, energy, spirituality, minds were driven with the same intensity. When the shackles, the teachings, of society were cut free from man and woman and the million variations on slave/master, beauty/beast were left to history.

Anton knew who Mom was. Mom could be this equal for him, if she'd only let herself go—forget what society had taught her to be. Doris Day. Grace Kelly. Whichever the case may be. "I am you. You are me." He believed that there wasn't anything they couldn't do together. Together they'd get lost just to get lost together. They saw the world in the same way: as theirs. They found things that others would never find: red, white and blue flowering Joshua trees in September; strangers by the roadside who'd become their children; a traveling utopia with ten kids; a way of life, to live life that was all their own. It was 1970. You could do that.

He could fill her in. She could fill him in.

There had been that time once, at home, when Anton had gotten mad at Mom because he'd been terribly jealous. "Terribly" was the word Mom had used. My sisters and I weren't there. We'd been at school. It was late May, not too long before we ran away to California. We'd never seen him mad so it was hard to imagine him swollen, face puffing the way we later saw it could. The veins like worms rising beneath the skin.

Mom was in the driveway in front of the house, alone and crying, when we returned from school. Her body folded over a smoldering heap of slides. The slides were of our trip, as a family, to Scotland the summer before Dad left. The slides burned and the negatives melted together into one gooey mass.

"He was just jealous," Mom said to us, the three of us looming over her. "It was nothing. He was just terribly jealous. Terribly."

People. So many people. They waltzed. Cynthia hosted a party in the Dunes Room for the convention of doctors and some artists, several of whom were her good friends. Anton swirled me around. He sucked on my ear and then he set me down. I was afraid he would think I didn't love him because of the fight with Mom. It had been two days since she'd spoken to him.

"Money's never a problem as long as there's plenty to go around," shouted Cynthia Banks, pouring champagne into the top glass of a champagne fountain. She had six going at once. She wore a long red dress of chiffon that was tight and showed off her fat, and her thin hair was twirled into a skimpy bun crowned with a rhinestone tiara. Her head nodded to one side from having had too much to drink.

"She looks like she's going to the junior prom," a voice said.

"What an adorable girl you are," said another voice, looking down on me, the face close to mine, big in my eyes. Mascara clogged her tear ducts and she smiled wide. Very white and crooked teeth. Anton took Cynthia in his arms and they danced. Lots of couples danced. Everyone in elegant clothes. I'd had my nightgown starched so it was stiffer than usual, and prettier. I wore my clip-ons and pink lipstick. I moved in and out of the couples. Mom wore a black dress with straps that sliced across her shoulder blades, showing off her tanned back. Sofia talked with the English doctor, who commented on our beautiful family. She told him about her four sisters, five brothers, two mothers and her father. I loved the way that sounded. He was so handsome I was afraid of him. Sofia wore patent leather shoeboots that rose to her thighs and a pink mohair minidress that must have been hot. I loved hearing Sofia include me as a sister. Jane danced with James. Me now with Finny and now with Timothy and then back to Anton. All the tables were pushed aside, napkins were strewn over the floor along with cigarette butts, and waiters in white suits made efforts to clear the plates off the tables. Mom waltzed with the English doctor, which soon bothered both Sofia and then Anton. Anton's eyes were red sockets and his lids kept closing. He had smoked and drunk a lot. He tried to cut in on Mom and the doctor's dance to offer the doctor a smoke. But Mom wouldn't have it and she swirled the doctor away, feeling strong, like she didn't need Anton.

The evening was cool, and through the doors I could see a net of stars and the silver moon. Water from all the fountains pricked in my ears. I'd had too much champagne. I was tired. "Kate," Mom said. She came up to me from behind and wrapped her arms around me. In her arms I felt like a little child and wanted to collapse and have her carry me to bed. When she had cocktail parties with Dad the three of us would sing songs for the guests and weave between them offering up hors d'oeuvres and when we got too tired Mom wrapped around us like now and carried us off to the cool, tight sheets of our bed. "You've had enough to drink, Kitty." She took the glass from my hand and set it on the floor. Sometimes she seemed very young and far away, but now she didn't. She felt close and like my mother, like all the mothers of my old friends. Mrs. Campbell, Mrs. Conquest, Mrs. Tiller, Mrs. Fritz and Mrs. Fitzpatrick, Mrs. Love. "You should run on up to bed, little Toad," Mom said. "But if you stay a bit longer do dance with Anton so he doesn't feel left out. I'll tell Jane too." I didn't want to dance. I slumped against the door and watched her dance back to the Englishman. People began to leave. Nicholas was drunk. He had thrown up in a cholla garden and come back with a vomit-stained shirt. Mom told him to stop drinking and to go and change his shirt. Nicholas ignored her so she told him again. Her voice rising, angry.

Anton tried to cut in again on Mom, but again she wouldn't let him. I felt bad for him. Even Jane felt bad, and danced with him.

His eyes were big and sad, bulging—almost, it seemed, with fear. We knew what it was like to be punished by Mom. She could make it feel as if things would never change again. The world would end and you'd still be standing there, waiting for her to forgive you.

Once more Mom told Nicholas to clean himself up, told him he shouldn't drink so much. He told her to fuck off and they started fighting until Nicholas stormed out.

Smoke stung my eyes and clogged my nose. I was tired. Some more guests shambled outside carrying candles and glasses of champagne and the party spilled out to the pools. Their voices clinking. I could hear splashing. The room emptied out. Jane took my hand in hers to lead me to bed.

"Don't you ever tell my kids what to do." We heard Anton's voice, sharp and sudden. That muffled anger, coming to us as if underwater. Jane's hand clutched mine more tightly and we stopped. We looked at each other. The walkways were lit with Japanese lanterns and the night was velvety dark. "I'm pissy mad," he hissed. "I won't have you bullying my kids."

"Fine," Jane said. "He tells us what to do, but she's not allowed to tell them what do. Nice combination, for all his talk about equality."

"Nicholas is drunk," Mom shouted. "He should take care of himself and if he can't, you should, damn it." Jane turned back toward the Dunes Room. I didn't want to go. Afraid. The underwater lights made the pools electric. I chewed on my tongue.

"Stop doing that," Jane said and linked her arm in mine. "It makes me nervous." I stopped. She held me close, in front of her like a shield. Mom and Anton were on either side of a table, alone in the room. He was big and swollen. I thought about him raising his hand to strike Jane. I wanted to go away. I turned around, but Jane held me hard.

"This isn't what I wanted," Mom said. "I didn't chose this life. I never would have chosen this life." Her eyes penetrated Anton. He just stared with those big eyes and his swollen head. Silence for a moment and then they were fighting again. About Nicholas and the drinking. About the Englishman and about Dwayne. About how she didn't know how to love him. About how incomplete their union was. About the beauty of his wife's mind. Screaming quietly, then, "Fuck off," Mom said. Silence. Bad silence.

"What did you say?" He articulated each word slowly. He was enormous, standing over her. She thought for a moment.

"I said fuck you," Mom said and she threw a champagne glass at him and his hand came down and smashed into her face. His eyes closed with the blow. His lids quivered, struggling to stay shut as if he couldn't bear to see.

On the road, heading east in the Eldorado. Everything inside raced. The four of us crowded together up front. No one wanted to be alone in the back. Julia, wrapped in a blanket stolen from the hotel, shivered between Jane and me. Mom drove calmly, holding a washcloth against her eye. The interior light was on so that Jane could read the maps. My maps. It was bright inside and almost cheery, just us. It had been a long time since it was just us. Outside was black, no one else on the road. I wished someone else would be on the road. I could hear the wind rushing against the windows. I thought I should cry, but couldn't. Jane talked evenly, though quickly, making plans about how to get home. Her palm pressed into her cheek. Mom's thumbnail rubbed her lip. I thought about Anton pointing out our tics so long ago and I felt sad. Jane's skin was blotched a nervous red-white. The maps crinkled and she couldn't find the one for Arizona, but she didn't get frustrated. "It's fine," she said. "Everything's fine. We're going to be all right."

"We should find a hospital," Julia said. Her eyes were big and blue and smart. Her body thin and frail. She'd lost a lot of weight. Mom's eye bled and the washcloth was almost drenched red. "I bet you need stitches. You're really bleeding. If you need them and don't get them you'll get a scar, Mom." Julia sat forward and leaned over Jane and took the cloth to refold it, but Mom wouldn't let her. I was glad. I didn't want to see the eye.

Mom laughed lightly. "It's nothing. Really. It's . . . " She said it didn't hurt. We could tell she didn't want to talk about it so we didn't. I thought about Finny for a second and wondered who'd speak for him, with me gone. The high beam pierced the blackness. Even the moon was small and dim. The spine of a mountain chain appeared and then vanished. We were quiet for a while. I imagined Dad at home, standing at the front door, waiting for us and then he vanished. I felt scared.

"I'm doing the right thing?" Mom asked.

"It'll be okay," Jane said, becoming Mom's sister again. She patted Mom's shoulder and again there was silence. We drove for awhile in the silence. Air leaked in from the hood. The convertible top hadn't been put up right. I imagined that was Dwayne's fault. I thought about renting Dwayne the Eldorado for his mission in the desert with the girl. Jane turned on the radio and we listened to some old songs.

We took turns sleeping on and off and it was cold and I snuck under Julia's cover and we held each other. She was all bones. "I love you," she whispered. I knew later she'd be asking me for the details of the fight. She'd be mad she hadn't been there.

I thought of Finny waking up in the morning and discovering that we were gone and I wondered if he'd say something then. "Where's Kate?" He'd want to ask and when he found out that I was gone and that he'd never see me again he'd be sad. I tried hard to imagine this. It made me feel good inside, grand, then it made me feel bad. Then I didn't care. I thought about all the things I'd charged to our room and was relieved I wouldn't be there when Anton paid the bill. My eyelids were heavy and my eyes burned beneath them. I had a headache from the champagne. I saw our home, all the lights on, lit up bright, every window glowing in the dark night. Dad standing in the front doorway, waiting. Dad used to scream at us for leaving the lights on. But I saw it that way anyway, with him at the front door screaming at us, "Eve, we can't run up bills carelessly. Girls, I've told you a million times." Outside, the seventeen-year locusts would be singing up a storm the way they had been when we left. They'd just been beginning then, and their tiny holes poked through the yard as if it had been perforated by some kind of giant perforating machine. During the day you couldn't see them, but you could hear them. A haunting sound, like that of crickets only with the volume turned up full blast. The last time I'd spoken to Dad at home, he'd said there would be millions of locusts before the summer ended. He said their bodies would cling to the trees like barnacles and at night the noise would be so loud you'd have to plug your ears to sleep. He said when they died their bodies would fall to the ground and there'd be so many of them they'd crunch beneath our feet like eggshells. By that time we'd be long gone to California, but I didn't know that then. He said that the last time the locusts visited was the summer he'd met and fallen in love with Mom. I wondered about seventeen years from now. I'd be twenty-five. I wondered if we'd still know Anton. I wondered if any of us would be dead.

"Kate?" Mom asked. Jane had turned off the interior lights and now only the dashboard was lit. It was a big dashboard with lots of things to light up. The clock read 2:48. "How much money do you have?" A jolt surged through me and immediately I was very awake. Jane and Julia sat up too. Their eyes beamed at me. I didn't say anything.

"About how much, Kate?" she asked again.

"How do you know if I've got any money," I asked.

"I know my little Kate." Mom turned her face away from the road to me. The washcloth bunched over one eye, but the other held me for a second. I thought of Allison's mother with the Vaseline and the patch over her eye. Mom turned back to the road.

"What?" I asked. I wanted her to say it again. I pretended I hadn't heard.

"I know my little girl," she said and I could see a smile on her lips. I had $347.57: the $7.57 scrounged from the fountain and the seats and floors of the Eldorado and camper; the hundred from Anton; eighty from Dwayne and the rest from charging.

"Enough," I said. "Enough to get us home."

Julia and Jane screwed up their eyes and asked a million questions, but Mom told them to be quiet. She didn't ask any questions and I didn't tell her how much I had or how I'd gotten it. Then Mom started laughing and so did Jane and Julia.

"We can sleep in hotels," I said, laughing too. "And no two-dollar limits. 'Two-dollar limit, babe.' " I imitated Anton's drawl. I thought for a moment and a wonderful idea occurred to me. "We can go to the Grand Canyon and stay in the best hotel and eat steaks for dinner!" I said. It was on our way, not too far from where we were now. By tomorrow we could be there. I got excited inside.

"Fine!" Mom said. We all got happy inside.

We drove until Mom couldn't drive anymore, in and out of mountains on some small state road. We stopped at an Esso and parked near the bathrooms, but it was lonelier this time. There were no trucks and it was locked up tight. No Coors or Coke signs flickering. No ice machine churning. No hotels across the road. We peed at the edge of the parking lot. We didn't brush our teeth. I heard a dog bark, but even that came from far away. The air was cold. We pulled some clothes from our bags and piled them on top of us and nestled into each other. Each breath like a stitch pulled us toward sleep.

I wondered what home would be like when we got there. I remembered once when we went away to Europe and Dad had forgotten to tell the milkman. The stupid milkman had come every day while we were gone and left the bottles of milk on the front steps. When we came home, over a hundred glass milk bottles stood on the steps with the milk swollen up and exploded, and some of them had broken. Mom had been mad at Dad, but it was such an ugly sight and so smelly with all those bottles oozing sour milk that they laughed. I wondered if someone had remembered to call the milkman. I thought he must have been a pretty stupid milkman to leave the bottles in the summer heat. In my mind I started making a list of the things I'd do when I got home. New clothes for school. Call the milkman. Clean the house. I wanted to do it the way Mom liked, leaving everything shining so you could see your face in it, from the floors to the chandelier. I got so excited I couldn't keep still. I couldn't sleep. I wanted to get there right away. Things would be ordinary. We didn't need Dad. If he weren't there it would be fine. He could drive us to school. That would be enough. It would be just us again. Jane was right. We needed to protect Mom. Inside me filled, though I was a little scared. I took out my money and counted it even though I knew how much was there. I wondered if Sofia would miss us.

"Sleep, Kate," Julia said.

I wondered if I'd ever see Finny again.

When the first light cracked the east Mom awoke. "Jane," Mom whispered, and nudged her. The blood had dried and her eye was swollen and would not open. I saw Anton's hand come down. I couldn't think about that. My mouth tasted dirty. My eyes weighed heavily and a dizziness made me queasy. "Jane?" Mom asked again. She just said her name. She didn't have a question. Kind of pleaded her name. She folded her arms over the steering wheel and leaned her head into it. There was an incredible silence like I hadn't heard in months. Jane held Mom. Mom cried. I'd only seen her cry once. It hurt her to cry. The tears stung the cut.

"I don't know how to do it," Mom said. Jane told her we could do it. Told her how. Julia made a joke about me being the bread-winner.

"I have enough money," I said. "I can get us home."

Julia wanted to know how much. I loved that she was curious. "Enough," I said. I was glad that I had the money and not her. She would have charged us interest. "Like a bank," she'd said. Now with the light I could make out the wound.

"It'll be all right Mom," Jane said. "We'll drive home. It's our home, Mom." And Jane said encouraging things about home and everything being all right and Julia chimed in and then so did I. Julia crawled over Jane to Mom and started cleaning up her eye. She got water from a spigot outside. She rinsed the washcloth of blood. It was cold. You could see your breath.

"You don't know what it's like to be left," Mom said. Her

thumbnail pressed against her lip, rubbing it. "I kept thinking Ian would come back." I was afraid she'd start getting mad about how he left her. But she didn't. "I must have been really awful to make him leave his three little girls. He never explained why, but I must have been really horrible. He said I didn't love him. Perhaps I was too young, I don't know." She was tired. Her words came out in one tired string. She broke down again. It was unbearable to see her cry, to see that bruised eye. Her wound was purple laced with veins of red, and it puffed like a small popover. The lid stretched down over the eye and the puffiness, sealing it. She stopped crying. "The thing about Anton is that he knows how to live. Your father didn't."

"We don't have to think about this now," Jane said. "All we have to think about now is getting home." Jane was excited in a way I hadn't seen her in months. She loved taking care of Mom.

"Work, work, work, that's all Ian understood. With Anton there's never a dull moment, is there?" She smiled eagerly and looked at us. I couldn't look at her. My legs were sore and aching as if I'd been running for a long time. I fiddled with the buttons on my sweater and then I felt my holster to check the money. "He's spiritual too. I like that he's spiritual. Your father wasn't spiritual."

"It doesn't have to be a choice, Mom," Jane said. Her face quivered. Palm in cheek as if to steady it. Then, as if suddenly remembering, "He hit you, Mom. He hit you."

I thought of Anton. He appeared in front of me, bending down and kissing us. "You forgive me, babe?"

"Your father doesn't enjoy his life. For him it's work. How could he have enjoyed me? Us? I wanted more. I wanted to be a writer, but he never took me seriously. He didn't want to share with the raising of the kids. The daily stuff. Changing diapers, feeding." She used "kids" as if we weren't *her* kids. "Equally caring." She paused. "He never explained anything to me. He never gave me a chance to discuss it. He never said, Eve there's trouble. Eve, I'm leaving. I've fallen in love because you didn't give me what I needed. He never explained. I never imagined that he'd leave his three little girls. With Ian there was no equality. Our relationship wasn't about equality."

The sun lifted on the horizon and outside turned gray. The Esso station stood lonely, glowing white. Mom said something about it being much easier to be unhappy than to be happy and I knew we'd be heading back.

"He hit you, damn it, Mom. We can't turn back. You're stronger than that," Jane pleaded. She was almost crying. Mom held Jane, hugged her.

"It was just his ring," she said. "If he hadn't been wearing that ring it wouldn't have been so bad. I shouldn't have flirted so much."

Blood clotted around her eye. Blood stained her black dress with a darker shade of black. She licked her finger and patted away some blood that had dried on her hand. She put on dark glasses. We sat there staring out the window, thinking what to do. Jane insisted we go home, almost angrily. I thought they'd get in a fight. I saw his hand come down and I shivered.

"He just had too much to drink and I provoked him," Mom said. "Anton needs us. Nicholas and Timothy and Finny and Sofia and Caroline, they all need us." She stared hard into the morning.

"But *we* don't need them," Jane said. "Think about yourself. Think about us."

"We need them too, Jane. I think we should go back, at least for a little while. At least until the end of the trip, just to give him a chance. Everyone deserves another chance."

"When's the end of the trip?"

"Oh please, Jane. Please."

We drove for hours into the darkness of the west and down into the desert again, the air cool from night and the world so empty-seeming, waiting to be filled in.

We stopped at a diner and I bought us all eggs and Mom a cup of coffee with cream. With the sunglasses on, you couldn't tell she'd been hit and her face even looked less anxious, as if she knew that Anton would be coming for us. She put on some rouge and lipstick, holding her compact out in front of her. Julia said she was feeling better even though her coloring was white and yellow. Jane said we were making the wrong choice. We all drank a cup of coffee. It was bitter, but good. I felt grown up.

In the distance, in the wet mirage of road, the turquoise camper came toward us. Mom stopped the car and when the camper arrived Anton got out, rising tall with his cowboy hat perched on the top of his head and he came to Mom who'd gotten out of the car to meet him and he lifted her up and hugged her hard.

"Eve!" Anton screamed and Mom looked so beautiful, hugged there tight in his strong, big arms. His lips pressed gently into her hair. "I love you, Eve!" I thought of the water tower that loomed over town. He folded in half and started crying and watching him cry made me want to cry.

Mom turned back, looking at us in the car. A smile cracked her lips and her hair blew this way and that across her face. The dark glasses made her glamorous. She turned back to Anton.

"I'm leaving," Jane said to Julia and me in the car.

After several days they were engaged to be married. Anton bought her a moonstone from an Indian as an engagement ring. We had a family meeting. All of us, including James and Cynthia—one of us now. She'd paid for the Desert Princess so Anton had invited her to join us. I was glad she'd paid; I knew she'd never notice my charges. Dwayne was gone. Anton had asked him to leave. Mom sighed when Anton told her, sorry she hadn't been able to be more generous.

We sat at a picnic table at a roadside stop and Mom and Anton asked our opinion of marriage, if we thought they should marry.

Nicholas said they fought too much and Sofia asked about their mother. Jane ignored the whole meeting. Caroline said it was a beautiful idea. James said Anton needed to work through his anger first, which I thought would make Anton mad, but it didn't. And though some of us thought they should not, the matter was decided and we had a small ceremony that night. Anton read a few prayers from his red book and also the marriage blessing, and their marriage was decided. Mom wore a beautiful dress without a bra, the way Anton liked. Some good bottles of wine were opened for the toast.

"He's not going to marry her," Sofia said. "Look at Finny's mom. You can be sure she wanted to marry Dad. And they had a kid together." She sucked on the end of her hair and held me with her beautiful eyes. "If Eve's in it for the money, she'll be disappointed. You see, if Dad marries he doesn't get any of Mom's money." She looked at me tenderly as if we were in this together. As if I were her partner, on her side. "Dad only gets the use of the money as long as he's married to Mom. It's their agreement."

A few days later we saw Dwayne hitchhiking again, dressed in his orange robes, and we picked him up. All of us kids ignored Dwayne, tolerating him. But he didn't seem to notice. He was one of those types who would never notice, even if the whole world hated him.

Mom said, "Let our home be a haven for those in need."

A WHOLE FAMILY

The December after Dad left, and several months before Mom met Anton, Sal and Sam—a novelist and his wife—and four of their seven children had moved into our house. The novelist had been a college friend of Dad's. His novels weren't yet successful and he was broke, so Mom offered him part of our house as a way for all of us to cut costs.

They had arrived in a beat-up old yellow station wagon and took over the house. A baby boy, two girls—one almost my age and one Jane's age—and a boy Julia's age. The two girls, Belva and Sala, moved into my room and I moved in with Julia. The parents and the baby, Saki, made a bedroom of the study and the boy, Pursey, slept on a mattress in the dining room. Boxes and suitcases and a strange smell of spices and breast milk overwhelmed the house. Mom was in bed a lot, getting over Dad, but their arrival made her happy. She said she wanted "a whole family" in the house, not "a broken family." She said the house wasn't a home without "a whole family."

The novelist had droopy, sad eyes and he always moped around, trying to work, but not working very much at all. He stared out the window, paced, ate, slept and sometimes he cried. His head was balding and terror flooded his light brown eyes. Sometimes just staring at him was enough to spook you. He had the saddest voice, as if the whole world were collapsing in on him. I felt sorry for him. There was nothing in the world as bad as seeing an adult cry. He was short. He dressed in khakis and oxfords like Dad.

Sam, for Samantha, was the exact opposite: tall and thick-boned with long black hair which she kept tied back in a rubber band she'd pull off the newspapers. She had black, black eyes. Her hands were always on her hips and it wasn't long before she started ordering us around as if we were her own children, organizing us with dinner jobs and house chores as if we'd never had them. She kept whole-earth food in abundant stock and tried to teach us to love tiger's milk and tofu. We were prohibited from seeing Mom while she slept, which was all the time. "Off limits," Sam would say, guarding Mom's door. Her mouth opened wide when she spoke so you could see all the pink inside. Her thick tongue ran over her big gray teeth. Only Jane was allowed to visit Mom when she wanted.

"Jane only has your mother," Sam would say. It had been a couple months since Jane stopped seeing Dad. Since she'd taken Mom's side, Sam liked Jane best.

Julia popped Mom's lock with straightened-out hangers and knitting needles. She kneeled at Mom's door, working fast. I kept on the lookout, leaning over the banister to watch the downstairs. The brass chandelier hung in front of me, dangling down from the ceiling, thick with cobwebs. Mom didn't care about cleaning anymore. A giddy feeling rushed through us. I'd whisper excitedly whenever I thought I heard Sam's heavy feet marching over the downstairs hall. Julia concentrated, sliding her tools in and out of the lock until it popped and we broke in.

"Do something, Mom," Julia complained. At first Julia couldn't stand Sam. Julia divided the refrigerator in half with cardboard. One side for our creamed chipped beef and normal food. One side for Sam's weird food. Julia told me she saw Sam lick her baby's poop off her finger while changing his diapers. We weren't going to eat any of her food, no matter what. Jane cooked creamed chipped beef for us every night. Sam said our food had nitrates and preservatives inside that would rot our stomachs.

"She means well," Mom said, lifting herself to lean against the headboard. Her hair fell all over the place and her breath was bad. Big dark circles formed half-moons beneath her eyes. The room smelled stale. The windows were closed. Outside was pouring rain. Mom always hated when it rained in winter. She felt gypped of snow. Snow made the whole world perfect—the way it fell, so softly and lazily, made her feel there was a lot of time. The rain streamed against the windows as if we were inside a tank.

"She's tired. She's recovering," Sam would say. "She's been through a lot with the separation. Your father hasn't treated her very well." A favorite subject of hers were stories about Dad. Her body inflated, leaning toward ours as she listed all his crimes. "Crimes," that's what she called them. She talked for hours, sitting there at the dinner table. Mom in bed. Sam's big black eyes beamed. I felt alone. I put my hands beneath me and rocked in my chair. The leftovers dried on our plates. Her kids made remarks, agreeing with their mother though they'd never met Dad. Saki cried and Sam lifted him from the floor to her lap to give him her enormous breast. He sucked noisily and burped.

"Your father had been fucking Camille for over a year." Fucking. She accentuated *fucking*, making it really hard. "They had it all planned out, their escape," Sam said. When Saki finished she gave her breast to Pursey. He was eleven, three years older than I. His bushy head of hair fell down her chest. You could hear him slurping, as if through a straw.

"Do you want some?" Sam asked, catching me staring.

"Do you eat your baby's poop?" I asked.

"It's the best part of him," she said, and smiled.

Mornings Dad's little white VW appeared in the driveway outside the kitchen window. Julia and I rushed out to it with our lunch bags and book bags. Dad had the court order that allowed him to drive us to school three days a week.

"Hello, Ian," Sam said, leaning out the kitchen door. Half in, half out. It was cold outside, but she wore a sleeveless nightgown. Her fleshy arms drooped and no goose bumps rose on her skin. Thick black hair emerged from her armpits. Steam issued from her mouth. Her hands rested on her hips. The two of us kissed Dad and piled into the car. Jane had already caught the bus. Dad would ask us about her. He'd ask Julia what he could do to get her to ride with us.

Sam's kids crowded at the kitchen door eagerly, hoping for a ride. Wild creatures, I thought. They had hair all over the place and Pursey's was longer than mine. And their clothes were all hand-me-downs, rattier than the clothes we gave to the Salvation Army. I hated that they went to my school and that kids and teachers would know they lived with us. Mom told Jane, Julia and me to treat them like we treated each other, as if they were our own sisters and brothers. The only sisterly thing I ever did was chop off Belva's hair to make her look better. Chopped it all off in the bathroom until she had short, short hair. "A pixie," I told her. She was six months younger than me.

"Would you mind giving the kids a ride to school? They've missed the bus," Sam asked Dad. They'd missed the bus because they'd taken such a long time getting ready. They could never find anything of their own and were always borrowing from us, and now I couldn't find anything of my own. Sam's voice was strong. She never flirted to get her way, the way Mom did, smiling up at men with her curly blond hair and that gap between her teeth. Mom even flirted with Sam. Sometimes I thought Sam thought she was Mom's husband. "Jealous husband," Julia would add.

Dad's face became long. Sam's eyes held him, unblinking. The kids rushed from the house and piled into the car with us. One up front next to Julia, two squooshed in the back next to me. Dad said nothing the whole drive to school, while the rest of us talked and shouted.

The next time Dad said something to Sam. "I drive fifty miles to spend a few minutes with my children before school." The words came almost visibly with his hot breath in the cold air. Her kids stood behind her at the door, peering around her, big hopeful faces. Belva reminded me of a rat with her short hair. I was glad I'd cut it. Julia and I sat in the car while Sam screamed at Dad. "You're a calculating man, Ian Cooper." She listed the things he'd done, "his crimes," but I didn't listen. I covered my ears and sang and Julia sang too. But even through the singing I just knew Sam and her children were hating Dad now and I knew they would tell Mom and soon enough she'd be hating Dad even more than she already did and then so would Jane. Everybody'd be hating Dad. I wondered if I could ever hate Dad as much as that.

A snowfall from the night before covered the ground and the limbs of all the trees. Icicles hung from the eaves of the house. The windows were frosted. Mom's bedroom blinds were down. I wondered if she'd heard Sam. The temperature was way below freezing. Inside Dad's car was warm. The engine vibrated. Sam stormed into the house, slamming the door. A few icicles fell and stabbed the ground. Dad leaned his head on the steering wheel. I looked at the house, our big white house in the woods. Dad and Mom had built that house. They bought the property together and moved out here from New York when I was just born.

After awhile we grew used to Sam and even came to like her. There's nothing quite like it when someone mean warms to you. Makes you feel special, like you've conquered something, you alone, because you're grand. She taught us to sew in the basement and took us to fabric stores to buy material. I made five halter tops for summer and also a skirt. Sometimes Sal would come to the basement and mope and then Mom would come down and mope and they made fun of each other for moping. We'd make bets and have competitions to see who could mope the longest. Sal and Mom would stare at each other, faces long, eyes drooping, until one of them erupted in laughter. The sewing machine churned and Jane laid the patterns on the fabric and cut it out. Seeing Mom laugh was like nothing else, her body alive, moving inside her nightgown. Sometimes I'd just hug her, cling to her until she'd tell me not to. Sam would take care of all of us by making enormous amounts of whole-grain bread and hot oatmeal. For a bit it was like a family. The basement floor was filthy with black centipedes.

At the foot of the driveway, strung taut between two trees, Sam rigged up a metal chain. On the mornings that Dad came to take us to school she marched down the driveway and fastened the chain.

"Your father is not a good man." At the dinner table Sam told us stories of affairs he'd had before Camille. Affairs with his secretaries and once with a whore. I imagined a whore and laughed.

"A whore?" Julia asked, laughing too, and then so did Sam, and then the whole table was laughing. Even Jane was laughing. It was great to see Jane laugh. She was always so serious. Mom would tell her she'd get wrinkles around her lips if she didn't lighten up.

Sometimes the way Sam went on confused us, made us feel she was speaking about someone else, made us want to join her, made us want to hate Dad too.

"It disturbs your mother too much to see him, to know that he's here picking you up. It sets her back," Sam said, interrupting the laughter.

Sam stood at the foot of the driveway in big clompy boots and her nightgown. A shawl draped her fleshy arms. Her nose was pink and it dripped. Julia and I stood by her side, bundled up in duffle coats. Our cheeks bright red. Julia's nose never turned red and that made her proud.

"Hello, Mr. Cooper," Sam said excitedly to Dad when he arrived. Black hairs sprouted from a mole near her lips. Exhaust from the car filled the air. I gulped a few deep breaths, loving that smell. I could have put my nose right up to the pipe, the way I did with the nuzzle of a gas pump, and sniffed for a good long time. The snow had melted and frozen again and icy patches glistened in the strong sun. Ice coated the branches of trees, forming a canopy of icicles over the road. I thought about sledding. Afternoons, Sam took us to the roller-coaster hills. That's what we called them. Hills in the Sourlands. Enormously steep hills, and because of the ice the sleds tore down them. If you stayed low, sometimes you'd make it halfway up the other side.

"What's the metal chain for, Sam?" Dad asked patiently.

"To keep you from driving up the driveway," she said pleasantly. Her black eyes sparkled.

He thought for a moment. Looked at the gloved back of his hand, fisted and flexed it a few times.

"What are you doing to me?" he asked, the words coming out slowly.

" 'What have I done?' is what you should ask yourself," Sam said.

"How was your weekend?" Sam asked. Sunday around the dinner table. Sal was there looking sad, a look that reminded me of a sadness I saw in my father's eyes. Sal's novel was going terribly. He had absolutely no money left, no prospects of earning any soon with his work. It looked like they'd live with us forever. It occurred to me he should get a different job.

"Why don't you get a different job?" I asked.

"Be quiet, Kate," Sam said. I shut up, but it didn't make any sense his being unhappy all the time for a job that paid him no money and that he didn't have to do. "Now how was your weekend, girls?" she said to Julia and me.

"Good," we'd say, afraid to say something wrong. Each time we came back from a weekend with Dad was the same.

"Well, what did you do?"

We'd tell them about where Dad had taken us, or what he'd read us or a dinner that Camille had cooked.

"Camille?" Sam would say, her eyes brightening, head leaning toward us. "Tell us about Camille."

We'd tell about Camille, that she was beautiful, with long ginger hair, and generous. That she walked around the house in her underpants.

"In her underpants?" Sam asked.

That she was very organized and her house was filled with so much of everything. We searched for something that would interest Sam, wanting to please her as if by doing so we were pleasing Mom.

"Camille says that they fuck like rabbits," I blurted, laughing nervously, imagining rabbits fucking.

"She said they make love like rabbits," Julia corrected. Julia had asked Camille about sex and about babies. Camille had said that when you had a baby the doctor slit your vagina all the way back to your poop hole. I had closed my ears. Julia loved knowing details like that. Camille was filled with them.

"She talks to you about sex, does she?" Sam asked, puckering her lips together.

All around us, like islands floating in the desert basin, were small black mountain chains with jagged, jagged spines. Jane, Julia and I alone in the camper. Now that Anton had announced to his kids that he was going to marry Mom, she tried harder than ever with them, trying to get their love. For the most part, it made us sick the way she'd ooze affection all over them. Especially over the boys. Sofia said that was because she didn't have any boys. Sometimes, now, the three of us liked it to be just us, and when the others would go off to town we'd stay behind.

Julia brushed the knots out of my hair. Her fingers searched for them, rolling them, pulling them, examining them. Jane read.

"Ouch," I said.

"Your hair hasn't been brushed in days," Julia said. She had a comb and a brush on the table and a little bowl of water to dip her fingers in. She hovered above me, looking into my scalp. Her knees pressed against my back and I could smell and feel her clean clothes. They were stiff and lemony, not like mine, which were soft with dirt. It was quiet. Her concentration was intense. All I could hear were Julia's fingers pulling my hair gently away from my scalp and the wind outside flapping the sheets that Mom had washed and hung up to dry.

"I like the quiet," I said. Jane put down her book and straightened out of a slouch.

"I like the quiet too, Kitty," Jane said.

"Me too," Julia said.

Out the window an infinity of power-line poles receded over the land. I thought of all my telephone calls and of all my letters. I thought again of the foolish hope that Dad would trace them across America until he found us. His little white VW appearing on the horizon.

"I hate Dad," I said.

"No you don't," Jane said.

"Yes I do," I insisted. "I do." I hated it when she told me how I felt, especially since I was saying something I thought she'd like to hear.

"All right, you do." She looked at me. "Why?"

"For the same reason you hate him." I didn't really know why she hated him. I examined my hand, the scars I had from picking at my fingers. I looked up at Jane and I thought of her reading and cooking and acting like Mom and I thought, I am not like that. I thought of Julia knowing everything and showing it off. I thought of her flirting with Nicholas and Anton and I thought, I am not like that either. I felt suddenly lonely.

"I'm leaving," Jane said. Her whole face flushed and she pushed her palm into her cheek.

"No you're not," Julia said, taking her fingers out of my hair. She slumped down into the booth.

"Do you have any of that money left?" Jane asked me.

"No," I lied instinctively. I didn't want to give up any of my money. "Yes, I mean yes."

"You can't leave," Julia said. The indoor-outdoor carpet was stained with old food, crusty in spots. I smelled old milk. The wind banged the screen door.

"I can't protect Mom anymore," Jane said, getting up to stop the door from banging. "Anton would be nobody without all these people. He gathers them around so he can tell them what to do and feel like somebody. James agrees with me. James and I have talked about this. He's going to leave soon too."

"Anton's just weak," Julia said. Jane gave her a look.

"Mom says you'll get wrinkles if you keep your face so serious all the time," I said to Jane. I didn't want to protect anybody but Finny.

"Can I borrow some of your money?" Jane asked. I didn't feel lonely anymore, but scared instead.

"Where are you going to go?" Julia said, suspiciously.

"To Anna's." Anna was her best friend. She was Eurasian, with long, silky black hair that she could sit on. Her eyes were green—greener than Mom's or mine—and almond-shaped. Her skin was pale like Jane's. She was the most beautiful girl I had ever seen. "How much do you have?"

I lifted my gun from its holster, twirled it on my index finger. They weren't impressed. I pulled out my wad of cash. That impressed them.

"You have a bloody mint, Kate," Julia said, counting it. "You've got over three hundred dollars." She counted it again. The money was beautiful in her fingers. "You could go to the moon with all this, Jane. Where'd you get it?" she asked me suddenly and suspiciously. Her left eyebrow rose, slowly.

"I stole it." I didn't like admitting that, but I didn't feel like lying anymore. They laughed. They couldn't stop laughing and then I started laughing too and told them how I had stolen it and as I talked pride rushed through me, making me exaggerate. I told Jane she could have the money because I knew how to get more if I needed it and they laughed at that idea too. We heard the Eldorado coming back and we turned serious. I scrambled to tuck the money away.

"I don't hate him. I don't hate Dad," Jane said. "It's just that he left us to take care of so much." I knew she wanted to say "Mom" and that made me sad. Jane seemed so grown-up to me then. Her hair was neatly braided and she wore a yellow peasant blouse with different-colored flowers embroidered around the yoke. I didn't think I was like her but I wanted to be. She was almost thirteen.

"Why doesn't he come get us?" I'd wanted to ask that forever and knew I could now. There were a million questions I wanted to ask my sisters.

"Because would you really go back with him? Could you really ever leave Mom? He knows that, Kate."

"I love you, Dad," Julia said. "No matter what happens, I love you." She kissed him hard as she got out of the car at school. All around kids screamed, tearing off school buses. It snowed fiercely. I wore a pair of Julia's Dr. Scholl's with wool socks. I couldn't find my boots and knew I'd probably find them on Belva at school. My feet were wet and cold. After that morning Julia stopped coming with Dad.

Sam had said it would be better for Mom if we didn't see as much of Dad, especially Jane and Julia, because they were older and knew more, could see more. Hearing about Camille's sex life disturbed Mom. Sam changed our telephone number to an unlisted one so that Dad couldn't call. Each time Dad learned it, she changed the number again. Again and again and again. So many times in only a few weeks that we couldn't remember it ourselves.

I walked down the driveway alone. Late February. Spring was coming and the forsythia were just beginning to bud. Crocuses hid in the woods, low to the ground, a flash of purple here and there. The driveway was alive and cheery even though it was a gloomy day. Dad's VW waited, the engine running, and Dad's eager face watching for me. My feet slid around in Julia's shoes. My dress was uncomfortable. I'd outgrown it. I wore wool tights that made my legs hot. My hair was unbrushed, but I liked it that way. I thought it looked curly. There were so many smells, bitter and sweet, and a loud chorus of birds.

"Is Julia coming?" he asked.

"Next time," I lied. It annoyed me that he wanted her to come so badly. I wanted to go to the Chocolate Shoppe and have a hot chocolate, stay there until I was late for school. The windows were rolled down and the air was soft and velvety and filled with all those smells. Clusters of children waited for the bus at the foot of their driveways and I felt lonely with Dad, thinking of my sisters and Sam's kids all together on the bus. I was afraid I was missing something. Patches of snow lay in heaps by the roadside. Dad didn't speak much. When he did, he sometimes erupted. "You're just your mother's marionettes," he'd yell. I thought of the marionettes we had from Spain, dressed in lacy red and black Spanish gowns. I stared straight ahead. Bugs and blue veiny bird droppings spotted Dad's windshield. Two weeks passed in this way.

I waited at the foot of the driveway. When Dad arrived, he got out of the car and quietly shut the door. Quietly, he went up to the metal chain. He was carrying a canvas bag that he set down on the ground. He fiddled with the taut chain, which was secured by padlocks to rings poking from trees on either side of the driveway.

"We're going to have a good old morning," he said. There was something scary in his voice. "Oh yes sirree." He took a small ax from the canvas bag and hacked out a wedge of tree where the ring was fixed. Chips of wood flew this way and that, and with a *thunk* the heavy chain landed on the ground. He lifted the chain and tossed it to one side of the driveway. He lifted his canvas bag, dropped the ax in it and carried the bag back to the car and told me to get in.

"It's a beautiful day," he said. Then he said he was moving back to town. He was going to live in Camille's house and they would build an addition so that we'd each have a room. It would be ready by fall and that's when he'd move in. He wanted to be closer to us so that he could see us more often. He smelled of sweat and coffee. "Yes sirree."

"We shouldn't do this," I warned. I thought of Sam and started picking at my knuckles.

"Oh we shouldn't, should we?" He stopped the car and leaned over to me. He held my arms tightly and I worried something had gone wrong with him, but then he hugged me. An awkward hug that hurt.

We crept up the driveway. I thought again of Sam and knew she'd be mad. Then I thought about the Chocolate Shoppe and I asked Dad if we'd go. "We'll go, Katy, once we get your sisters."

"You think they'll come?" I asked getting happy inside. Dad wore a forest green wool sweater and khakis. His thick black hair was graying. I noticed the skin on his hands was wrinkled and I thought about Mom complaining about wrinkles around her eyes, wrinkles you could hardly see. But she'd pinch the skin at the corner of her eyes and lift it. "One tuck," she'd say. She did that when she was happy, when the only thing on her mind was her eyes. Dad's hands clutched the steering wheel, his knuckles red, fingers white from pressure. Sun poured through those trees.

Dad got out of the car and walked through the kitchen door into the house. Julia and Jane were at the table with Sam's kids. Sam stood at the stove concocting something that smelled terrible, like liver. All the windows were raised and a breeze raced through the kitchen. Julia looked up from her cereal bowl and smiled and then, remembering something, stopped smiling and her face dropped.

Sam turned from the stove. Her baby clung to her hip. "Let's go, girls," Dad said. "I'm taking you to the Chocolate Shoppe."

"You're forbidden by the court of law to enter this house," Sam said. "Leave this house immediately or I'll call the police, Mr. Cooper." God, I hated that she called him Mr. Cooper, as if he were a stranger. The baby smiled a big toothless smile and Sam patted his back and he burped. Dad walked over to the table and told Jane and Julia to get ready.

"Over my dead body," Sam said. I could almost smell her pleasure, as if it was sweating from her. I wished just this once Jane would give in.

Dad put his hand on Jane's arm. Her face darkened, at first bewildered. "I have to get ready for school," she said softly. Her voice faltered. For a second, I thought that meant she'd come with us. But then I felt distant from Jane, as if by going with Dad I no longer belonged to this side of the family. Inside the house was different now. Sam's world. Nothing was familiar anymore. I smelled that liver smell again.

Jane shook Dad's hand off her arm. Her face turned a nervous red. Her chest would have been splotched with red and white patches. Sam's kids stopped eating. The baby laughed. I wished Dad would just forget about Jane. I bet I could get Julia to come and I thought maybe that would make him happy enough. I could bribe Julia with my nose, let her bite it as much as she wanted.

"I'm not coming with you, Ian," Jane said. My stomach fell. The kitchen was dark and everyone seemed like a shadow.

"I'm your father and you are coming. Now get your things. Come on, Julia." Dad held Jane's arm again, tightly. Julia stood up and Sam picked up the phone.

"Let me go," Jane said.

"I'm calling the police, Mr. Cooper." Dad let Jane go and went to the phone and yanked it from Sam's hand and then he yanked it from the wall. The baby started crying. Dad's face remained constant and determined, a slight smile on his lips. For a moment Jane stood in a daze.

The next thing, Dad was chasing Jane down the hall up the stairs to her room. Jane's room was bright and neat, painted yellow, and her bedspread was yellow printed with evening primrose. She always kept everything so neat, the way Mom liked it.

"I only want to drive you to school," Dad said. "You can't give me this? You have to take that away from me too?" His voice was more desperate now, but restrained trying to be patient, that weird angry controlled tone, that yes-sirree tone.

"I'm not going," Jane said, trying to shut the door on him, but he pushed it open, knocking her against the wall and out of the way. "I'll be late, Dad. Leave me alone." She scrambled to the bed.

"Let's talk at least," he said. "Give me that at least." He pulled her from the bed, but she refused to speak. "I love you, Jane," he said. He started shaking her. "I love you," he shouted. His face flushed and now Jane's went white. Her big eyes wide. She flung her arms free of him, but he grabbed her again and shook her some more as if he could shake her into loving him and then he held her, squashing her against his chest.

"I hate you," she hissed. Then there was utter silence. He held her out from him and stared at her and she stared at him, trembling, and I thought somehow things would be all right, but in a flash they were wrong again and Dad picked Jane up and heaved her onto the bed. Julia was on him at once, but he shook her off and went after Jane.

I crawled beneath the bed and closed my ears and started singing. I could feel the box springs on me and dust balls beneath me. It was dark under there with light just barely seeping in from beneath the bed skirt, and messy. I wanted to laugh, thinking, This is how she manages to keep her room so neat. Papers from old school years and books and pictures and junk and then I saw a whole bunch of Wendy dolls, that's what we called Madame Alexander dolls, a whole world of them. I loved playing with them. I had a wicker basket filled with dozens of them. They were beautiful dolls, with the little eyelids that roll up and down and their costumes from foreign countries. Among the dolls was a new box and inside a new doll, played with or held once or twice, one that came from Spain. It was the doll that Dad had sent in August. She hadn't thrown it away. I never thought of Jane playing with dolls. I never imagined there'd been a time when Jane was my age, doing the things I did now. Then it occurred to me that Dad and Mom were still together when she was my age.

"Ian," I heard Mom's weary voice say. The bed stopped moving and the shouting stopped. A silence settled down. I was relieved it wasn't Sam. I could hear Dad crying and I crawled out. Jane was up at the head of the bed pressing her body into the wall. Julia crouched over her, wiping Jane's hair away from her face. My wool stockings felt very hot now and dust balls stuck to them and the crotch had come down between my thighs. I thought about school and how late we would be and how the teachers would ask me questions again. They loved taking me into their offices to ask questions about home. Then I wondered how we'd get to school. I wondered, if Dad drove us, would Sam's kids come along?

"Ian," Mom said again. That "Ian" seemed to say a million things to Dad. He dropped his arms. His face was ugly, smeared with tears, and he drooled. She came through the doorway, wearing the nightgown she'd been wearing for months. The skin around her eyes was wrinkled from too much sleep and I thought about her pinching it. I hoped she didn't smell. Her arms reached out to Dad as she glided past me to him. She hugged him and he held her hard, clutching. Jane watched, holding a pillow against her stomach, shaking, while Julia petted her. Mom smoothed Dad's hair and he continued to cry, hugging Mom, holding on to her hard as if she would vanish.

Sam let us have this. She stayed away. It was hard for her, surely, but she let us have this.

In early March, Sal and Sam and the four of their seven children piled into their yellow station wagon and drove away. They moved to England, where Sal had found a publisher, their lives receding from ours. By then, even Mom was glad they left, and for a while she was strong.

THE BEAUTY OF
CHRISTIANITY

Sometimes it was like drowning, like what I'd imagine drowning to be—bobbing up, gasping for air but breathing in water, arms flailing, attempting to crawl higher above the waves. Body heavy. Weak. And when you do give up, it's supposed to be a magnificent feeling, of total and final relaxation. Tingles run through your veins easing you, soothing you slowly, slowly until you are finally absorbed.

We weren't ever going home. Our father wasn't ever coming to pick us up. Jane, with her plans to run away, wasn't going home either. Otherwise I might have gone with her. Instead I started feeling religious. A wonderful sensation, like I was being absorbed by something grand. Something big. The arms of God stretched down and enveloped me, hugging me like the arms of my friend Allison's mother. I thought this was what feeling spiritual meant. I wanted to feel spiritual like Mom. I had to find God. Everywhere I turned He appeared like a premonition. Chapels and missions and churches popped up by the side of the road in the middle of nowhere. PAUSE, REST, PRAY read a sign in Sultan for the Wayside

Church, horribly lime green and small, small. Every town had a religious store selling biblical figurines so colorful you'd want to believe: Mary in prayer, Christ on the Cross, Saint John the Baptist—they were the ones I knew. There were religious candles and religious balms. Rosaries and prayer books and Bibles. There were "evil away" air fresheners and special dried religious leaves and twigs that when burned attracted the Holy Spirit. I could have spent a lot of my money in these stores. On the radio, ministers of the faith proclaimed miracles they'd performed like magic, curing paraplegics, giving sight and hearing to the blind and deaf, wits to the dumb, raising the dead like Lazarus. I believed. At camp one night a religious woman rode up to us on a bicycle and handed me a religious pamphlet that told me Jesus loved me. On the highway, billboards appeared: CHRIST IS ALIVE, ARE YOU?

I thought God was trying to tell me something and I wanted to hear it. I prayed. Began praying all the time on my knees, looking up to heaven with my mind and heart opening for God. I'd fold my hands together and press my knees into the dirt, waiting to be filled. At first I kept this to myself. I didn't want to be made fun of. And I'd squeeze my eyes shut tight and wait and pray to God. And He'd come down and fill me until I thought I'd burst inside. Fill me with the desire to be generous and good and giving. I was awake, alive. I thought about the religious kids back at home going to parochial schools and felt blessed and more aware, like I understood because I was choosing this. No one was choosing or had chosen it for me. The arms of God came down and wrapped around me from behind, protecting me. Instructing me to be good, telling me what was out there when it seemed that there was nothing. We weren't ever going home.

Peter asked Jesus, "Sir, how many times should I forgive my brother if he keeps wronging me? Up to seven times?"

Jesus responded, "Not just seven: seventy times seven."

Anton said, Forgiveness is an attitude not an action. Anton said, Forgiveness is an openness of heart. He lit a joint and I looked up to him. We were camped in Arizona on our way to the Grand Canyon, finally. Ocotillo surrounded the field like barbed wire and flycatchers and woodpeckers drilled holes in the saguaros. "Forgive us our wrongs as we forgive those who have wronged us." Forgiveness is the beauty of Christianity.

"The beauty of Christianity is that it is based on life on earth and the reality of our world more than any other religion," Anton said.

"Except that you're not allowed to enjoy any of the pleasures of life on earth without sinning," Cynthia Banks said and laughed.

"What about Zen Buddhism?" James asked in his sweet, deep accent.

Anton's eyes glowed red and the campfire burned fiercely, the flames twisting and righting and as night came we heard a coyote and then a plane flying through the stars overhead. Anton talked about the Jesuits and sex and the Virgin and his visions of the statue in the courtyard outside his cell. He talked about making love to Mom for the first time in the onion grass outside his therapy farm. Cynthia laughed and no one else paid much attention, except for me and Julia, who asked questions about sex. Then she went away to join the big kids, who were having a taste test of bad wine to see which was the worst: Mad Dog 20/20, Wild Irish Rose, Boone's Farm Strawberry Hill, Thunderbird.

"For if you forgive others their offenses, your heavenly father will forgive you." In my holster I had the three hundred dollars I'd collected. For a little while I wanted to give it all back, hand it to Anton and have him take it from me and bless me and forgive me and tell me I was good. His hand would be warm and soft, sweeping over mine and he'd hold me and comfort me and love me. I wanted him to help me find God.

I'd promised the money to Jane, though, and when I thought about it, I figured if Christ and Anton would forgive me now they'd also forgive me later.

Anton said, Love is a vital part of forgiveness. Anton said, Christianity is centered around the mystery of Divine love and man must learn to respond to that love. I saw the back of his hand come down on Mom. I saw the enormous turquoise ring and the pinched skin and the little hairs which emerged from beneath the silver setting and I saw Mom take it, standing strong, her body wavering only from the impact. I saw him asking, begging, pleading with her for forgiveness. "He hit you, Mom," Jane had screamed over and over. I could still hear her. He said, "Thou shalt love the Lord thy God with all thy heart, and with all thy soul, and with all thy might. This is the first and great commandment. And the second is like unto it, Thou shalt love thy neighbor as thyself. On these two commandments hang all the law and the prophets."

"Anton loves me the best," Julia said. "Of the three of us he loves me the best. I can feel it." She wasn't saying it competitively. She was simply stating fact. I thought of the way she sat in Anton's lap sometimes, plopped herself in his lap and wrapped her arms around his neck. I thought of the way he always chose her to be on his football team. The way she flirted up to him like a smaller version of Mom. It hadn't occurred to me that he could love her differently from me.

"I'm going to convert," I said. I liked using the word *convert*. It was sophisticated. Julia was the first one I told. I wanted to test it out.

"You can't do that," Julia said and screwed up her eyes. She understood absolutely nothing about God. Then I thought she didn't want me to because she was jealous. She'd wished she'd had the idea first.

"I can too," I said and told her Anton was going to help me, which was a lie, but I knew that Anton would help me when I asked.

"Why?" she asked.

"For the same reason most people do," I said.

"Most people are born Catholic."

"I know," I snapped. "But I wasn't." I thought for a moment. "I want to know what's going to happen to me." I thought about Dolly, my Catholic friend whose mother had said I treated her like

a priest. She trusted God would take care of her and she didn't
think about the future because He thought about it for her. When
she was six years old all her blood was removed from her body
through a tube plugged into her navel, sucked out as if through a
straw and there was a moment, before the new blood was put back
in, when she was bloodless and could die and she hadn't been
afraid. She said God protected her and if He chose to give her
death then she would welcome it. I didn't want to be afraid.

"What if you knew you were going to die tomorrow?" Julia
chewed on a twig she'd picked up off the ground. We squatted,
thighs pressing into shins, rocking. I heard Sofia bossing Finny and
Timothy, telling them to do dinner jobs and I heard Timothy tell
her to fuck off and then I heard Dwayne try to arbitrate. I hated
Dwayne. Then I felt bad for hating Dwayne, ungiving, and started
loving him. I loved Dwayne. Home flashed before me for an instant. The sky turned indigo and the air cooled.

"If that's what God wants I'll welcome it," I said. Actually that
too was a lie. I'd started thinking about dying a lot now and was
afraid. Sometimes I thought there were so many of us one of us
would die soon. Sometimes I'd be so afraid of dying I wouldn't
leave the camper in the middle of the night to pee. I'd hold the pee
until morning, afraid that someone would be out there in the dark
to get me. But I liked saying that I'd welcome death. It made me
feel better than Julia. I saw her in Anton's lap again and wondered
if she'd stolen anything.

"You can confess to me," she said and flexed her left eyebrow.

Anton's love for Jane wasn't obvious love, that's the way Julia
put it. "Obvious love. A love/hate relationship." But Jane's love for
him wasn't "obvious" either. She still didn't speak to him and he
gave her this disgusted look when he told her to do a dinner job or
some other chore. It was a "You're-gonna-do-it-babe-and-not-
complain" look. We felt sorry for Jane. We wanted her to get on
with Anton because we knew that somewhere inside she wanted to
get on with him the way we did. We thought she was jealous. I
didn't believe that Anton loved Julia better than me.

"Look at how Anton and Julia get on," Mom had said to Jane. Julia and Anton had been playing a game that Julia said he had invented especially for her. She was wearing one of her outfits, a polyester minidress with blue sailboats floating on it. Her hair a bunch of curls. Anton called their game "Uncle." She ran and he chased her. First slowly and lazily. His pants fell down his hips and his cowboy hat flopped on his head. He wore no shirt. At first he let her believe she was faster. In poker he taught us to play like that, to lose a few hands to fool your opponents. Then suddenly he'd grab her and she'd scream and we'd stop what we were doing for a moment to watch them flirt, Mom watching with her pleased smile. Anton bent Julia's fingers back as far as they could go until she coughed up more screams and looked at him with her eyes opening and closing and smiling and pleading. Julia had told me that Anton made her feel sexual. I thought about that now. Thought about the bulldog ants oozing infertile eggs. I wanted to play "Uncle." She loved Anton and her eyes beamed and she slipped down to her knees. "Say 'Uncle,'" he'd say. At first, giggling and still struggling to get away, she'd refuse. "Come on, babe." His body loomed over hers, casting her in shadow. And her fingers went back further and her knees pressed harder into the dust.

"Uncle," she'd finally say, and with "Uncle" the game would end.

Now Julia stared at me, really seriously, trying to figure me out, see if I were convinced about converting. Her look made me nervous. You could just tell something smart was forming in her mind.

"Do you believe in the host?" she asked, suspiciously.

It took me a minute to remember what the "host" was, but I did and felt relieved.

"Yes," I said. "It's symbolic. I don't really believe it's Christ's body and blood. It's just a beautiful part of the ritual." I had heard Anton say that, so I knew it was all right.

"You mean transubstantiation?" I didn't know what she was talking about. "How about original sin? You can't possibly believe in that." I didn't know how Julia knew all this stuff and I was beginning to feel annoyed. I didn't know what original sin was. I just wanted to be Catholic.

"I feel the same way about that as I do about the Host," I bluffed. "It's symbolic. A beautiful part of the ritual."

We were silent for a bit, squatting there in the late afternoon heat, watching the camper. Anton, James and Mom sat at the table, talking. Mom had draped the table with a cloth and it flapped in the light breeze. Anton's classical music played from the cab. He was telling a story, his arms gesturing a lot. A bottle of Jack Daniel's stood on the table. Cynthia Banks walked from the camper to join them. She carried a bottle of wine. Then Nicholas did too. A few of them laughed as Anton told his story, probably a story from his childhood. Anton was big and animated sitting there, the leader of our world.

"I like to protect Anton," Julia said suddenly, eyes far away. "He's like a child, a scared child. He needs to be protected."

I liked the miracles the best. I liked the way Jesus or someone acting for Jesus could make the dead rise, or cure an incurable disease. I liked drinking the wine from the big metal goblet and eating the wafers that dissolved on my tongue. The water and the sign of the cross. The kneeling. The praying. Confession. I thought of all the things I could confess to and be forgiven for. I was impatient for forgiveness.

At a store selling religious things I had Anton buy me a strand of mother-of-pearl rosary beads that I wore like a necklace.

"You're not suppose to wear it like that," Sofia said. But I didn't listen to her. I counted the little, beautiful beads, saying Hail Marys and Our Fathers in my head, trying to memorize the words.

Mom liked that I wanted to become Catholic and encouraged me to talk to Anton. Converting would bring me closer to him, make us whole, more of a family. I could tell she would have liked for Julia and Jane to convert too.

"How long does it take to become a Catholic?" I asked Anton.
"Not very long, babe, if you listen carefully to me." He smiled.
His gold caps sparkled. He squeezed my elbow. There was nothing
better than after a fight. He held Mom near. All that had frightened
me turned soft and you'd forget that he could ever swell up. You'd
forgive. Forgiveness was easy for me.

Sometimes when we stopped for lunch or parked early for the
night Anton would take me for a walk, just the two of us. We'd
walk away from everybody else, entirely alone. His big hand en-
veloping my tiny one, soft like a mitten. I'd feel awkward at first.
My knees would tremble and I wouldn't be able to think of anything to say. It would all seem stupid. I remembered Finny on his
birthday being led away and I'd get scared that Anton would be
leading me to something bad. I'd hear the other kids doing their
own things, laughing, whatever, and my world would get very
small. Inside would feel funny and I'd forget to breathe properly.
I'd feel dirty inside. My stomach would knot and I'd think he was
going to tell me that I was dying.

I had had several friends who had died just like that, and I told
Anton. Felicity, the English girl, hit by the school bus. Mary Gains,
who drowned trying to skate on her neighbor's swimming pool.
The skates became weights on her feet, anchoring her to the deep
end. I hated thinking about that, but that's how the teachers had
explained it in school. Edie Miller died of bone cancer in second
grade. One day she looked fine. The next month she was pale,
yellow-looking like an enamel doll, and bald. The tiniest hairs
sprouted from dry and flaky skin and her eyes widened, receding
in the sockets. Wise dark eyes that didn't flinch. On her lips she
wore a little smile, a little almost mean smile. The next month she
didn't come to school. The next after that she was dead. In the
courtyard behind our classroom the teacher planted a cherry tree
for Edie, as she had for Felicity and Mary. There was a whole orchard back there for kids who had died. I wondered if I died out
here would I get a tree in that orchard?

Anton listened to me, his playfulness temporarily suspended. I'd feel large and important. He looked at my hands and my feet, almost shy in his seriousness. "But why do you want to become a Catholic?" he asked.

Because *you're* Catholic, I wanted to say, but didn't because I wanted to think of something smarter to say, but couldn't. He was always talking about people who weren't smart and people who were smart and I wanted to be one of the smart ones. Then I just wanted him to understand.

Time passed. I pretended to be thinking. I thought of Caroline standing calmly at prayer, hands folded, and of how Anton loved her and of how I wanted him to love me the way he loved her.

"Because I'm afraid of dying and don't want to be. I have bad thoughts that I don't want to be having. I want to be good and spiritual," I said. I spoke fast. That's what Mom said all the time, *spiritual*. He asked me what my bad thoughts were and I told him. I wanted to confess to him and be forgiven and loved the way Mom was. The way Cynthia Banks was and Mark Bitar and all those other patients. I told him I thought about stealing. I didn't tell him I had actually stolen. I told him I thought about Dad and Mom getting back together all the time. For a moment I was afraid he'd get mad and jealous, but he didn't. He said some tender words about my parents and how this wasn't the way families were supposed to be. He said he understood how hard it was on all of us kids.

"You aren't the kids you used to be," he said. "All of you, we've all changed. Pain does that to you. But you go forward, babe. You can't look behind. In some ways that's what Christ's Resurrection is all about." His eyes were warm and soft and I could feel that everything in him was focused on me, trying to make me feel better. I loved Anton. I didn't really know what he meant about the Resurrection, but I loved him so absolutely. We were quiet, still walking.

"When my father was sick and dying, I thought a lot about death too, babe. Death makes you think more about God, Whom I'd forgotten about after leaving the priesthood. Thinking about death made me think about life, coming to life and the surprise of it. Death can be just the same, a surprise. We don't expect to be born. We don't expect to get sick. We don't expect to die. It's comforting to realize that existence is a miracle. But, Katy . . ." I loved that he called me Katy. Dad called me Katy. His mouth had that dry unsticking sound. He cleared his throat and spit. "Jesus preaches that salvation is in this world. Try focusing on being here, on this trip, in this desert. Each new experience unlocks a new part of your self, opens you up." The way he spoke, it was as if there were all these mysteries inside of me that hadn't yet been revealed. In a way it was exciting to think about that, and I did as he talked on about some other ideas that I didn't understand or pay attention to. I wondered if he were loving me more than he loved Julia.

"Why did you become a Catholic?" I stubbed my sandal into the ground. Dust rose and sank again, blowing. I thought of Mom in love with Anton's spirituality and how good that made her feel. I wanted to feel like that, all good and pure inside like the inside of a potato. I wanted Anton to save me. I wanted to stand there forever with Anton.

"I was born a Catholic, babe," he said. "It wasn't a choice." His eyes squinted.

"You believed, though. At some point you had a choice to believe or not. And you wanted to become a priest," I said. I pressed my pocket to check for the money. It was still there. I wanted to tell Anton that Jane was thinking of running away. I thought if he knew he could make her stop and love her and forgive her. Then I filled inside, thinking maybe I could get Jane to convert too and that would make them love each other in an obvious way. I'd speak to Jane. We could convert together.

"St. Augustine said, 'I believe because it's absurd.' I always loved that. And I think it was Sartre who said, 'I believe because if I'm wrong I'm the loser.' I always loved that too." Anton laughed so I laughed, though I had no idea who he was talking about. "When I became a Jesuit I wanted to help people see the love of God. I thought it could help make their lives better. More peaceful. But also it was an intellectual, a philosophical quest. I suppose that's why I wasn't suited for the priesthood." He paused to light a joint. The smell was first sweet, then large. I hated when it got large. It took over every other smell. I felt confused. I no longer understood what I wanted. "It's not a small choice to change religions." That actually hadn't occurred to me. I didn't think it was such a big deal.

Anton recited some prayers to me from his red book. We meditated for a while and then Anton guided me through one decade of the rosary. I liked the chanting and the meditating. It made me feel in touch with something. I didn't know what, just something. The sun was so orange and big on the horizon, sinking. We'd walked a long way. I didn't want to turn back and repeat the same steps. I hated repeating things. I didn't listen to the prayers. I thought about the Resurrection and becoming someone new and of all the mysteries locked inside me. I wanted to be Catholic.

Sometimes when Julia and Anton played "Uncle" he'd take her shirt instead of bending her fingers. That made Julia yell louder. He'd chase her, sneaking up on her from behind, catch her and yank her shirt off, giving her that wink and smile.

"Julia's flirting with Dad again," Sofia would say, tossing back her hair.

Julia laughed and her knees sank into the dust and the dust rose and settled on her legs and her arms crossed over her chest, covering the pinkish knobs.

"I like protecting Anton," she'd say.

"I can't protect Mom anymore" is what Jane said when she ran away. Jane ran away in Lake Havasu City—Home of the London Bridge. One moment she was with us. The next she was gone, as if she were dead. Anton and Mom tried to go after her. They drove off in the Eldorado all the way to Los Angeles, but they couldn't find her. It was late October.

Julia and I knew Jane would be leaving. Julia packed Jane a bag of clothes and I made some sandwiches. We had stopped in Lake Havasu City at a park for a swim and had ended up staying a few days. The park smelled of motorboat exhaust and gum wrappers and cigarette butts; straws and bits of paper littered the shores. Motorboats cruised at fast speed, spitting up a wake that tumbled, foamy, to the shore. "They dammed the Colorado for this?" James said, his arm gesturing toward the water.

Jane took a bus from downtown Havasu at the Esso Station, back to Los Angeles. A five-hour trip. In Los Angeles she'd catch a cross-country bus, a Greyhound, to New York City, where her friend Anna would meet her. Julia and I walked with her to the bus. I felt as if we were all the same age. In fact, as if I were the oldest, because I bought the ticket. I bought it from the boy selling gas, feeling sorry for Jane that she was leaving. I thought she didn't feel part of the family and that made me sad. A lump caught in the back of my throat. I coughed. I wasn't going to cry. The boy didn't seem that old either. His face was thick with pimples so sore they certainly must hurt. The gas station was on a hill above town. You could look down toward the river and see the London Bridge.

"Are you sure you guys don't want to come?" Jane asked. Her big eyes held us. I looked away from her. It was a new town and the black roads shone and smelled of tar. The air was hot.

"Why do you think they bothered bringing that bridge all the way over here?" I asked. It had only recently been erected. I wondered if we'd seen it when we were in London. We'd been there with Dad two years before, in 1968. That seemed like a million years ago. I tried to remember Dad and Mom together, but couldn't.

Jane asked again if we'd come.

"We have a bloody mint with all Kate's money," Julia said.

"We could stay in hotels," I said. I imagined the three of us in a hotel like the Desert Princess, sipping cocktails or sodas by the pool, charging up a storm. I almost wanted to go. It felt as if something tremendous were about to be ripped from me. From my insides. My throat choked again and my nose ached. Jane and Julia laughed again, a nervous kind of laughter. I handed Julia all my money, digging it out of my pockets and holster. It was crumpled up, but Julia straightened it out and then gave it to Jane, neat and ordered. Now the air smelled of exhaust. A car skidded to a halt in front of the gas station, giving us a start. For a moment we thought it was the Eldorado with Mom and Anton. We almost wished it had been. The car left rubber tracks on the new asphalt and vanished.

"I can't protect Mom anymore," Jane said again, looking at us as if to apologize. The bus pulled in. An old-looking bus. All soft angles. I thought it might fall apart.

"Some rich guy not knowing what to do with his money, that's why the bridge was brought over," Julia said.

"What if the bus breaks down in the middle of the desert?" I asked.

"I've got your money," Jane said. The bus waited impatiently. I wondered if I'd ever see Jane again. I gave her some special twigs that she could burn for good luck.

"Good luck, babe," I said, my voice shaking, my eyes filling with tears. Jane winced.

"She's going to convert," Julia said and wiped some tears from her eyes.

"God be with you," I said and smiled. I felt bad for making fun of God, but I thought He'd forgive me.

"And also with you," Jane said, and winked. Then Jane stopped smiling and her face became serious. "Don't do that, Kate. Promise me." I didn't understand why everyone made such a big deal out of converting. She grabbed my arms suddenly and her nails bit into my skin. Her big eyes held me. "Don't do that." The bus door opened and the boy selling gas said it was time for the bus to leave.

The entrance to the bus was dark. You couldn't see what was inside. Everything went silent, fast and sharp like a slap. I grabbed Jane, clinging to her. "Don't cling to me," Mom would say when we held on to her like that. I thought of small things, of Jane cooking creamed chipped beef, of Jane braiding my hair, of Jane making food-shopping lists, keeping us in order. I was suddenly afraid. Terrified. All my fascination with God hadn't prepared me for this. I couldn't hear a thing. It was as if we were submerged in water, with the world becoming all blurry and funny-seeming. Inside me shattered. Julia tried to pry me away from Jane and the boy gestured for her to get on the bus. There were a thousand things I needed to say to Jane. I thought of Siamese twins and what it would feel like to be severed. I wanted to scream. The sunlight blinded.

"You'll be home before you know it, Kate," Jane said softly in my ear. "I promise."

Julia took me in her arms. The bus sucked Jane inside and the doors closed. I shut my eyes. My nose and throat ached. The engine started, bursting exhaust. I thought of standing at the foot of the driveway waiting for our school bus, of Anton's Cadillac hidden down the overgrown lane. I thought of Dad picking us up and the Chocolate Shoppe and the sticker store, how that was all gone. I looked down at my dress. It was filthy. I had bare feet. Then Jane was gone.

It took the others a while to realize that Jane had run away. James noticed first, but not until dinner. She was long gone by then. "Where's Jane?" he asked. We were all at the table. Everyone looked around. Julia and I stared at each other and then away, pretending to be just as confused. But our faces kept twitching and our nervous tics gave us away. Julia twirled her hair and I fiddled with my knuckles.

"Where's your money?" Mom asked, getting up from her chair to come toward me. She grabbed my arm. Suddenly everyone was talking. I thought of Jane on that rickety old bus, chugging through the desert. I wanted to cry.

"This is crazy," I heard James say. His face was dark and shining, lit only by the light from the candles on the table.

"Answer me," Mom said. I couldn't.

"Brilliant. This is just fucking brilliant," James said, shaking his head slowly. There was a look in his eye, like he could see what had happened, like he knew Jane had run away. As if he were understanding something large, and that scared me.

Mom dragged Julia and me into the camper. The overhead light was on, drowning the inside in yellow. Mom's bruise bulged purple and black, making her left eye appear smaller. The cut from the ring sliced down the center of the swelling, healing now, a light pink. We were camped at a public spot and other campers and tents stood nearby, lit up, older people preparing for bed. A baby cried. A dog barked. I didn't know what to say. Outside, the others milled about, waiting for the fight to be over. Anton and James were talking loud. I was afraid they'd fight. Julia sat next to me. Her skin was pasty and pale in the bright light and she was still very thin from her disease.

"Do you realize what you've done?" Mom cried. Her face messy with drool and tears as she screamed at us about all the horrible things that could happen to Jane. I was afraid the crying would cause her cut to sting. Anton came into the camper and for a moment I was afraid he'd get mad, but he didn't. "Raped and killed" kept repeating itself in my mind. "Anything could happen to her. You girls," she looked at us and her face dropped. Her brow creased. "You girls don't know. She seems old to you, but she's just a little girl. She's not even thirteen! She's not even thirteen years old." Mom was crying hard, heaving. I'd never seen her cry like this. Not even after Dad left. I imagined Jane with her hair neatly braided sitting on the bus, the perfectly straight part running down the back of her scalp.

Then Mom fell silent, dropping her head in her hands, catching her breath from the crying. It seemed like a long time passed before she spoke again. Anton held her, stroking her hair. She collapsed into him. He asked us where Jane had gone and what her plans were. Julia told him. Jane would be keeping in touch with Anna as she crossed the country. Anna would meet her in New York City. It was close inside the camper. Under the table Julia twirled her right leg around my left leg. She was warm.

"Anna!" Mom said and sat up. "What are Anna's parents going to think?" Then she was at it again. Furious. Shouting. First at us. Then at Jane. "Jane doesn't want to make me happy. I just want a family, a happy family, but she'll do her best to destroy that. I'm a failure as a mother. I was too young when I had you kids. I was only twenty-one when I had Jane. Eight years older than Jane is now." Her eyes pierced us. I shut my eyes so that I couldn't see her and prayed to God. "Stop that, Kate," Mom snapped and grabbed my hands. Julia pulled me into her arms to protect me. "Jane's wretched. Daughters? Ha! I no longer have daughters. They've deserted me. You should have gone with her. I've spent all this time creating and raising them, been through hell for them and look what I get in return." She said *them* as if we weren't her daughters.

Julia and I sat there stiffly. Anton said it would be all right. Then he took Mom and they left for Los Angeles. They were gone for two days. When they came back, we got a day of the silent treatment, but then we were forgiven.

Finny slipped the rock back into my hand. At first I didn't know what it was. The ugly gold rock, the rock that gold comes from. His blue eyes gave me a look that said it was mine, he was done with it. I didn't really know what to do with the rock. I didn't really want it back. I didn't want Finny to be done with it. The tiny flakes glittered in the sunlight as I held the rock in my palm. Finny studied me. I thought of my father 6,800 feet down in the ground getting that rock, of him traveling all that distance in an elevator. I tried to give it back to Finny, but he wouldn't take it.

Traveling again. Route 66. Black-eyed Susans. Indians selling jewelry by the side of the road. Anton bought us each a gift and Mom suggested I barter and I did. The Indians hated me and I felt bad. I felt deceptive, afraid I'd done wrong in the eyes of God.

Yellow fields with green bushes. Hot though lush. Towns with two gas stations colored white and a beautiful jade green with great old-fashioned cars in their lots. The sky filled with thousands of cottony clouds. Anton couldn't decide if we should go to the Grand Canyon or Las Vegas, so we went to the El Mojave bar to think.

The El Mojave bar was on a wide street and inside it was dark and smoky, with a few rickety old tables. Anton and the big kids had beers and there were a few Mexicans drinking. One was with his girlfriend, sharing a beer, and another was drunk though it wasn't yet noon. Finny and I shared a glass of milk. We were hungry, hoping Anton would decide we could stay there for lunch.

Anton stood at the head of the table, loud in his lime-green Bermudas and the long-sleeved shirt that was an explosion of colors. An outfit that, when we were all loving each other, we'd have teased him about. I could remember Jane teasing him about that outfit. "I'll have to teach you a little something about style, I suppose," Anton had said, flirting with her, and she had smiled, that soft, almost shy smile of hers.

Family meeting to discuss where we were headed. To discuss Jane. Everyone said a prayer. Mom had called Anna's parents and they said they would pick Jane up in New York City. She was safely on the Greyhound now and fine, and would be home in two days. Mom had arranged to be in touch with Jane through Anna's parents twice a day to make sure that nothing went wrong. I imagined Jane eating the sandwiches I had made for her. Wondered if they'd all squooshed together and gotten soggy. Finny sat by my side and held my hand.

Anton told us the story of the Prodigal son, from the Bible. Nicholas burped. I laughed. I looked around the table. Sofia sucked on the ends of her hair. No one seemed to be listening to Anton's story except James, who fingered his chin, staring at Anton and then at us. His expression soft but irritated, with that look from the night Jane left coming back to his eyes, as if he could see something we couldn't.

Anton went on and on, and when he was finished, James said, "You make your own rules, don't you?"

"No. Before making any rules I ask God. I believe in higher authority. It would be too much responsibility to make all the rules myself," Anton said, flirting with James.

James smiled and tipped his head in a nod, but that look didn't leave his eye. He wore a pair of jeans with holes in the knees and a T-shirt with the sleeves rolled up to his shoulders. His arms were very tanned. He hadn't shaved.

"Sometimes people have to go off and figure out for themselves what's right," Anton said to all of us. The waitress asked if we were ready to order. She was short and Mexican with silky, long black hair. Her teeth were surrounded with gold. Anton said two-dollar limit and we all ordered something. Some Mexican music played on the jukebox. Everyone started talking about this and that.

"What kind of rules does God make for your children?" James asked, interrupting the chatter. Anton raised his eyes and looked at James, realizing he wasn't making fun. The waitress came over with some nachos. Everyone took one. Anton slipped one in his mouth without taking his eyes off James. Another fight, I thought, and shut my eyes.

"I love you, man," James said. "You've been more than generous. You've helped me out a lot. You've helped out Dwayne. You've helped Cynthia. You've helped out everyone. But Anton, we've got a problem." The way James talked I thought our world would end and I got scared inside. I opened my eyes to see if Anton were beginning to swell, but he wasn't. Nothing. Only that flirtatious smile lingered on his face, drooping there, fading slowly. He tried to hold it, as if trying to maintain the inscrutable face, but even the bluff didn't seem to come. I wanted him to swell.

Mom ran her thumbnail over her lip. "Jane will be all right. I've arranged things. In two days she'll be home." She spoke quietly and then tried to change the subject. She asked whether we'd prefer the Grand Canyon or Las Vegas.

"I don't just mean Jane," James said. "I mean Finny. He isn't speaking. I mean Nicholas, who's always drinking."

Nicholas burped again and then smiled. "Don't get me in trouble," he said in a teasing sort of way. Cynthia Banks laughed.

James ignored them. "I mean Kate, who's becoming a religious freak. I mean all these kids who should be somewhere." A new song played. The singer, a woman, had a whiny voice.

"Looky here, babe. I appreciate what you're saying," Anton said, softly but quickly, stuttering a little.

"These nachos suck," Timothy said. He sipped some of Nicholas's beer and burped. Anton told him to be quiet.

"It's not about getting someplace," Mom said. "You've got to think about . . . "

"Eve, babe, I'll speak for myself," Anton said.

"I'll say what I please," Mom said. I was afraid he'd get mad at her, but he didn't.

"You're missing the point, James," Anton went on. "It's about being where you are. You can't always be thinking about where you'll be next. Didn't one of your countrymen, Leonard Woolf, write *The Journey Not the Arrival Matters*?"

"When are we going back to Europe, Dad?" Sofia asked.

"Sofia, babe."

"This is their business," Dwayne said to James. "Don't interfere." He wore all black and his white hair seemed yellow, shining in the inside light. I hated him. He was a parasite, that's what Julia had said.

"You've been teaching us that," James said to Anton. "But it can't keep going on like this. What I'm understanding is that it may be fine for you and Eve to live like this, but it isn't for the children." He paused. He chewed on a toothpick. He seemed old and smart, yet he spoke cautiously. "At some point you have to have a plan for them. None of us has wanted to pay attention to this because, when we do, this world you've created, no matter how beautiful the good parts of it are, will be over. But Anton, it's childish to continue like this."

I thought of what Julia had said about Anton being a child and felt scared, afraid we'd have to protect him the way Julia wanted to. The waitress brought the food and we ate. Mom said nothing. Anton said nothing. His face changed. He was uncomfortable, shifting in his seat, then standing, but still he wasn't getting mad. Mom studied him, hoping for something, for him to pull us out of this mess as he had done a thousand times before. Dwayne talked about some theories and Nicholas told him to shut up. James seemed to be waiting for an answer. That creepy look in his eyes; something lifted in him and for the first time he could see inside us. A heaviness settled down on all of us. Everything felt incredibly complicated. One moment you thought everything was one way, the next everything was completely different for no apparent reason. I ate a nacho. I wasn't hungry.

I remembered Anton on the phone at Mark Bitar's calling a relative in San Diego to ask if he and Eve and their eight kids and a friend could visit. I couldn't hear what the person said of course, but on his face you could see that that person was saying no. No. We weren't wanted. "I see," he had kept saying, unsure of what to do with the *no*, shrinking in it. In the world he had created there was very little *no*. The only one of us who ever said *no*, who ever questioned him, had run away.

The door opened. A blast of noon heat rushed in. Outside was bright and hot and vast. The camper would be an oven. I wanted Anton to get mad. We were all staring at him, I could feel it, all of us wanting him to get mad, even Mom, as if his getting mad meant that he was in charge. His eyelids quivered. He glanced at Julia, who gave him a comforting look. He fingered his ring and stared down, into the table. There were eleven of us looking up at him from that table. He took a nacho from the plate and ate it slowly. He seemed alone and scared, as if he suddenly realized what he had on his hands—eight children, one of whom had run away, three strangers and a woman who wanted to be his wife. As if for the first time we were real. We were all frozen. It seemed Anton would break in half. Just looking at him made me feel terrible. He was big and vulnerable. His blue eyes flickered. Our world emptied, drained. No future and certainly no past. Get mad, I wanted to scream.

I tried to pray to God and then something awful occurred to me, fast, cut through my mind and then was gone. It occurred to me that Jane was right. "He's a nobody," she'd said. "Nothing without us." I saw nobody in the place of Anton. I saw him stripped of everything, of his big and swollen self. The Almighty Leader of Erehwon. A blowfish without the blow. Get mad, I kept thinking. His invincibility was disintegrating fast, the cops were catching up with him, and even God, even Jesus, was gone from his side. I saw him now, ridiculous in those stupid clothes.

"Where are you driving us to?" I asked, trying to sound like Jane. I wanted to make him mad.

"Kate," Mom said. She said my name quietly, but sharply, using it alone to tell me to shut up. She rose from her chair and made her way to Anton. Her white blouse was pressed—I imagined from our days at the Desert Princess. Her jeans stiff. Hair loose. She linked her arm in Anton's and he pulled her to him, suddenly not so alone anymore. Anton held Mom close and we all stared up at them, waiting.

Slowly she started to speak. At first saying only, "I think . . . " She paused. Her hair hung in her face. I imagined she was thinking about Jane. She lifted her head to face James. "You're right," she said. Then to Anton, "James is right about a lot of what he's saying." She said some comforting things about home. She said that going home didn't mean the world we'd worked so hard to create would be over, that we'd still be able to live the way we wanted to there. She was tender, pouring love all over Anton. Her eyes were determined and strong, looking up to him. Her voice soft, but emphatic. "Doesn't Paul say in the First Letter to the Corinthians that when he became an adult he had to put an end to childish ways? James is right, Anton. It is childish to continue like this. But it doesn't mean we can't find a new way. Together we will."

Quietly Anton withdrew his eyes from Mom and stared at the ground. I was afraid he might cry. I didn't want to see him cry. Instead he pulled a joint from his silver cigarette case and went outside, off by himself for awhile.

When he returned he told us that he'd decided we would go home to Jane, back to New Jersey, that he had a practice under way there. Mom encouraged us to all hug and love each other and we did, in the parking lot of the El Mojave bar, trying to make Anton feel strong and in charge again.

I pictured Jane on her bus, lumbering along on Interstate 40, paving the way through Needles and Flagstaff, Albuquerque and Amarillo, Memphis, Nashville, one bend north just past Knoxville to 81 up through the Appalachians to New York City. I saw Jane on that thread of road, up there ahead of us with flags and trumpets leading the way, leading the caravan, the utopia, as if we were tethered to her by some invisible force, as if Jane alone were painting that bright red road onto the map. "You'll be home before you know it," she'd said. I wondered if somewhere Jane knew that by leaving she'd get us home, as if she knew Mom wouldn't leave her. "Could you really ever leave Mom?" I remembered Jane asking me. And then I smiled because it occurred to me that if Jane were leading us, it would be my money that was getting us home after all. And not just the four of us, but the whole damn family.

THE DAY THE MEN LANDED
ON THE MOON

"In the beginning God created the heaven and the earth."

In the beginning there was nothing and from nothing came an explosion which created the heaven and the earth, and the emptiness filled, and the earth was a formless mass and void, and this happened all day Monday and until noon on Tuesday, and each day was seven hundred and fifty million years long.

"And God said, Let there be light: and there was light."

And by Tuesday afternoon the earth took shape and a chemical reaction happened to form water and the earth was covered with water, a globe-girdling sea.

"And God said, Let there be a firmament in the midst of the waters, and let it divide the waters from the waters."

"And God called the firmament Heaven."

And Heaven held the sun and the moon and the stars, stars so far away it could take four hundred years for their light to reach the earth.

"And God said, Let the waters under the heaven be gathered together unto one place, and let the dry land appear: and it was so."

And all day Wednesday and all day Thursday and all day Friday and until afternoon on Saturday the scum accumulated on the waters and gathered and amassed until the scum became dry land and vegetation appeared, flora to feed the world.

And there was salt and sun and time.

"And God called the dry land Earth; and the gathering together of the waters called he Seas: and God saw that it was good."

And when there was plenty to eat, fauna appeared.

"And God blessed them, saying, Be fruitful, and multiply, and fill the waters in the seas, and let fowl multiply in the earth."

And the fauna evolved, and by Saturday afternoon the reptiles appeared, and by midnight something mysterious happened on Earth and the reptiles vanished, and by early Sunday morning man appeared, and all day man evolved, and minutes after eleven P.M. on Sunday Christ appeared, and seconds later my father and Anton were born and with them our family came as a zillion families had come before—here for a millisecond, brief and at once both so important and insignificant, then gone.

The day the men landed on the moon, our father left us. I was seven. Julia was nine. Jane was eleven.

I wondered what it would have been like that day if Brian Cain hadn't come to our house. If our father had come home.

That morning Dad left in his white tennis outfit, with a windbreaker in case it rained. He had a tennis racquet under his arm and his thick, curly black hair was a mess. Mom said he looked like a poet with his hair all wild and messy. He kissed us and drove off. We played on the lawn, running through a sprinkler. Mom gardened.

"*Eagle* has landed," Armstrong said that afternoon, and we would have heard it on the crackling radio. We would have run inside to the TV and seen the spaceship landing on the Sea of Tranquillity after a near miss in a crater field. Dad would have returned in the early evening and we would have had a late dinner on the front lawn, watching the TV Dad had promised to bring out on the end of a long extension cord.

It would have happened like this: The cord snaked through the wet grass to the house. We sat on a tarp and a plaid blanket that Dad had laid down. The wool scratched our bare skin. Fireflies blinked crazily over the front lawn like stars. Dad's eyes were sad. Inside he had a choice to make: Camille or us. We could all tell he was sad. He was a million miles away. Dad never could hide his mood. He was like Jane. They didn't have inscrutable faces. Bad moods settled on them like a black cloud.

Mom ran back and forth to the kitchen nervously, talking about nothing just to talk, bringing out the chicken and the salad and the rolls. At the end, Dad's moods could do this to her. A bottle of red wine stood open on a cutting board, next to two glasses, beautiful like tulips, half filled with Burgundy. Up again. Mom dashed to the kitchen for the forgotten knives and Julia crawled on top of Dad and Jane started to tickle his hair and I pushed Julia off and crawled on him myself and as I did I knocked over the wine. "KATE!," Dad screamed, his insides ripping apart. "Look what you've done. Can't you ever be more careful?"

The image of Camille stood in front of him, her arm reaching down to him. Her ginger hair blowing across her face, her eyes pleading her love, their happiness.

"Kate, look what you've done," Mom said, repeating Dad. Jane and Julia chimed in with Mom. Mom rushed out with the chocolate-wafer icebox cake and a sponge. She was all over the place mopping up the spilled wine. Mom knew how close she'd come to losing him. She was trying to keep his secret, ironing their life back to something flat and clean that she could handle.

"I was only playing," I cried.

"It's all right," Dad said. He patted my hair down and pulled me into his arms and hugged me. It was a hard hug, like I could go away. He smelled of sweat because he hadn't showered. Usually we'd never let him near us after exercising, he'd smell so bad.

"Come on girls, your father's tired. Let him be," Mom said. Dad looked up at the moon. We nestled into him, gently, trying, still, to pry attention out of him. A little exhausted because it was so late and the evening, despite the storm, was that hot summer kind, swelling with a new storm that could break just as easily as it could pass. Crickets hummed in chorus with the tree frogs. All the windows were lit in the house, and it glowed. Mom knelt down and sliced the cake. Her hair was a perfect mess of curls and she wore navy slacks and a short-sleeved, white cotton shirt that buttoned up the front. Her cheeks were gently burned from the sun. She talked about our plans for the trip to Maine and Nova Scotia, trying to excite Dad. We used forks and knives to eat the fried chicken and the cake. All of us a little nervous, waiting for this day, this week, this month to pass.

After a while Camille would have passed. A trial. A glitch in life. And life would have settled down again, normal again. The same. I would have grown up in the pink room. Julia in the blue. Jane in the yellow. The three of us growing bigger until we were all the same size. Each year a pattern, a diagram to get through. Very little memorable. Mom would have gardened and continued to have made us clothes. We would have all succeeded in school. No teachers taking us into their offices to talk about home. No mothers canceling play dates because they feared divorce themselves. Years made different by nannies from foreign countries. By vacations we'd take. By my father's appointments and scientific discoveries. Normal. We would have been the Loves, the Fitzpatricks, the Campbells, the Coopers.

"How dull," Mom would say later, sighing as if relieved.

On July 20, 1969, two men landed on the moon. All year long in science class we discussed, read and saw films about the first landing and all the others that followed. We read the papers. We did reports. Discussed it so much and there were so many landings that after awhile it took a tragedy for people to pay attention.

On the day the men landed on the moon, fourteen-year-old Jeffrey Ward was voted Mr. Teenager 1969 and was sent to Saigon to "assess" the war as a guest of the South Vietnamese government. For breakfast we had cottage cheese pancakes, light like soufflés. I drenched mine in maple syrup and then complained I couldn't eat them because they were too sweet. David Robb of Missoula, Montana was in Stockholm, Sweden, after defecting from the U.S. Army. On the planet a woman was being raped every ten seconds. I was still mad from the night before, when Mom had made me eat liver and I'd refused. She'd sent me to the laundry room as punishment and I'd had to stay in there until I finished the liver. I hid it at the bottom of a hamper filled with dirty clothes. Many Americans had long since traveled the distance to the moon—238,857 miles. It turned out the liver had stayed in the hamper for weeks, smelling up the place. The dirty laundry was still dirty, and by the time the liver was found no one cared that I'd hid it. Every twenty seconds someone was dying of starvation. On a sunny summer Sunday Americans covered 340 square miles of their own flesh with suntan lotions. My sisters and I ran through a sprinkler on our front lawn, waiting for our father to come home. Rehoboth Beach, Delaware, was infested with a slimy, rust-colored jellyfish called *Cyanea capillata*. Brian Cain drove up our driveway mad drunk, flailing a letter. My father and Camille were in Dad's white VW driving north, believing it was the right thing to do. Two men were walking on the moon. My sisters and I were sent to the laundry room. The liver didn't smell yet. Hubert Humphrey was on a bear hunt in Russia; the Mets were in Montreal splitting a double-header with the Expos; Randy Geise of Keyport, Washington, was sailing a bathtub to Vancouver in the Great Canadian Bathtub Race; the Henry Fords were cruising the Aegean Sea; many millions around the world were listening to the television and radio; three wars were being fought—Vietnam, Middle East, Nigeria; Mom was trying to calm Brian Cain; Reverend Edward Zeiser read of the miracle of the loaves and fishes to eighty-five parishioners in St. Paul's Lutheran Church. But his sermon focused on the astronauts: "Through these three men in orbit today, Jesus is announcing that something of tremendous value is about to be offered—the Kingdom of Heaven."

But this is how it happened: Camille stands in front of Dad. She's thin but fleshy, and her skin is pale and pinkish and her pubic hair is ginger like the rest of her hair, which falls over her shoulders. Her breasts are pert and her nipples erect.

Dad's laid a tarp down in the woods because the ground is wet. The men are about to land on the moon. On top of the tarp is a wool blanket and on top of the blanket is Dad. His arm stretches out to Camille, who wants an answer. Her hands are on her hips. She tells him that Brian has found their letters. That he's drunk, gone mad, has a gun. The expression on her face challenges Dad: "Are you going to leave?" The tall trees hide them. At once the air is both warm and chilly and though the birds have been chirping all along it's as if someone has suddenly turned on a switch and Dad and Camille can now hear them, as well as all the sounds of the woods, and they can see the overcast sky. Dad decides. He sees us slipping away, as if being pulled by suction, the suction of water pulling more water down a drain. Swirling. Gone. He cares and he doesn't care. This is his life. He wants his happiness. He cries. Camille comforts him. Her ginger hair, silky, all over him. He cries hard because everything is wonderful and horrible.

At the pool at the Desert Princess I watched kids. Little kids, younger than I, who didn't need to be in school. I'd see a mother go away for a moment and leave her child with a friend and the child would cry and cry until it was annoying and you wished the mother would hurry up and return. I saw fathers return from a day on the golf course and I saw the little children throw themselves at their fathers, hugging them, strangling them as if they'd been gone forever. A day is a long time then.

The night Dad didn't come home we didn't turn on any lights and the house became very dark and my sisters and mother had pillows over their faces and they cried into the pillows and I didn't know what it meant. At first I just watched and then I took a pillow from the couch and pushed it into my face and tried to understand, but couldn't.

While Mom and my sisters cried, the men were walking in the silence of the moon and I kept looking up, straining to see it, thinking if I strained enough I'd be able to make out the tiny figures of the men. Thick clouds crossed the moon's path, blotting it out, but then suddenly it reemerged, blasting through the darkness. It was silent because there is no air on the moon, an incredible silence, like the silence you can only come vaguely close to in the desert. But in the desert you hear the wind and you hear planes overhead and the ubiquitous dog and you hear each other.

"When's Dad coming home?" I finally screamed. I screamed it a few times like a brat. "I'm not going to bed until Dad comes home."

The men went to the moon to conquer the impossible. They went because it was there and they'd figured out a way to get to it. Behind them they left an earth that was decaying and at war. Sometimes it is easier to tackle the impossible than to fix the possible.

"And God said, Let us make man in our image, after our likeness: and let them have dominion over the fish of the sea, and over the fowl of the air, and over the cattle, and over all the earth, and over every creeping thing that creepeth upon the earth."

THE GREAT UNCONFORMITY

God was all over the place. As far as the eye could see and beyond. I looked down on a thousand painted layers. Burgundy. Black. Red the color of blood. Above, a rose sky was broken with lakelike spaces of blue. It was morning and we didn't have the clothes for this cold so we bundled into all the clothes that we had, all twelve of us, with Cynthia Banks yawning, "Simply divine." As the sun rose it seemed to lift pyramids of stone into the air, revealing gulches and plateaus and more pyramids and pinnacles. A dusty cinnamon path snaked its way into the Grand Canyon.

Anton said he'd been to the canyon before. He lifted his cowboy hat to wipe his forehead. He cleared his throat and spit. "Almost died when I was here last. It's true. Some friends and I got lost hiking. Had no water. My friend's tongue turned black. Almost died," he repeated proudly, setting his hat back on his head. He squinted and winked.

Timothy yelled to hear his echo. His voice bounced around and then was swallowed up. Solomon Temple. Shiva Temple. Krishna Shrine. Vishnu Temple. Apollo Temple. Venus Temple. Jupiter, Juno, Thor—out to eternity and farther.

There was a stiff breeze and the strong scent of pitch pine. We were quiet. Other tourists, two elderly couples, arrived. They were noisy and then they too were quiet and then they left.

We'd arrived the night before. At the last moment Anton had decided we should in fact see the Grand Canyon, that it would be educational. He said we'd just have a "little" look. Since we were so close it would be a shame to miss it. We were just into New Mexico when he turned around. I was afraid we wouldn't catch up with Jane if we didn't keep driving. Everyone had an opinion. We pleaded, but Anton had decided, in charge again.

A Bordeaux sky reigned on the horizon and we drove into it until dark. We drove all evening, arriving late. All of us asleep. The sound of cars suddenly silent, all motion stopped. Outside Anton spoke with someone. I heard only voices. No words. One by one we awoke and emerged, our figures in silhouette in the dark. The screen door clapping. It was colder than it had ever been on our trip and I wrapped some dresses around my shoulders and slipped into a pair of Julia's jeans that were too big for me. There was a vast and moonless sky, very dark and very cold. All around was the smell of pine and the air was thin and breathing it in felt good, like drinking ice-cold water in the desert.

Anton spoke with a ranger, a skinny man with a huge ranger hat on his pinhead and big eyes that shone in the dark like a cat's. His chin was sharp and he kept fingering it while talking. He seemed to like talking and talked for close to an hour.

"How many of you are there?" he asked with a friendly and astonished voice. We stood all over the place. Caroline came up and hugged me, trying to keep warm. Her hair fell over me. It smelled clean. The ranger was tall and wore a parka. I had bare feet. Mom was asleep in the cab and Cynthia Banks stood by Anton's side, pretending to be his wife.

"Now let me see a second," Anton said. He counted us up in his head. "We're thirteen."

"Boy," said the ranger. That's all he said for a minute until Cynthia corrected Anton's figure to twelve and reminded him that Jane was gone.

"Boy, that's swell. Twelve of you?" He stopped to think, searching for something more to say but only said "swell" again.

A wind was in the trees and the cars made settling sounds. The ranger drove a truck and he'd left the engine running and the lights on in the cab. I shivered in Caroline's arms. I was happy she was holding me.

"You see out there," she whispered and pointed in the direction of an even deeper darkness that I hadn't yet paid attention to. My eyes were still adjusting. "That's the Grand Canyon."

"The fucking G C," Dwayne said.

For a moment I felt large being there simply because we'd finally gotten somewhere we'd planned to go. Caroline linked her arm in mine and we walked to the edge of the parking lot. I stared hard trying to make my eyes see through the dark, but only the vaguest forms appeared. Since I didn't know the shape of what I was looking at I had a hard time discerning it, but I could feel it somehow and the feeling made me momentarily afraid because it was so big and infinite and dark. There was no moon, no stars. The black pit and the night blended together into one great void, and you couldn't tell where land ended and universe began. I was frightened. This was what I had been wanting to get to for so long. This was what Dad had wanted to bring us to. Caroline wrapped my dresses closer around me and pulled me into her. Her body was warm. My teeth chattered. We moved away, back to the others.

"I don't recommend it with kids that little. You really have to be expert hikers," the ranger said. He chewed on something and spit. I agreed with him. Usually I didn't like to be referred to as too little, but this time I agreed. I was too little. "Some of them trails haven't been hiked on too much and there's slides and such." He paused. "Say, we have mules. You could go down on mules. Or if you wanted to hike, you could go partway down and explore a little. You could go to Horseshoe Mesa say, or Plateau Point. But I don't recommend going the whole way down or on an extended hike with eight- and six-year-olds. Besides, this time of year storms aren't too predictable."

"Nah-nah-no," Anton stuttered, determined. "The kids are tough," he said. "I've been down before. They can do it."

"I don't know if you're impetuous or adventurous," Cynthia said.

"We're not going in there," I said. Suddenly I had a premonition, I saw us getting lost.

"Looky here, babe," Anton said, his body beginning to swell. Then everyone started giving Anton their opinion—James and Dwayne and Caroline and Nicholas and Cynthia and Sofia. James was easy on Anton now, after the El Mojave bar and Anton's decision to go home. James had decided to go back to England once we returned East. Everyone speaking at once. Anton told us to quiet down, but Sofia continued.

"I'm warning you, babe."

"The trails are rustic," the ranger said. A quick smile flitted across his lips. He seemed to like the fact that he was causing a commotion. "And there are scorpions and coyotes and rattlesnakes and even cougars down there. I don't mean to be so cautious, but it's me that's gonna have to come in after you all if there's any trouble. And let me tell you that ain't easy. We lose a lot of people down there. More than you'd think. Just this summer we lost a girl, only twenty-five years old, and she was hiking on an easy trail. But there are no easy trails in there." He shook his head. "She must have tripped on a bootlace or something, but she fell. She fell a good five hundred feet and splattered. Well, okeydokey." The ranger tipped his hat, backing away. "Make sure you bring plenty of water." He flashed a smile, got in his truck and left.

It was spooky descending all that way, as if the trail would never stop and you'd never come to a bottom. You'd keep sinking, so deep you'd never be able to get out. My knees ached. I kept thinking about hell and prayed to God, descending into hell, but the canyon was too beautiful for that.

Sheer rock faces dropping hundreds of feet. The rim scalloped with side canyons and terraces, amphitheaters and promontories. I was dazzled, understanding, absolutely, why Dad had wanted to bring us here. And then I understood too why Anton had had to come here. All chaos and beauty. Temples soaring above us. The colors changing constantly. We'd be wandering through a passage of rose and then suddenly a cloud would cover up the sun and the whole world would become beige and blue and you couldn't hear anything except maybe the river or the wind if the wind were blowing or a jet sailing past overhead, leaving a wake like a boat and sometimes you could pretend you were deep beneath the ocean looking up at the world. This was the world, the most exquisite I had ever seen.

Some days we'd hike together, the big kids taking the lead. The little kids, Mom and Anton lagging behind. At first we had plenty of everything, but the hike lasted longer than we'd anticipated. Cynthia Banks had bought out a camping equipment store, stocking us up with freeze-dried foods and things we needed for our packs, for the nights. Boots for those of us who didn't have any. She bought a backpack and all the appropriate equipment and anything Anton said we would need.

When the sun was at its highest and the shadow of the rim vanished we'd find spots in the shade to hide and we'd eat some food. In these nooks the air was still, but you could hear the wind racing through the canyon. In the afternoon we'd hike on. The twelve of us marching, spreading out, into the land.

We hiked backward through time, traveling two billion years to the river. I loved that idea. Time with those wonderful names my father had loved to list, repeating them like a mantra or a song: Kaibab, Supai, Muav time, Bright Angel time, Tonto and Vishnu time. The trail dust on our boots changing from beige to red to white to gray, depending on the color of that time. I thought about Dad talking about time and the slate being wiped clean. I tried to remember everything he'd taught us about the canyon, as if somehow through his words I could understand him. This land didn't feel very clean, with two billion years of the earth's history recorded here in the canyon walls. You could see it in the layers of rock, the beds of limestone, sandstone, shale hundreds of feet thick. Dad had said that the Grand Canyon itself was an infant, younger than I was, it had been cut in the rock so recently. He'd told me this a year ago, when I was seven, but I'd known what he meant. He said some geologists believe the canyon is so young that human beings, standing upright, walking on the earth, could have seen it being carved. So young and fresh, "like a scalpel cutting through skin," he had said. Now I imagined man standing upright there on the rim, watching the river cut through all that rock and time like a knife. I imagined Dad standing up there too, at Thanksgiving the year before, waiting for Julia and me to arrive. Five months had passed since we'd last seen him.

Dad had said that the famous time in the Grand Canyon was more interesting for the time that wasn't there than for the time that was. The Kaibab plateau of the canyon's rim was from the Paleozoic era and 250 million years old. "The Grand Canyon quits in the Permian. Where did the Mesozoic and Cenozoic formations go?" he'd asked. "Did they erode or were they never there?" As if 250 million years both had and had not happened in this one spot on earth. Time like a thief outmaneuvering time.

Dad had said that the Great Unconformity of the Grand Canyon's inner gorge represented one of the most extreme examples on earth of that famous missing time. He said that two rocks of vastly different ages meet there, indicating a gap of close to one billion years. "Imagine a multivolume set of encyclopedias missing everything from Carthage to Harvard. The remaining volumes are standing next to each other, but even so the gap is there. A lot of information that should be there is not. Where did the time between those two rocks go?"

For a long while after my father left, I thought time had stopped for him, that he was back there on that day when the men landed on the moon. Frozen. His life static as our lives moved forward.

And whenever we saw him, on the weekends or holidays that belonged to him, we would go back and meet him in that frozen time. Time that both did and did not exist. It was easier to imagine this than to know his life had moved ahead.

I wondered if it were the same for Dad, if our lives remained frozen, static because our time didn't exist for him.

We got lost slowly. Julia, Sofia and I. On the fourth day of our hike, when we had nearly run out of all of our supplies. We got lost after starting the ascent from the river, on the plateau above the inner gorge. Lost in the Grand Canyon Super Group somewhere near the Great Unconformity, one level below Bright Angel time. It was late afternoon. The sun and the moon were up there together, brilliant in the sky.

"We're nearly out of the Precambrian," I said. I had a field guide I kept referring to that Anton had bought for me.

"Oh Kate, shut up," Julia said. She had a baseball cap on. Sweat beaded her face. We had been looking for the trail up for a few hours. The trail we were on was several hundred feet above the river, but ran parallel.

"It means we're making progress," I said. "We're out of the Vishnu Schist and into the Tapeats Sandstone."

"I don't give a shit," Julia snapped. "We're lost."

"We are not lost," I said. I wanted to cry. It was my fault we were lost. I had had a knee ache. A terrible one that involved my entire leg. I was stiff all over and it was hard to walk. Julia and Sofia had stopped to rest with me while the others went on ahead.

"I'm sorry," I said, my voice cracking. Julia and Sofia walked in front of me and I looked into their backs. Julia said nothing. Sofia said nothing. The path was narrow, and to our right there was a cliff and to our left a drop and below it the river. I could only hear the river. We were hot. Our boots crunched the ground. The straps of my pack sliced into my shoulders. The bottom of it chaffed my hips. The path climbed and descended, endlessly. Each time we went around a bend, we got excited, hoping for some path up to be revealed, but there was nothing. We'd be walking toward nothing forever. The world felt empty, and though I was with Julia and Sofia, I felt entirely alone and that feeling frightened me. We were tiny down there, microscopic, with the monuments rising all around. A wind blew.

"Ka-te." My name reverberated a hundred times, loud and bellowing, alive throughout the canyon. We stopped.

"That was Bone's voice," Sofia said. We looked around. Ahead and several hundred feet above us, we could see Mom pull Finny back, away from the edge of the trail. We saw Anton and Cynthia Banks. A shear rock face separated us, impossible to climb, but I wanted to climb it anyway.

Only Finny noticed us. Mom and Anton and Cynthia Banks hiked forward and away from the edge. I couldn't see them anymore. I started to race inside, thinking they'd hike on without noticing us and we'd be stuck down here forever. At once I started hollering.

"Mo-m," I screamed. My voice echoing. I wanted to climb the wall. I thought we could do it. I started to try, but Julia yanked me back.

"Don't be a fool," she said.

"Shut up," I snapped. I hated her.

Little Finny reappeared, pointing down to us. "Mo-m," I yelled again. Then Sofia started yelling and then Julia too. The distance between us seemed impossibly large, an ocean, a universe. We were all yelling at once. The echo of our voices merged. Then Julia said we should all be quiet. I heard laughter. Cynthia Banks. I hated her. Everything was funny for her as if nothing bad could really happen. More laughter. I imagined Mom was laughing with her and hated Mom. For Mom it was that way too, as if nothing bad could ever happen. "Are you happy? Aren't you happy?"

The four of them stood up there on the edge, a family, looking down at us. So far away their figures were tiny. I wanted to be with Finny. I wished I'd never stopped to rest my knees. I wanted Jane. She was probably at Anna's now. I imagined her making creamed chipped beef and felt hungry. I wanted us all to be back in the camper again.

"Come get us," I hollered. A piercing cry. Julia held me from behind and put her hand over my mouth. Quietly she tried to speak up to them, asking how to find the trail. Anton tried to explain the route, gesturing with his arms. I looked up to them as if I could make out what he was saying by the way his arms moved. He seemed to be pointing in the direction we were going, but the wind carried his voice away.

"They're going away. They're going away," I shouted, shaking Julia off. I started crying, hard like a child. I was scared. I felt stupid standing there with that gun in the holster belted around my hips, trying to be so cool, so grown-up. "We're going to die down here. I feel it. I had a premonition." I hadn't had a premonition, but I said I had anyway because it felt as if I had. I wondered what Dad would do when he found out we were dead. I wondered if Jane would be with him. Everything seemed hopeless. I slumped to the ground. We waited, hoping Mom and Anton would return, hoping they'd appear on our trail in front of us.

"We need to be strong," Julia said. She started organizing us, taking charge, surveying our supplies, calculating the time and the sun to see if we'd be able to find our way before dark. Sofia didn't like that Julia took charge and started saying how difficult everything would be and how dangerous it was out here with all the coyotes and cougars and rattlers. She said we'd never have enough water to get out of here alive. Just looking at Sofia frightened me.

"We need to pray," I said. I took the rosary beads from my pocket and started counting them.

"Grow up," Julia snapped. "The sooner you realize that God's like Santa Claus the better off you'll be." I stopped crying and just stared at her.

"That's mean," Sofia said, and suddenly the two of them were fighting. They were crying and screaming. Tears made their faces ugly. They fought about this trip and Anton and the strangers and Cynthia Banks. About God and money and home. About Mom and how she was using up all of Sofia's Mom's money and how it was this money that was supporting us. I shut my ears to their voices. The past few months rolled in front of me like a dream. It seemed so impossible that we'd ever become a family.

"Stop," Julia hollered, her face a burning red. That *stop* echoed a million times through the canyon. We heard it ringing even after they stopped fighting. Julia apologized and then Sofia apologized and they hugged each other.

"Okay, so we won't pray," I said. I wanted to make them laugh. They laughed.

Sofia took me in her arms. Her arms were big and strong and warm, like a mother's arms. I wanted to stay in them forever. I wanted to fall asleep and not wake up until this was all over and we were out of here. My face burned from tears.

"They're gone," I said flatly. I looked up at the spot where they had been. Nothing was there and once again we were alone and I realized that we really were lost. Sofia ran her fingers through my hair. Julia used her T-shirt to wipe my face. "I can tell you one thing about Dad," Sofia said. "He isn't going to leave us down here, Kate. And even if he did, do you really think Eve would let him?"

We were quiet for a moment; everything was quiet, brown and dead. A vast expanse of brown parched land spread out in front of us and behind us, above us. All the colors seemed to be gone. It was as if we were the only life out there. My sisters and I were alone in the desert. Our whole lives had been funneled toward this. The only difference was that Sofia had replaced Jane.

But then I started noticing things I hadn't noticed before. A line of ants crossed the trail, methodical, busy carrying crumbs. Two ants to one crumb. A few white-throated swifts. James had said they spend most of their life in the air. The light changed; a purple haze colored the canyon. A variety of cacti poking from the rocks, prickly pear. I remembered Sam's baby taking a bite out of a prickly pear. Hundreds of prickers stuck into his tongue and I'd been glad. The dirt, sandy and soft, a cushion beneath us. A splash of red from a lone Indian paintbrush. A few tiny ground-cover flowers, sapphire blue, rising from the dry earth, thriving with life.

The horror of being lost was in the first realization, not in the knowledge of it. Once we knew we were lost the horror dissipated and a calm settled down on us. We sat there for awhile, exhausted, resting. The difference between us and Anton was that Anton had become so used to getting lost that the surprise of first learning it was no longer chilling. Now the trick was to be found, to find our way out, and that task loomed in front of us like a pissing competition or a poker game that was just within our grasp.

"They were in Bright Angel Shale," I said lazily, staring off blankly. "That's just one level above us." I wanted some of that greenish rock. I was going to hack some out as a present for my father even though the field guide said you couldn't: "Take only pictures, leave only footprints."

Julia fanned me with her baseball cap and Sofia asked me how I knew so much about rocks. I explained where we were now, how between the Vishnu Schist and the Tapeats Sandstone a billion years of rock is missing. "Like missing volumes in a set of encyclopedias," I said. I explained that Anton and Mom had been on the Tonto Plateau in Bright Angel Shale, a greenish shale deposited in a Cambrian sea that covered that area about 570 million years ago. "The trails of marine animals are fossilized in that shale," I said. "Along with trilobites, brachipods, hyolithes, mollusks and crinoids." I didn't know what those things were—they came from my field guide—but I used them as if I did. I told them that Bright Angel was the name of a creek, named by a one-armed geologist who first explored the Colorado. "He named it that, you see, because the creek was so clear in contrast to a muddy one upriver that he'd named the 'Dirty Devil' in honor of the great Indian chief of the 'Bad Angels.' "

"You see, our father is a geologist," Julia said. "That's why Kate knows so much. Dad used to bore us to death, giving lectures about rocks. We were supposed to come here with him last year." It sounded funny hearing Julia explain about Dad. We were supposed to love Sofia like a sister, yet she knew very little about our father.

A hawk flew toward the other side of the canyon, getting smaller and smaller, receding in the distance. We got up and started hiking again. We had more energy than before. My knees didn't ache so badly. We walked for a good hour, while the sunlight faded and night filled in the canyon. The colors changed again, and the forms of mesas and buttes and cliffs became distinct. We walked until it was too dangerous to walk anymore.

A gap broke open in the cliff and we took our packs off. My back was sweaty, but the air had a chill and the sweat dried. Sofia gave us water from her canteen. It tasted of iodine, but good. We took little sips. We didn't have much. For dinner we shared the remainder of a chocolate bar and the remainder of a beef jerky stick. We set up camp. Julia took our packs away from where we would sleep, the way Anton had taught us to do, in case some animal smelled something and wanted to eat it. We laughed at that. We were hungry. Before long we got into our sleeping bags. There was nothing else to do. Sofia and Julia talked about the stars and then Sofia made plans for each of us to take a turn keeping watch, since there were so many dangerous animals down here. She agreed to go first. I said it was a good thing I had my BB gun. I took it out of its holster and spun it on my finger. I was glad now that I had it.

"I should hold on to it," Julia said. She cracked a smile and brushed her hair away from her mouth. I thought she was beautiful. She looked just like Mom.

"I'm a better shot," I said and she couldn't say anything because she knew that was the truth. I set the gun above my head, within easy reach. The wind was gentle and a canopy of stars illuminated the sky. I felt good and tough like John Wayne, in my bedroll in the desert beneath the moon. For a moment I felt all right, as if everything were fine. The velvet wind caressed my face and I think I almost fell asleep.

There was a story my father used to tell about a time when I was two years old and had almost died. It was a story my father loved to tell because he'd saved me.

We were picnicking at the foot of an observation tower in a pine forest. I crawled away from my sisters and parents and climbed to the top of the tower. There was no railing, and the tower was over eighty feet tall. I'd heard this story so many times that I believed I remembered the experience. I remembered the sunny day and the strong scent of pine and my sisters and mother and father sitting around a checked blanket below, laughing and eating. I remembered that being up there was like being on top of the world because you could see the Atlantic Ocean and the endless forest of pine cut here and there with small rivers. You could see the curve of the earth.

Whenever my father tried to pick me up, I had this little thing that I did: I would giggle and jump back from him. When he realized where I was, he was afraid that I would do just that when he approached me. On the top of the tower there was a metal grate that you could see through. I saw my mother and sisters below, looking up with fear, wondering what I'd do. The ground was sandy and from the sand came all those millions of pine trees and the whole world seemed white, bathed in sun. My father dashed up the steps, two at a time. Then, cautiously, he approached, praying I wouldn't giggle and jump back. My father had always said that nothing worse could happen to a parent than to lose a child.

When I was little I was afraid of losing my father. Joshua Shapiro's father died and his mother didn't have a job and suddenly they were poor and his mother had to work in our cafeteria at school, collecting money from the kids who bought hot lunches. Joshua Shapiro had a very white tongue and he dressed entirely in black and punched kids when he felt like it until he punched too many and got suspended. He was a grade ahead of me. The next year he was gone because he couldn't afford private school. He had to go to the public. I was afraid Dad would die and sometimes I'd tell him I was afraid. "I'm not planning on dying anytime soon," he'd say. "When I die you'll be a woman and I'll have lived a long life and at my funeral I want you to celebrate. I want you to have a party after the funeral and I want you all to eat the biggest, juiciest steaks. I'll be watching you." He'd describe his favorite steak with peppercorns, rare, slicing into the thick slab of meat. The beautiful rose color, the juices. I thought of all of us sitting around a long table, all grown-up eating steaks with peppercorns, big steaks like the ones we used to eat when Anton was courting Mom. I wondered how I'd look all grown up. I hoped I'd look like Mom. Dad's dying didn't scare me anymore.

"Kate," Sofia whispered gently. "It's your turn." A few hours had passed. Julia slept soundly. Sofia shuffled in her sleeping bag, getting comfortable. I wondered if she'd really been awake all that time.

The sky was thick with stars, cutouts against the night, and the moon was gone. The stars so thick like the lights of a far-off and enormous city called something-or-other, and I was warm. I thought of my children and my children's children and their children's children seeing these same stars. I made plans for what I'd do when we got out of here. I'd wash my clothes. I'd help Mom clean out the camper. I'd be good. Incredibly good.

I was almost nine. I had a gun. I was awake, warm in my sleeping bag. I had faith. I could take care of myself. I wasn't tired anymore. I was racing inside, could feel the blood in my veins. I could earn money. That made me laugh, earn money. I heard sounds and saw beautiful shapes. I wanted to stay awake. I never wanted to fall asleep. I felt big, grown up. I could cook. I could take care of myself. I was almost nine.

I crawled out of my sleeping bag and went to my pack and from the top pocket of the pack I took the gold rock that Dad had given me. I had the urge to throw it. I imagined someone, a geologist, finding that nugget of rock that gold comes from. He would think he had discovered gold and soon there would be a whole gold rush in the bottom of the Grand Canyon, an excavation of the whole damn thing. I laughed. No, better: the rock would hide somewhere, becoming a fossil of gold, and a hundred million years would pass and it would metamorphose to form gneiss. It would become a million different things. The possibilities were infinite for that rock, that rock had life. And so I threw it with as much strength as I had. My legs were cold. I could feel goose bumps on my skin. I listened. I wanted to hear it land.

Julia and Sofia were black silhouettes, a few shades darker than the night. I loved Sofia for having stopped with me. I loved little Finny, who broke his silence to try to save us. I loved Caroline and Timothy and Nicholas and Anton. That's all that Anton and Mom wanted, for us to love and trust one another. I held my rosary in my hand, fingering the beads, counting them. I tried to remember how to say Our Father and Hail Mary and then said a few. It felt as if God were really close, as if He could hear me or I could hear Him. I pressed my ear into the ground, the way you can press your ear into sand and hear the whole ocean, and listened.

"You still awake?" Sofia asked. Her eyes glowed. Head on arms as if on a pillow. Her hair long and wild, frizzed out the way it did. I closed my eyes tight and kept listening. Hearing things. Night-creeping things. I thought of all that time surrounding us, cupped here in the canyon. I felt both small and insignificant and large. Very large. I thought of all the fossils that must be trapped in the strata of the canyon, recording time.

"It's your turn, Kate. You better watch. What in the world are you doing with your head to the ground?" I thought of the three of us as fossils, curled in our sleeping bags wedged up against these rocks with the trilobites and the crinoids, with the brachiopods and the mollusks. Lost. And even that didn't bother me. Of the ledge overhead sliding and trapping us and of where we'd be a billion years from now. In another Great Unconformity? "Are you praying again?"

"Shsh," I said. "I'm listening. Shsh."

"For what?" She sat up quickly, scared.

"For God."

"Oh, Kate," she sighed, and slumped back down into her sleeping bag.

But I could feel God, inside, embracing me and I filled. Mom and Anton were one level above us, on the Tonto Plateau in Bright

Angel time—in that time that seemed to be named by God, that seemed to hold a promise. In the morning we'd hike out of here to them, one way or another. I knew that absolutely, like you just know some things.

And then we'd head home to Jane, who was waiting.